LOSS OF LIGHT

DM STONE

This is a work of fiction. Any resemblance of the characters in
this novel to actual persons is coincidental.
The town of Lewes has been adjusted a bit to avoid confusion.

This novel is for M and J.

1. A LONG TIME AGO

There was someone behind the tree. She saw a boot swing out, saw it connect with something on the ground, and then there was a crunch.

Emily stood quite still, her stiletto heels sinking into the mud. She was sobering up now, but her mind wasn't working quickly enough. She looked around, wondering whether to run. On the other side of the Steine the cars carried on past. Their lights grew without penetrating the green, and then faded away. It was the busiest night of the week, but here, in the dark space separating the roads in and out of town, she felt invisible.

The thing on the ground coughed and turned on its side. A dark shape stepped backwards from behind the tree.

'Hello, Em,' he said. It was Dougie Tate. He smiled, pleased to see her.

'Hello,' she said.

'Going to the Norfolk? I think it's closed luv.' He rearranged his quiff, stroking it back into a smooth line.

'I forgot my jumper.' She looked around, seeing the spike-haired silhouettes of Dougie's friends, waiting for him at the edge of the road.

'Did you?' he said. 'Best go and find it then. You can see what you had for breakfast through that dress.'

Emily smiled back and tiptoed past, concentrating hard on her satin stilettos. She did not look around until she had stepped over the fence on the other side. When she did, she saw Dougie's foot swing out again, then, pausing for breath, he looked up and over towards her. He raised his hand in a wave and she waved back.

2. MANY YEARS LATER

'The thing is,' Tim took another bite of bruschetta and continued to talk as he chewed, 'the thing is, I know it's smug, but you can't help being fascinated, can you?'

'I can,' said Mark.

'Oh shut up Mark, I want to know. Go on Tim, how much?'

Tim swallowed, taking his time, savouring the look on Emily's face. '320', he said.

Emily slapped her hands on the table, '320! Can't be. The asking price was only 300.'

'Yeah, but they got into a bidding war.'

'A bidding war! In Lewes!' Emily rocked back on her chair, beaming.

'It's true,' said Clare. 'I talked to her. She seems very nice. Very open. They've moved down from London, you know. I think it was more, umm, what do you call it . . . gazumping? Is that right?'

'Well that's shit.' Everyone turned to look at Mark. 'How would you like it if it happened to you?' They turned back to each other.

'It needs loads of work.' said Clare. 'It's not even as big, is it? As either of ours.' Her dimples twinkled.

'I know. I mean, you've got the conservatory and ours is just bigger all over. And we've done the attic.'

Mark got up and brought over a new bottle of wine. 'We should invite them next time,' he said. 'Welcome them to the neighbourhood.'

'Ooh yes,' said Clare. 'Show them what you've done, Em. They said they're going to gut the place. I think they both earn quite a lot. They work in the city. Both of them.'

***

Emily stacked the dishwasher carefully and then looked around the kitchen. The sight of it gave her a warm glow inside. The oak kitchen doors matched the long oak table, which, in turn, drew your eyes though the room, out of the

French windows and down to the garden. Inside, the granite surfaces shone and the new appliances sparkled. She brushed an imaginary speck of dust from the cream Smeg fridge, and sighed with satisfaction. It was worth every penny.

Mark brought some more glasses from the dining room.

'I think we should have it soon,' she said. 'Wednesday maybe.'

'Have what?'

'The dinner party. The new neighbours. God Mark, keep up.' She glanced at him in irritation. 'Anyway, why were you so funny tonight? You were really bloody rude.'

'Excuse me if I can't get excited at yet another discussion about house prices.'

She ignored him and placed the glasses inside the machine, marvelling again at the ingenious moorings and the satisfying 'thunk' as she closed the door.

'And what was all that about, as well?' He imitated a woman's voice. 'He's upstairs playing his video games. We hardly ever see him ourselves.'

Emily picked up the sponge and wiped the kitchen surface, keeping her back to her husband. 'You're the one who said that we should act like everything's normal. Just wait until he's ready.'

She took a kitchen towel and gave the surface another wipe. The granite was gleaming. She could almost see her face in it.

3. THE NEW ARRIVALS

Lewes sits in the folds of the South Downs, about eight miles outside Brighton. It is a Nice Town. It has historic buildings (including a castle), antique shops, pubs selling real ale and good schools. It also has a Waitrose and a direct train link to central London.

It even has a river. The river Ouse runs dark and muddy straight through the centre of town. It is never, even on the brightest summer day, any colour other than snot green or grey but is still considered to be rather picturesque. At the time of this story, however, the people of Lewes were still recovering from the flood of 2000, which had devastated the centre of town, leaving many people with ruined houses that could not be sold or insured. Every heavy rainfall and resultant swell now made the townspeople nervous.

Apart from the flood, the town only ever makes the news for two other reasons: its county court (and associated prison) and its bonfire night celebration, which is massive, unique and completely takes over normal business. For the rest of the time the town is blissfully unnewsworthy: a peaceful, civilised, nice place to live.

Emily's house was far enough from the river to have been unaffected by the flood, apart from the temporary inconvenience of living with a flooded high street. It was also high enough to have excellent views of the castle from the bedroom windows. The houses were large Victorian terraces with huge bow windows and high ceilings. The value of these houses had gone up and up, and Emily's house was the most valuable in the street.

Now the new couple had arrived. They were younger than Emily and Mark, and city types apparently. Still, Emily thought, they might provide some much-needed new blood to the street.

The new couple, however, had not seen their arrival in quite the same way.

***

'The sofa's too big.' Jenny gave it another shove but there was nowhere for it to go. It already took up all the space between the bow window and the hall door.

James sighed. 'It'll have to do. It's virtually brand new.'

Jenny looked around the room. 'It looks a lot smaller in here with the furniture in, doesn't it?'

They sank down onto the oversized sofa and stared at the fireplace. Sunlight was just beginning to penetrate the dirty windows. Apart from the sofa, a large silver TV, and an ethnic effect coffee table, the room was bare. Jenny didn't go in for ornaments and knick knacks.

'We can't get new furniture, Jen. We said we wouldn't. It'll be better when we've had the extension done.' He took hold of her hand. 'It'll be fine.' He put his arm around her and they snuggled together. He tried to think of something that would please her. 'Why don't we go for a run? I feel like my muscles are seizing up after yesterday. Feel like I could do with running it off.'

Jenny looked more cheerful. 'We could see if we can get as far as the riverbank. Come on then. Before it gets too busy.'

They started up the stairs towards the bedroom, already aching as they climbed. Jenny lowered her voice.

'Don't forget dinner next door tonight.' She turned to look at James and pulled a face.

'What are they like?' he said.

Jenny gave a half smile and shrugged her shoulders. 'I only met her. In the garden. Bit hippified looking. Not really . . . We have to go though.'

'I suppose,' he answered. 'Keep it polite. Leave a long gap before we ask them back.'

She smiled back at him. 'Keep on the right side . . .'

A few minutes later they were doing their stretching exercises outside the house. It was cold, but bright, a chalky blue sky, the sun already clearing the clouds. They set off in the direction of the high street.

The downs gave everything a slightly disorienting feel. If they looked upwards, they could see the green roll of hills rising up above some of the rooftops. Looking downwards they could look right into the front rooms of the houses perched on the side of the hill. In one, two women sat reading, curled up at opposite ends of an antique sofa. For a second one of them caught Jenny's eye, and they both looked away. Further down the hill they could see the sprawl of new housing spreading the town towards the hills.

James waited for Jenny at the corner of the road. He was jogging up and down. 'It'll be great in the summer,' he said.

The high street was steep and the pavements narrow. An old couple turned right around to 'tut' at them as they sped past and a woman in a Range Rover opened her door out at James so that he nearly ran into it.

By the time they got to the river they were too tired to run. They walked along the path, holding hands, looking at their new town.

'I suppose we'll get used to it,' said Jenny. 'Remember we didn't really like Clapham when we first moved in.'

James looked disheartened. 'You're not saying you don't like it now? Jen, you were the one who said we should come here.'

'No, no, don't worry. Look, it's going to be fine. I just need to settle down and get used to it. It's just different, that's all - small town living. God, I did it for 18 years, I'll get used to it again. And I know Dad was right, if we do it up and everything we'll be able to get what we really want next time. It's just that . . .'

'What?'

'Well, when we came down to look at house, it really reminded me of Rodale. But it isn't is it? It doesn't seem to be the country at all here really. I thought we'd kind of meet the same sort of people. You know what I mean? Go pony trekking with our kids and country fairs and all that stuff.'

'They'll have all that here too. We couldn't live in Rodale. Unless you want us commuting for three hours each way a day.'

'I know we couldn't. It's not that. It's just that the people here aren't . . . They're a bit . . . Oh, I don't know. I can't explain. A bit 'right on' I suppose. Not really like country people.' Jenny's face was still bright red from the run, but she was beginning to feel cold. 'Let's start again,' she said, 'Maybe we'll meet some more people at dinner tonight.' She set off with James running behind her.

4. SPYING

Emily observed the couple from her bedroom window. She watched as they warmed up and then set off down the road and her mouth set into a thin smile. So they were that type, were they? In Emily's mind the world was sharply divided: there were those who jogged and those who read. People did not do both. People who read might ramble or swim, or even cycle, but they did not jog. If people who jogged read at all, they read magazines. They did not even read newspapers. Not even the bad ones.

She had guessed as much when she met Jenny. She was wearing deck shoes, for example, and tasteful little diamond earrings. She probably even had a wax jacket. No, they were not her type, and not just that, they were not 'Lewes' either. Emily now saw their arrival in the way that many people would view the presence of a string of gypsy caravans. People like that were going to ruin the area.

A noise from upstairs made her start, and she sat down on the bed to listen. Yes, Sam was definitely up and using the loo. She heard the chain pull and then his footsteps as they crossed back over the room towards his bed. Then there was nothing. She sat and waited, not willing to make any noise that might disturb him, might stop him from getting up, coming downstairs, acting normal. That was all she wanted: things to just go back to normal.

Mark said to give him time. He'd come out eventually if they didn't hassle him, but every so often the strain of waiting would get too much and she would make her way up to the attic door again. Then she would shout or cry or wheedle depending on the mood she was in. None of it made any difference. What was he doing? Even more worrying, where did he go at night? She knew that he sometimes slipped out, but had never managed to stay awake long enough to catch him.

***

At that precise moment, Sam was dozing. He didn't want to tell her though. He didn't actually want to talk to her at all today. Sam was aware that he hadn't wanted to talk to her for quite a few days now, he had lost track of how many, and he knew that this was causing some consternation. But he couldn't help that. It wasn't planned. The first few days had been kind of accidental. He just didn't want to face people after what happened, wondering how long it would be until everyone in the town knew. He'd certainly had enough texts about it and now his phone was permanently turned off.

At first he just kept to the house. Then he started getting up later and later and in the end just hadn't bothered to come downstairs at all. Couldn't face it. This went on for a few days and then he'd begun to feel a little bit funny about it all. He knew there would be a fuss as soon as he appeared and he couldn't stand that. The longer he stayed up there the bigger deal it was going to be when he came out. And every day he thought the same thing: he didn't want to talk to them today and he would think about it again tomorrow.

Today, what he wanted to do was sleep, but his bottom sheet had become untucked and it was twisted and uncomfortable. He thought about getting up to sort it out but he was not quite uncomfortable enough for that. In the meantime, he lay there, unable to sleep but too sleepy to do anything about it.

He listened to his mother downstairs. He knew her patterns, she would make the bed, then she would go downstairs and make a coffee, then she would go up to her study and he would hear the sound of the computer starting up. The day would proceed with typing noises and the occasional phone call. The phone calls were the worst bit. She sounded so awful on the phone. Her voice changed and she got all greasy with the people on the other end: her clients. It would be all 'Great catching up with you, Steve' and 'Say hi to Philip,' and 'No, no, really, thank you for the opportunity.' Sometimes he put his headphones on.

This was one of the reasons why it was best to be up when everyone else was asleep. He hoped that she would sleep tonight, he needed to go out. The good thing about his mother was that when she slept, she really slept. Nothing would wake her. Even the time his bike had fallen over. And you could always tell when she was asleep because she snored really loudly.

Today seemed a little bit different, though. The smell of coffee drifted up to the attic, delicious, proper coffee. She was going to take her time this morning then. Maybe work was slow. He was glad to be upstairs if this was the case. It made her snappy, or rather, even more snappy than usual. But then he heard the front door slam. The car alarm beeped off and there was the sound of the engine starting. Sam got up and made his way to the window. He stood to the side of the Velux and peered out as the car moved down the road. He wondered where she was going and how long she would be.

***

Emily was going to Tesco. She should have gone later, after she'd got some work out of the way, but she felt restless. It was hearing Sam move around. She couldn't quite settle and thought she might as well get the food in ready for the evening. At the back of her mind, she was also wondering whether Sam might come down while she was out, perhaps to get something to eat or some coffee. She'd made his favourite to try to tempt him.

She treasured any sign that Sam had left the attic, even if it was just to deposit some filthy clothes in the linen basket. It made him seem as if he was really there. Sometimes she felt in danger of forgetting about him altogether, and this made her feel panicky and desperate. She wanted anything that gave her concrete evidence of a living boy. Not this ghost-like attic-dwelling presence.

14

As she turned the corner she caught sight of Jenny and James on their way back from their run. Too late to pretend she hadn't seen them, she gave them a smile and a wave and carried on past. When they were safely behind her she allowed herself a real smile. Well, she thought, the girl might be younger and fitter, but she still looked bloody stupid when she ran.

She switched on the radio and The Ramones 'Sheena is a Punk Rocker' blasted out. Emily sung along as loud as she could.

***

Her good mood did not last long after her return. She searched through the bags and then went through the fridge again. No, she'd forgotten it. The bloody soy sauce. She held the old bottle up against the light. Nowhere near enough to make the soy braised chicken. She'd either have to do something else or get Mark to pop out to the shop.

She remembered standing at the Chinese condiments section very clearly. She remembered examining the different bottles and their respective prices. But then she'd seen him: Dougie Tate, wheeling a trolley loaded with cat food and lager.

At first she thought that she was imagining things. How could he appear like that after twenty-odd years? Where had he been in the meantime? And what was he doing in Lewes? As far as she could remember he had no connection with the place. She pretended to stare at the bottles of soy while sneaking looks over towards him.

He had a strange way of standing: ramrod straight, but with a slight pigeon chest. He wasn't tall, but the posture gave him a presence. That was how she had recognised him. His hair was still dyed jet black, in the fashion of twenty years ago, but now she could see some silver roots around the temples. And although he was surprisingly fresh faced and healthy looking, he looked old, the wrinkles deep scored.

Otherwise he was just exactly the same. Maybe his trouser legs were a little less aggressively skinny now, and he wore thick soled work boots, not pointed winkle pickers, but he had kept the essentially the same style down to the quiff and the leather jacket. Some people did this, she knew. People found a style that they felt suited them, and stayed with it, no matter what. Maybe it was a way of hanging onto their youth. If they never changed what they wore, they never felt that they had changed. She, on the other hand, looked totally different. After all, it was all twenty years ago. She had become a wife, a mother, a freelance website designer. An adult.

She moved away, but then felt stupid. Of course he would never recognise her. She wasn't even blonde any more.

Emily had a strong urge to get out of there as quickly as possible. She paid for her shopping and then walked back to the car feeling rather vacant. On the way she caught sight of her reflection in the automatic doors. Yes, she really did look totally different.

She packed her shopping in the boot of the car and then sat for a long while with the keys in the ignition but the engine off. What had happened to her? When had she given up on herself? Why the hell did she look like that?

5. IMPRESSING THE NEIGHBOURS

Emily's bad mood worsened when she found a tiny chip in the kitchen's granite surface. It was supposed to last a lifetime, granite.

She wasted quite a bit of time in looking at the chip from different angles and increasing distances. It showed. As far as Emily was concerned it actually ruined the effect of the whole kitchen. Someone must have dropped something hard onto it and then not owned up. There were only two suspects of course. And both of them could be broken under interrogation. But she didn't think it could be Mark, he wasn't looking guilty enough, and Sam was hardly likely to come down and be interrogated. This made her feel crosser than ever.

Then a client phoned, demanding to see progress on the estate agency web site and she set about work in a fury of embarrassment, only stopping when the prototype was on line. Then there was chicken to marinade, napkins to iron, and last minute cushion fluffing to be done. All the same, her mind kept returning to the chip in the granite surface.

Eventually she heard the front door open and then Mark's footsteps in the hall. He opened the kitchen door, holding a clinking carrier bag aloft.

'I remembered the wine,' he said, a relieved smile on his face.

'Did you do this?' She pointed at the granite.

The smile disappeared and he edged towards her.

'What is it?' He bent down to look right at the surface. Then he looked back up at her face. 'I didn't. Honestly.' There was a silence. 'It hardly shows. Really Em.' He studied her face for a few seconds and then pulled her towards him, putting his arms around her and holding her close. She let herself be held and suddenly realised that she wanted to cry. The chip felt like the end of the world, all

17

her hard work ruined by someone's carelessness. Crying was out of the question, though. There was no time to redo her make up. Instead she rallied, pulling herself away from Mark and putting out some more coasters.

Jenny and James were the last to arrive, and by that time Emily was pleased to see them. Clare had been in full flow on her favourite topic, her daughter, and had spent a large part of the preceding half an hour telling them about Tamsin's progress at school. She had covered all the relevant information: what the teachers had said at parents' day, what she had said to them, the girl's projected grades for each subject, and a full analysis of any extenuating circumstances or displays of inherited genius.

She was just working her way around to asking about Sam when the doorbell went and Jenny and James appeared with a bottle of Turning Leaf. Emily was a little bit annoyed immediately. At least Clare had made an effort, with her annoying flowery skirt from Fat Face. Jenny had obviously not bothered at all. She had a little bit of white paint on her blonde fringe, and was wearing jeans that had splashes of magnolia on them. Emily studied the splashes intently, wondering whether they would transfer to the upholstery.

Clare and Jenny seemed to hit it off straight away and had soon arranged to go to a Yoga class together. Jenny turned to include Emily, but Clare said 'Oh, don't bother asking Em. She thinks Yoga is for bored housewives.'

Mark and James also seemed to be getting on. James and Jenny both worked as project managers for a city firm and James was explaining something called PRINCE, which after an embarrassing and confusing couple of minutes, Emily gathered had absolutely nothing to do with the pop star and was, in fact, something rather boring to do with work.

She felt herself receding into the background of her own dinner party. The room looked fantastic, the row of candles on the island unit had worked beautifully, the outdoor lighting made the garden look like a fairy grotto, and the blue of the dinner service accented the cushion covers on the sofa. She had created this evening, but now it was running without her. She was like a stage hand, useful, but excluded from the action on stage.

Only Tim seemed to notice when Emily wandered towards the kitchen area and began to serve the chicken. He went over to join her and started trying to help.

'You really did a good job on this place, Em,' he said. 'You should show Jenny and James round.'

She smiled at him. Actually she was feeling a little annoyed that neither one of the new couple had mentioned anything about the house. No one had even said 'What a lovely room,' which was the normal response, although some people had really endeared themselves by asking whether she had used an interior designer. Jenny and James hardly seemed to notice anything at all. Obviously they hadn't seen how it was before, so they couldn't be expected to know the difference. But they did live in the house next door, which was actually rather like living in the 'before' version of Emily's house. How could they not be interested?

She made a few conversational gambits, all of which fell flat and died in front of her. The first was to tell them where the library was. They looked at her in a confused way for a few seconds and then Jenny asked whether it loaned DVDs. Emily felt momentarily smug, realising that she had been right about their reading habits, but then felt excluded again as the group had a passionate discussion about whether Terminator 1 or 2 was the better movie.

She tried again: asking them what they thought of Lewes so far. This was the moment when they could have redeemed themselves by saying what a special place it was, how beautiful the countryside, how charming the town, how its unique character had drawn them towards it.

Instead, James said 'I wanted St Albans, but it was too expensive.'

And Jenny said, 'I just wanted a small town really. I grew up in a small town, and I didn't want kids to grow up in London.' She gave a coy, sidelong look at James. 'I want to start having babies as soon as we're settled.'

Emily could not keep the stricken expression from her face. They were going to have children and be right next door. And they think that Lewes is the same as other towns! It could not be worse. She attempted to recover herself.

'So there must have been something about Lewes that attracted you to it.'

They looked at her blankly.

'It is very nice,' said Jenny, looking a bit worried. It was clear that she didn't really understand the point of the conversation.

Clare and Tim looked back and forth from Jenny to Emily. They're enjoying this, Emily thought.

'It's just that I think Lewes is quite an interesting town. Don't you Clare?'

'Oh yes,' Clare looked aghast at being put on the spot. 'Though I do quite like Uckfield as well.'

'Uckfield!' Emily was appalled. 'Uckfield is full of fascists! They all read the Daily Mail and think that Brighton is Sodom and Gomorrah.' She looked around the dinner table.

'Have you heard about Bonfire night?' said Mark. 'It really is amazing. Quite a sight.'

'Oh yes, It does sound good,' said James. 'Some of the guys at work went a few years ago. Said they burnt a giant Pope on a bonfire. They had a few problems getting home though. Got split up and put on different trains and it was raining.' His voice trailed off. There was silence.

'Brighton is getting a bit rough though, isn't it?' said Clare. She had something green stuck on her front tooth. 'You're always saying that Emily. Aren't you?'

'That's not the point, Clare,' she said. 'Yes, Brighton is getting rough, but that isn't why people from Uckfield don't like it. They don't like it because it's got homosexuals living there.'

Tim smirked. 'And you do like the homosexuals?'

Emily was controlled. 'I do actually. I think they make a great contribution to the town.' She paused. 'The reason that I moved out of Brighton was that there were too many drunken arseholes, peeing up against my front door and fighting in West Street.' She turned to Jenny, who shrank backwards, 'You see, that's what's so nice about Lewes. It's a really tolerant, open-minded place. And it's got loads of interesting people too. But it's still quite quiet. We love it here. Don't we Mark?'

Mark poured everyone another glass of wine and Jenny and James took large gulps.

'Yes, it really is a great place,' he said. 'It's got its own special character, you know. There's quite a few writers and artists and stuff. And some people who work at the BBC. And loads of teachers, though I suppose you get them everywhere. Mind you, we do seem to have an awful lot of them. I wonder why that is? Oh, and there's some nice restaurants too.'

'Is there?' said James. 'We like a good dinner, don't we Jen?'

'You know what you should do,' said Clare. 'You should go to that Thai restaurant. It's just off the high street. What's that little road it's on Emily, I can never remember.'

'Station Street,' said Emily.

'Yes, Station Street. The one up from the Station.' Clare brushed an imaginary crumb from her skirt.

'Oh, we will do! Thanks.' James smiled at Jenny who smiled back. 'That's a good tip, isn't it Jen?'

They've already been there, thought Emily. And they don't like it.

'What about pubs?' said Jenny.

The conversation blundered on until they had all finished eating. Emily caught both James and Tim trying to

21

look at their watches. She put the coffee on. It was only ten o'clock, but she didn't see how she could spin things out much longer.

At last she said, 'So Clare tells me that you're going to do some work on the house.'

Jenny and James exchanged quick glances.

'Yes,' said Jenny. 'Actually my Dad's going to do it as a wedding present. He's a builder.'

'Oh really! That's good to know,' said Clare. 'We need the damp sorting on the back walls. Perhaps he could pop round and have a look while he's here.'

Jenny went a little bit red. 'Um, he's not really that sort of builder. He kind of owns a building firm. Essbuild, it's called. I don't know if you've heard of it. They mostly do work in Essex.'

'I've heard of it' said Mark. He looked uneasy.

'So what are you having done?' said Emily.' We've had virtually everything done here. Would you like to look round?'

'That would be nice,' said Jenny.

Emily put the coffee back on the hot plate and went towards the kitchen door. Jenny and James got up to follow her out of the room but Emily turned so that she was standing in the doorway, blocking their exit. She was suddenly determined that they would comment on the kitchen.

'Well you've seen in here. We had the old kitchen ripped out. It's all brand new.'

'It's lovely' said Jenny. 'The worktop. . . is that granite?'

'Yes it is,' said Emily.

Jenny was looking directly at the chip in its surface. 'Granite's supposed to last a lifetime, isn't it?' she said.

'Shall I show you the rest? You've seen the cloakroom, haven't you?

They followed Emily out of the room. Clare waited for a second and then scuttled after them. She had seen it all before but would never miss an opportunity to have a look round someone else's house.

Left alone in the kitchen, Tim and Mark looked at each other.

'Essbuild, eh,' said Tim. 'Don't for God's sake tell Emily. 'She'll blow her stack.'

'I'm right, aren't I,' said Mark. 'They're the ones who build on green field sites and flood plains and stuff?'

'Yip,' said Tim.

Mark rubbed his forehead and looked at the table. 'She'll think we've got the devil himself living next door.'

Things were going little better on the tour. Jenny had complimented both the living room and the dining room, but Emily was certain that she was planning something rather different.

'You've still got the original fireplaces, too, haven't you Jenny? You're lucky. A lot of them were taken out.'

'Yes, it's awful when they take them out, isn't it? Sacrilege, I always think. What I was thinking though, is that they look a bit sort of dark and, you know . . . I was thinking of painting them white.'

'Painting them white?' Emily heard the squeak in her voice. 'They'd soon get dirty again, I can tell you.'

Jenny tilted her chin upwards. 'Actually, I wasn't thinking of using the fireplaces. I'm more of a central heating kind of girl. I thought I'd arrange some pieces of wood in them. Like logs.'

'Logs?' said Emily.

James coughed. 'Yes, um, we kind of like the sort of minimal look, you know. In fact if the fireplaces had been taken out, we wouldn't have replaced them. Some people just have a hole in the wall, you know. With logs or pebbles in it. I quite like that.'

'Pebbles?' said Emily.

Clare made a small choking noise and turned away.

'Shall we see the rest?' said Emily. They trooped out of the dining room and up the stairs behind her. 'I can't show

23

you the attic. Sam's up there with his video games. You know what teenage boys are like. We had the full conversion job though. He's even got his own little shower room. We hardly see him.'

They turned into the master bedroom. Emily was very proud of this room. The sash windows had been restored and the furniture had taken years to source from Lewes antique shops. 'You see we had our own loo put in here.' She opened a sliding door that looked like a wardrobe and everyone dutifully gasped and complimented the WC.

'Through here,' said Emily, leading them out and across the hall, 'is my study.' She opened the door and then closed it almost immediately. The shelving units were only IKEA. 'And over here is the guest room.' They all peered in. 'You see, you get quite a good view of the castle.' They all agreed.

'And finally,' said Emily. She paused. 'I think this is my favourite. The wet room.' She opened the door with a flourish.

Sam was in his underpants, kneeling on the floor and using the guest towels to mop up a pool of water. Looking up at the ceiling they could see a tile drooping downwards, indicating the source of the problem.

'Oh for Christ's sake . . .' said Emily. 'You've let the shower flood, haven't you? What the hell is the matter with you?'

Sam got up and squeezed past the crowd, but not until everyone had seen that he had tears in his eyes. Then he bolted for the attic and locked the door behind him.

'Well it's certainly a wet room now,' said Clare.

6. SOME VISITS

Emily exhaled with relief. The phone often went non-stop. There were the clients ringing to check on work, members of the Historical society and the Conservation society calling to ask about meeting times, but for once this was someone she wanted to talk to. Her friend Sally was the only person she would not have to put on an act for, mainly because it would be pointless to do so. Sally had known her for too long. Also, Sally was the only person Emily knew whose life was in a worse shape than her own.

She took the phone over to her armchair and settled in. After the first few minutes, which consisted of a run down on the problems of seeing a man who did more cocaine than even Sally thought advisable, Emily told her friend about Sam.

'Three months? Bloody hell Em. That's ages ago. Haven't I seen you . . . ? When was that? I would have been going out with Steve then, wouldn't I?'

'Possibly,' said Emily. 'Anyway, then last night, there he was, looking terrible and half naked in front of the new neighbours, and I shouted at him.'

'You shouldn't have done that you know. Now he'll never come out again.'

'Thanks Sal. Yes I know that.'

'I'm sorry, I'm sorry. I'm just saying . . . He must come out sometimes. How does he eat?'

'He gets up when we're asleep. I've tried staying up for him, but he seems to know. And then I worry that he's starving to death up there so it seems better to just let him get on with it.'

'Do you think he might listen to me? We always got on you know. Sometimes people can't talk to their parents. Maybe I should come down this weekend.'

Emily smiled. Sally had obviously already planned on a visit, probably needing some proper food and advice about her love life, but this way she could make out that she was doing her friend a favour. Emily wondered when exactly she had become Sally's mum.

'It's worth a shot, I suppose,' she said. 'Oh and there's something else . . . Do you remember Dougie Tate?'

'Dougie Tate, yes of course I do. Don't tell me you've seen him?'

'In Lewes Tesco. I haven't seen him for years.'

There was a brief silence at the other end. 'It must be over 20 years,' said Sally. 'God, that was a long time ago. Did he see you? Did he say anything?'

Emily laughed. 'Come on, he wouldn't recognise me now. I was a blonde then, anyway. Don't you remember? Blonde and spiky.'

They giggled and began to reminisce.

**

When Emily hung up the phone she tried to concentrate on work. It wasn't usually difficult. Emily liked creating web sites in the same way that other people liked doing jigsaws. Each time you solved one problem, a dozen others appeared, but at the same time you could see more and more of the end result appearing in front of you. Soon you were so engrossed that you could not tear yourself away. It blotted out everything else.

Today though, she couldn't summon up the enthusiasm. All she seemed to be able to do was to re live the awfulness of the night before. She had laughed off Sam's appearance, but it was unconvincing, and her guests had left almost immediately, declining coffee and collecting their things. Then she and Mark had gone to inspect the damage.

She could only imagine what the flood had all done to the beautifully converted attic. Of course they wouldn't be given a chance to go and check. She wondered what on earth could have made him let the shower flood when he was in the same room. Was he on drugs? Was that where he went at night? To get drugs?

Perhaps Sally would bring some blow with her at the weekend. The thought pleased her. She didn't often bother these days, preferring a nice glass of red, but right now getting really stoned sounded just fine.

She tried to concentrate again but then she heard an irritating scraping noise from outside. It was difficult to see out into the garden as the desk took up most of the space in front of the window, but she craned forward, pretending to reach for something on the window sill. A man in white overalls was in the garden next door. He was measuring something and talking to someone else who was not in view. Then another man, wearing a suit and talking into a mobile phone walked right out to the back of the garden and looked up at the houses. She ducked back down into her chair and pretended to concentrate on the computer. He finished his conversation and put the phone back in his pocket. She saw Jenny walk out towards him and they talked a little and laughed. Then they both looked up at Emily's window. Jenny smiled and waved and Emily waved back.

She sat for a few more minutes feeling rather exposed, then took her coffee cup and retreated downstairs to the kitchen. The man in the suit had to be Jenny's father. They both had the same wavy blonde hair and ruddy complexion, though he was slightly smaller and wiry looking. So they were going to start work soon. Emily realised that she had failed to find out their plans for the house. This made her quite cross. Had they evaded talking about it or had she been too wrapped up in showing them her own place?

Anyway, it looked like they were going to do something to the back of the house, which would be noisy and inconvenient. She and Mark had been lucky with their own building work. The previous next door neighbour had been in the hospice at the time, which was very convenient really. She wished that she'd asked Jenny what their plans were when she had the chance. Now she just wanted to avoid the woman.

***

Jenny and her father walked back into the house. She put the kettle on and they both sat down at the table.

'Well, you're supposed to talk to them, of course.' Alex Wheeler took the plans from a long cardboard tube and laid them on the table, using a set of candlesticks to stop the corners from curling up. He looked at his daughter. 'But, do you want my advice?'

'You're going to say don't tell them. But they'll find out in the end. Won't it cause bad feeling?'

'Are these people your best friends?'

'No, of course not, we've only just moved in. I kind of like the couple on the right though.'

'Which ones?'

'That way.'

'That's fine. Now come and look at this. You see the compass here,' he pointed at the corner of the drawing. 'This tells you the direction that the sun moves.' He traced his hand from the top to the bottom of the paper.

Jenny tilted her head and looked out of the window until she had found the pale yellow sun. It was a bright autumn day, cold but virtually cloudless. 'Okay,' she said.

'Okay,' her father then traced his finger round a large square on the drawing. 'The extension will block out some of the sun for the people on this side. Quite a lot of their sun, actually. And their view. Especially if you build the trellis on the roof terrace. The people on the right won't be so affected. You won't be blocking their sun, because they are between you and it. . . you see what I mean?'

Jenny nodded. 'But we'll cut their sun right out, won't we? The people on that side. From the whole of the top of their garden.'

'Yes. And the other thing that they can get you on is loss of privacy. It won't be such an issue for your friends on the right, but you're going to have the extension right

28

up against this wall here, so even if we don't put any windows on their side, your roof terrace is going to look right out onto to the these people.'

'Oh crap. I mean I knew about the roof terrace. I knew that it wouldn't be popular. I didn't think about the sun though.'

'That's why you've got me. Listen lovey, if you tell them, all you're doing is giving them more time to get their arguments together and make a proper objection. If you don't tell them, you don't give them much time to run around finding out what their rights are.'

'But we will be able to do it though, won't we. I mean we only bought the house . . .'

'Don't worry. Everything's going to be fine. There's already a precedent. It's on the other side of the street, but that doesn't matter. Anyway, it's numbers that count in things like this. You're only going to affect one household really. They'll be no petitions or letter writing campaigns. Plus I've already talked to people.' He winked.

Jenny smiled. 'Oh Dad,' she said.

Alex laughed and reached over to brush his daughter's hair from her face. 'So you should listen to your old father. I mean it Jennifer. Let me deal with this and keep your mouth shut. That goes for James too. OK?'

'OK,' she said.

***

For the rest of the week, Emily tried to concentrate on work. The weather was bright for October and she spent a lot of unproductive time staring out of the study window, gazing at small fluffy clouds and planning what to do with the garden next year.

Of course, as Jenny was the last person on earth that she wanted to see, Emily kept bumping into her, or catching sight of her in the neighbourhood. The first time was the day after the dinner party. They had walked smack into each other outside the corner shop.

They smiled and asked each other how they were and then said 'See you later.' The incident in the bathroom was not mentioned. Emily realised afterwards that this was a mistake. She should have made some kind of joking reference to show that it didn't matter. Now of course, it was obvious that it did.

Also, Jenny did not proffer a return invitation, and as the days slid by, Emily realised that she probably never would. That would have been fine; she would have preferred to forget the whole thing. Except that Jenny seemed to be everywhere. There appeared to be no part of Emily's life that the woman did not intrude. She would be daydreaming out of the window, for example, and Jenny would appear in the garden wearing jeans that showed off her athletic figure, her cheeks rosy from exertion and her blonde hair swinging in a ponytail. Then, if Emily walked to the shops, there she was again, cleaning the living room windows, hanging curtains (taupe, linen) or, on one particularly annoying occasion, chucking a bucket of water down her front steps almost hitting Emily as she passed.

Most irritating, though, was not being able to guess where she was or when she would appear. One day she saw Jenny in the garden, hard at work potting plants, and decided that this was a good time to nip out to the shops. In the time it took her to grab her coat and leave the house Jenny had seemingly beamed herself to the doorstep of number 32, and was holding the neighbour's baby in her arms and chatting like she'd known her for years. On Emily's return from the shop Jenny was on yet another neighbour's doorstep, quickly ending her conversation with 'See you tomorrow night.' Emily had never wanted to befriend these women; they were younger and their children were small. She had done all of that: the mess, the clutter of children's things and their leavings. She didn't want to be invited to their houses, because, naturally, she couldn't invite them back. Now though, she felt excluded and resentful.

By the evening Emily had worked herself up into a stew. She assumed that Jenny had taken time off work for the move and would soon be out of her way again. In the meantime, she felt under siege. She didn't like to think about what would happen when the woman started 'having babies' as she had put it, and was at home all the time. Perhaps she's infertile, Emily thought. You never knew.

As soon as Mark got home, she started. He was reading the paper at the kitchen table. She could tell he didn't really want to chat. He had been monosyllabic since he came through the door, but she didn't care. She needed to let off steam.

'Well, she'll be back at work soon,' he said without looking up.

'I know but . . .' she struggled for something to add. All she wanted was for him to make comforting noises. To feel like there was someone on her side. Anyway, he was only reading the Evening Argus. It never said anything interesting. She glanced at the article he was reading. The headline was 'Neal Street feels the Pinch'. The picture showed a man looking mournful standing behind a newsagent's counter.

'I know but she's really getting on my nerves. She's just everywhere and I just feel like . . .'

He slammed his hand down hard on the table, closing the paper. 'What do you expect me to do about it?' he said.

Emily, so shocked that she could not think straight, stood with her mouth hanging open.

'I mean, what am I supposed to do? Go round there and say 'Excuse me, love, you're getting on my wife's nerves. Do you mind stopping in a bit?'

'No, of course not, but . . .'

'No. No, Emily. I'm sorry she's getting on your nerves, but you're just going to have to put up with it.'

There was silence for a few seconds while Emily tried to decide whether to cry or storm out. Then he spoke again, a little more calmly.

'You want to know my opinion? I didn't like 'em. They're dull and he's really up himself. Going on about how he'll be made a partner by the time he's thirty-five. I could tell what he was thinking. What a loser, stuck in middle management. But it doesn't matter. They're nothing to do with us. And they won't be staying round here either. This is a stepping stone for people like them. They're just on a detour before the detached house in the county.'

Emily slumped down into the chair next to her husband and he took hold of her hand.

'Shall I open a bottle of wine?' he said.

She nodded and squeezed his hand. Then he took the newspaper and threw it in the bin.

7. REUNIONS

Emily could hear something outside the front door. Somebody was having a conversation on her doorstep and she moved closer, hoping to hear what was being said. It was Sally's voice.

'No, I will. I'll phone you. I just need to find out what we're doing.'

Emily could hear the low buzz of a man's voice, protesting, persuading. She opened the door and Sally fell in. A young man of about twenty-five, headphones swinging from his neck, backed away, disappointed. 'Hello Em,' she kissed Emily on both cheeks and pushed past. Emily smiled apologetically at the boy. He looked at her crossly and slunk away into the night.

'And he was?' she said, closing the door behind them.

'No one. Carried my bags from the station.'

Without realising how it had happened, Emily found that she was the new recipient of Sally's rucksack and she followed her friend, with difficulty, downstairs to the kitchen.

'Bloody hell, Sal. This is heavy. How long are you staying for?' Emily knew that she didn't have much say in the matter. Sally would stay as long as she pleased.

'Not sure. You don't mind, do you? Job's finished at the council.' She headed straight for the sofa and lay down, hanging her feet off the end so that her shoes didn't mark the upholstery. 'Wow. Looks great in here Em. Really. I'll have a look round in a moment. What a journey! How do people stand it? Any chance of a cup of tea? I could really do with a cuppa. That journey! There were all these businessmen and they all got on holding these little plastic bags with cans inside them. By the time they'd got to Haywards Heath they were all pissed. Honestly, totally pissed. One of them had to be helped off the train. I suppose they go back to their wives like that.'

Emily hung up Sally's coat and put the kettle on. There was no point interrupting. Anyway, Emily liked to hear her chatter. The house was too quiet these days. She made the tea and took the time to survey her friend. They saw each other at just long enough intervals to be able to spot little changes, a new wrinkle, another grey hair. Emily was always surprised that she didn't feel able to gloat at any of these signs of ageing, as she might have done if it had been another woman. Sally was so much part of her history that it was as if she was watching her own self get older.

Anyway, Sally was still a beautiful woman. She still had long red hair, but now it was pinned up in an ornate 'do' with pieces that stuck up and trailed down in a complicated but casual manner. And she still had her figure. Long legs, big bum and big boobs. She would be ninety before she stopped attracting men.

Emily felt small and colourless in contrast. It hadn't always been like that. When they were young it had been fashionable to be skinny and flat chested. Plus she used to bleach her hair and everyone said that with her tiny miniskirts and black makeup, she looked just like Debbie Harry. She didn't of course, but there didn't seem to be many other women around at the time to compare her with.

Now she was still skinny, but out of condition, and it showed. Periodically she would haul herself out to the swimming baths, but it always seemed too much effort. And her hair had long since grown out to its natural mouse. It was still cut in a bob, but she was aware that bobs were no longer the fashion. People had their hair cut all different lengths now. It looked complicated and expensive to maintain.

As for her clothes . . . well she always made a bit of an effort when Sally came down. She didn't want Sal to be ashamed. But really, what was the point? She was nearly always at home. Or doing something to the house. She needed to be comfortable.

The two women settled into their usual ritual. Sally pretended to be interested in the transformation of the kitchen. Then she told Emily the latest drama of her latest relationship. Then Emily wondered when Sally would find someone nice.

When Mark arrived Sally jumped up to kiss him and he blushed a little and gave her a hug.

'So have you made any progress?' he said.

The two women looked at him blankly.

'I mean Sam. Have you been up to see him?'

Sally glanced sideways at Emily. She knew that they had both forgotten all about Sam, and seeing her friend's stricken face, she knew she had to lie.

'I was just going up now. We thought we'd wait till you got back. In case . . . Anyway, I'll go up right now.'

She took a glug of tea and gave them both a cheery smile. Then she set off up the stairs.

Mark and Emily wavered by the open kitchen door and then slid out into the hall. Mark picked a loose bit of paint off the dado rail until he caught Emily's look.

Sally called out as she went. 'Sam! It's Sally.' She reached the top of the stairs and stood there, not knowing what to do. Then she knocked on the door. There was silence. She knocked again.

'Are you in there Sam?'

She paused and then knocked again. 'You alright, Sam?' she said.

There was another pause, then there appeared to be some kind of movement in the room. After that, there was a rustling noise as a piece of paper slid out from under the door. Sally picked it up and carried it back down to Emily and Mark.

The paper had the words 'Go away' written on it, and underneath there was drawing of a smiley face.

***

The next day was Saturday. Mark said he had to pop into the office, and Emily and Sally decided to go into

Brighton and have lunch in the North Laine, Brighton's supposedly bohemian centre.

A little further down the hill, Dougie Tate was also preparing for a day in the North Laine. He had a batch of Big Issues to sell and a mid-day spot outside Infinity Foods. He felt great, on top form and happy to be escaping to Brighton for a while. The weather was beautiful and the crowds would be out. He knew he would make some money today. He gave a last look at the tiny cottage as he set off. Life wasn't so bad, and you never knew what was round the corner.

He spotted the women as they got off the train. Brighton Station was a good place to spot loose pickings. It was ok to look at people in the station. You could be waiting for someone. And the big old glass ceiling meant that you could see everyone and everything as the light flooded through. They could see you too, though, which meant you had to be careful.

He recognised Sally straight away. It was only by association that he recognised Emily. It was never Sally he was after, not like the rest of them. Sally was a bit of a slapper. He couldn't stand that in a woman. It showed a lack of self control.

Emily though. He remembered how he used to fancy her. She had been a saucy mare. He remembered the little miniskirts she used to wear and smiled at the memory. But look at her now. Not taking care of herself. To Dougie's mind, women should always take care of themselves. It was kind of like a sacred duty. They should be clean and neat and smart and slim. Well turned out and preferably middle class. Nice girls. Emily was a nice girl. She could still be alright if she just took care of herself.

He watched them leave the station, leaning together, gossiping, and set off behind them.

***

The lift doors 'pinged' as they opened, but inside, the office was quiet. Mark was glad. Often at the weekend keen workers could be found finishing reports or tweaking web pages before joining the Saturday afternoon shopping scrum in Brighton. Now the office seemed kind of eerie, inhabited only by the traces of people who no longer felt like putting in the extra effort.

Sue's desk had a browning apple core on the keyboard. How could the cleaners miss an apple core? Adrian's Computer Weekly lay open at the job pages. And someone had interfered with Carol's teddy collection again. Very amusing. Mark had just about made it to his desk at the top of the room when Ted Harris appeared at the end of the corridor, wheeling a set of golf clubs behind him.

Mark stood his ground, dragging the corners of his mouth up into a smile.

'Mark!' Ted called out as he trundled the bag along towards him. 'How're you doing? Heard the news. Bad luck about all this.' He looked around the office and then fixed Mark with a sympathetic look, his head tilted to one side.

'Well, not much I can do about it,' said Mark.

'Suppose not. Shame though. Awful shame. You'll get something else though, won't you? Lots of jobs around these days.'

'So they say.' Mark tried to think of an exit line.

'Come to pick up your stuff?'

'No! Good God, no. Nothing's happening for three months.'

'Three months! Well that's good isn't it? That's plenty of time.'

'Yes it's not bad.'

'You probably won't want to hang around that long though, will you?' He paused, letting his words sink in. 'Okay then. Better be off. Meeting the guys up at Roedean. You a member? No, of course not. Never seen you there. You should join!'

Mark smiled and turned the handle of the office door.

Ted continued. 'Oh, you didn't have any trouble getting in did you? Did your card work OK?'

'Actually, I didn't have to use it. One of the cleaners was on the way out.'

'Ah,' said Ted. 'Okay.' He smiled again and turned around, wheeling the bag along behind him.

Mark made his way to his desk and slumped into the chair. So the bastards had stopped his weekend building access. How the hell was he going to look for jobs now? At home? With Emily breathing down his neck?

***

Emily and Sally took the road under the station concourse down towards the North Laine. Sally wanted to see everything, to see what had changed, because something always had.

When they were growing up in Brighton the North Laine was still a grid of run-down Victorian terraces. It was where you lived if you were poor or a student. Huge families were crushed into tiny houses. It was dirty and grim. A series of streets, cutting through the middle of the grid, held the neighbourhood shops: butchers, greengrocers and hardware stores.

Then, sometime in the late 70s, a shop appeared that sold second hand clothes: mohair jumpers, miniskirts, pointed shoes. Another shop opened selling bongs, pipes and smelly rugs. Then another opened selling rubber trousers, and that was that. The area became the alternative centre of Brighton, and Sally and Emily had a flat right in the centre of it. For a few glorious years it was a hugely exciting place to be.

Then it got a reputation for being 'bohemian'. One by one the butchers and greengrocers closed down and were replaced by more shops selling clothes, knick knacks or 'antique' furniture. Residents began to say that you couldn't buy an onion in the North Laine, but you nipped out for five minutes, you were quite likely to return with a stripped oak dining table.

Emily felt a twinge of regret as they passed their old street. At the same time, though, she could see her predictions about the area coming true. It was noisier, busier than ever. Loud music blasted out onto the street from every building and the shops had a samey look to them. Emily began to have a feeling of déjà vu as she was faced with yet another collection of candles and fluffy cushions. Had they already been in this shop? It was hard to tell.

Everyone around her seemed to be enjoying it all, so the problem was obviously with her. She was too old, that was it. She belonged in Lewes now. She confided as much to Sally as they pushed their way through the crowds in Sydney Street.

'Oh for God's sake. Why do you do that? Why do you do that to yourself? I'm the same age as you, remember.' Sally made a decision, and holding Emily's sleeve, she broke them away from the stream of shoppers and turned down the hill. 'Come on, we're going for a drink. The Basketmakers is still there isn't it?'

'The Basketmakers will always be there, I hope.'

It was still early so they were able to get a seat. Sally slid into one of the upholstered benches near the door while Emily went to the bar. It all looked the same as ever, the walls covered in old tins with quaint slogans on their lids, advertising tobacco or mints or biscuits. The clientele was the same too, a mixture of the young and the ageing young at heart.

When Emily turned she saw that Sally was no longer alone. Dougie Tate was leaning over her, his back towards Emily. Sally flashed Emily a panicked look.

'Emily, look who it is! You remember Dougie, don't you?'

Dougie turned and smiled, his pale blue eyes searching her face.

'Emily Fletcher. That's it, isn't it luv? Emily Fletcher. I remember you all right.'

'Hello,' she slid next to Sally before he could take the seat. 'How are you? Haven't seen you around for ages.'

'That's because I haven't been around. Been travelling. Travelled the world, as they say. But I'm back now.'

Emily smiled, wondering how to extricate them from the conversation. It was important not to ask a question, or they would never get rid of him.

'So where did you go? What were you doing?' said Sally.

'What was I doing?'

'I mean, did you work? When you were travelling, I mean.'

'Oh. Yes. You know. Bit of this, bit of that. Import, export, you know what I mean.'

'What did you import and export?'

Dougie's eyes flickered. Emily followed their direction to a tin stuck to the wall by the bar. 'Ambassador's Teas, rich and full of flavour.'

'Tea, mostly. Tea. Can't even drink the stuff now. Used to be a lot of money in it. Not now though. It's all coffee now.'

Sally's coat was piled on the bench between them. Emily slid her hand under it and pinched her.

'Ow.' She gave Emily an angry look. 'Dougie, sorry, would you like to join us. Look, there's a stool over there.'

Dougie smiled at them and said. 'Thanks very much. I'll just get myself a drink, you girls all right?'

As soon as he moved away Emily started whispering to Sally.

'What did you do that for? We'll never get rid of him now. You're mad.'

Sally began picking a beer mat to pieces. 'What was I supposed to do? I couldn't be rude, could I? Did you want me to tell him to get lost?'

Emily turned away in irritation. Dougie stood at the bar, occasionally smiling over at them.

Sally prodded her on the shoulder. 'Come on, Em. It'll be a laugh. D'you remember that time he turned up at the flat and we couldn't get rid of him?'

Emily didn't find the memory funny. The two girls had shared a flat with a couple of boys from school. One day, one of the boys turned up with Dougie. They hardly knew him, he was just someone who frequented the same pubs and clubs as they did. But they'd all heard stories of the violence that seemed to surround him. Whispered conversations in the kitchen revealed that Pete had walked around Brighton for hours, hoping to lose him, and then given up and sought safety in numbers.

It was before the incident in the Steine, so Emily wasn't quite as scared as she might have been, but she was scared enough. He seemed to realise and enjoy the fact that he set everyone on edge, taking exaggerated offence at non-insults, and picking up records and ornaments before returning them with a sneer, in the wrong place.

They were certainly too frightened to ask him to leave. At the same time, though, they wondered what on earth he was doing, hanging around with them. Dougie would have been around twenty two at the time, they were all eighteen. He seemed like a very old man.

Dougie returned to the table and laid his pile of Big Issue magazines on top of it, watching their faces as he did so.

'So you're selling the Big Issue?' said Sally.

'That's right. Life's dealt me some twists and turns. Life is hard, as they say. I've ridden the breakers and I've hit the deck. Always pull myself up again though. Some people just aren't born to live safe little lives.'

'No shame in selling the Big Issue,' said Emily. She took a sip of her wine and Dougie registered the large diamond ring on her left hand.

'So do you actually sleep on the street?' Sally was wide eyed.

'At the moment I'm staying with a friend in Lewes.'

'Lewes! Oh that's where Emily lives,' Sally caught a glance from Emily and bit her lip.

'Really? So you're not in Brighton anymore? Whereabouts in Lewes?'

'Oh, up near Shelley's hotel. What about you?

'Welsh Passage.'

'Welsh Passage! That's so cute. Are the houses lovely on the inside?'

'It's tiny. They're only meant for one person really. What street near Shelley's?'

'Pelham Street.'

'Pelham Street . . . that's just off Lancaster . . .'

'Yes that's right. So how long have you been in Lewes?'

'Off and on for a while. As I said, I'm staying with a friend. It's not permanent. I'm still homeless, officially, or they wouldn't let me sell these things.' He smiled. 'Do you still see anyone from the old days?'

'Not really. Sally lives in London now. Most people moved out, I suppose. Oh, there's Ken Baxter, he runs his dad's antique shop in the Lanes. D'you remember Ken?

'No.'

'He was at our sixth form. Used to hang around at the Norfolk. You probably wouldn't remember. Who else . . . ooh, Kevin McReady died. Do you remember him?'

'Yeah, I remember. Bleached hair. Skinny.'

'That's right. Smack.'

Dougie nodded sagely 'There were many casualties. Some people couldn't take it. Didn't have the mental strength.' He stretched out his legs.

'I live in London now,' said Sally.

Dougie smiled at her and turned back to Emily. 'You used to be blonde. Looked good on you.'

'I keep telling her she should go blonde again, Dougie, but she won't listen.'

'You should listen to your friend.' He smiled at her and had another look at her diamond ring. 'So are you married now? Kids?'

'Yes. Married, and I've got a boy. Sam. He's sixteen.'

His eyes locked onto hers. 'Happily married?'

'Of course.' She felt outraged. How dare he ask such a question? He barely knew her. She drank her wine and looked over at Sally's glass to see how she was doing. 'What about you Dougie, any kids?'

'No.' His blue eyes were blank.

There was a pause while everyone took a long drink and then Emily said 'Sal, we're going to have to hurry up.'

For once Sally wasn't being dense. She glugged the last of her wine and looked sheepish as she collected her stuff together and put on her coat. They said goodbye and Dougie smiled to himself as they hurried out of the pub.

One step at a time, he thought. The thing was, with women, you couldn't hurry them. He knew that now. And circumstances had made him a patient man.

8. LURKING

Sam was in a quandary. On the one hand, he knew it was dangerous to go out. Sally was in the house, which meant there was one more person to check. One more person who he had to be sure was asleep. And a person who did not snore, as far as he could tell.

On the other hand, he was feeling very restless. He hadn't been out for days. He wanted some exercise. He wanted to see something other than his attic, to feel the air, to smell something other than his old trainers, which really were beginning to stink the place up. And most of all, he really craved some junk food.

He also would quite like some new porn. He'd spent a lot of the evening on the Internet. So he could have been expected to have as much porn as he wanted, whenever he wanted. The thing was, though, that Sam was not really up on computers. He knew how to use them to do what he wanted and that was it. Computers were his parents' business, and he found their talk of terabytes and motherboards as boring as hell. He had heard that when you looked at porn on line it left files on your computer, nasty stuff that you couldn't get off; and which would eventually be found by his mother, who would know exactly what to look for.

Anyway, he had other stuff to do on the internet, and the people on the MerryPranxsters forum usually went on line in the evening too. They were night owls, like him.

So far, he hadn't actually taken part in chat sessions. He was a 'lurker'. He read other people's contributions but did not participate. He knew that lurkers were kind of frowned upon, but everyone did it really, at some point. And he was getting to know the other posters. It was modern. This was the way modern relationships happened, which was something you couldn't expect his mother and father to understand. They understood the nuts and bolts of the internet, but they didn't have a clue about how it was changing everything, and they wouldn't understand how the people on a web site could have become so important to him. Tizer, for example, might be a boy or a girl or a transsexual, blonde or brunette or bald, but so what? All that didn't matter.

What did matter was that Tizer was responsible for hanging a banner that said 'Wellcome to Hell' over the entrance to the Brighton Marina. Ok, so 'welcome' was spelt wrong and there were a few comments about that, but it made the point. Everyone except for Brighton's planning department knows that the Marina is a vision of hell (with a central car park) and seeing a picture of the banner on the front page of the Argus made Sam feel like he was part of something important, even though he wouldn't recognise Tizer if he saw him, or her, on the street.

Then there was Snoopy3 who climbed the front of Ambassador Heights naked except for a policeman's helmet. He was caught before he could finish the protest, and the papers just had him down as one of people who climb buildings for fun. Actually, as he later said on the Pranxsters' website, he was trying to spray paint a warrant for the arrest of the building's owner. Alfred Sterne was a notorious Brighton property developer who bought up blocks of flats, did no maintenance until the despairing tenants moved out, and then sold the blocks on at a huge profit. Unfortunately Snoopy3 had left the spray can behind in the pocket of his trousers. He said it was a media conspiracy that they had ignored his protest.

Some of the other stunts were a bit childish, graffiti and stuff, but people like that were discouraged. To get big time kudos, the stunt had to be funny and it had to do something. It had to point out the rotten core in the heart of nice, middle class East Sussex.

Sam knew that if he just made one posting he would stop being a lurker, and become part of the group, but every time he was just about to send a post, something stopped him. He wanted to make his first post really special. Nothing he had thought of saying so far seemed clever enough. And he had done nothing that might impress them.

He slipped on his Nikes and tied them, taking his time, listening hard for noises from downstairs. The low, groaning, almost grunting snore, came from his mother. Above that, he could hear his father's squeaky nasal whistle. So far, so good. They had come in late. They always did when Sally was staying. Quite drunk too, from the noise. It was totally sad.

He opened the door and waited, scanning the dark stairs. Then he started to make his way down, missing the third and fifth stair, which creaked, and gripping the banisters on both sides so that his full weight did not reach the floor. On the second floor, he could see that Sally had left her door slightly ajar. This really pissed him off. Was it to spy on him? He almost turned and went back up the stairs, but he was too keyed up, too desperate to get out.

He moved onwards, past the bedrooms and down the stairs to the ground floor, once again almost swinging downwards, from safe step to safe step until he reached the hall. Then he gently lifted his bicycle out from the hall cupboard, cursing at the hoover with which it had become entangled.

Out on the street he moved quickly away from the house, only stopping to take stock as he rounded the corner at the top of the hill. Looking downwards, he could see that Pelham Street was asleep. All the lights were off, save for a soft lamplight glow from the Dixon's front bedroom, and as he watched, he saw that turn off too.

On Neville Road, he turned south, heading towards Brighton. Cars were still passing, mostly in the other direction, back to homes in the countryside after a night on the town. The cars moved slowly and carefully past him and he kept to the small strip of pavement, as far away from the road as possible. He didn't really know what he was scared of. Part of it was that as he spent so long in one room everything in the world outside seemed threatening. Every movement, noise, sight, and smell was accentuated. So unfamiliar were the normal everyday scenes around him that it was as if he was in a foreign country.

Also there were practical concerns. The police might see him and take him back home. Or a car full of beered up wankers, looking for a fight, would stop him to have some fun. It wasn't just the porn and pot noodle that drew him onwards, though. He knew that he had to get used to the world again if he really wanted to be part of the MerryPranxsters. He was getting up his nerve.

Further down the road, things got a bit more difficult. The pavement petered out to a small pathway running along the side of the A27 and he had to watch out for potholes. His wheels caught on bits and pieces of rubbish that had collected at the side of the road. The lighting here was meant for drivers only: the streetlights paced well apart with long passages of darkness in between. The cars came faster too. And noticed him later. A Golf veered towards him, its passengers leaning out of the window shouting something incomprehensible amid their laughter.

He heard a rustling noise from the bushes and forced himself to look forward and concentrate on his destination. Five hundred yards ahead, the Esso sign glistened in the frosty air. He pushed onwards, thinking of the Twix he would eat on the journey back. How he would save a bag of Revels for when he got back, after the Pot Noodle, but he wanted the Twix badly. He wished they wouldn't give out those diaphanous blue bags. You could see straight through them. Once again, he cursed himself for forgetting his rucksack. Then he had an idea. If he bought an Argus he could wrap the porn in that. He wanted an Argus anyway. Wanted to see if they had printed any more pictures of the Pranxsters' latest stunts.

***

Dougie Tate had spent the evening in the pub. He went by himself, but that was OK. It was one of those pubs where men sat at the bar and you could always be sure of conversation, if you weren't too fussy about the content.

Dougie wasn't fussy at all. Julie had been whiny and clingy recently and it was best to knock that sort of thing on the head as soon as possible. The trouble was, though, she hadn't got the message and she was starting to make him angry. She was going to have to have a bit of further education.

The pub had a lock in, and he was enough of a regular customer now to be invited to stay, so he stayed as long as he could to make his point. When he got back to Welsh Passage and tried to get into bed she started to question him, where had he been, why hadn't he told her that he was going out, and all that bollocks. She had to learn.

So instead of taking the rest of his clothes off he had put them back on again. At first she sat up in bed, watching him, and whined some more. He filtered out her voice, so that he saw her opening and closing her mouth but did not listen to the words she was saying. When she saw him putting on his leather jacket she leapt out of bed, ran down the tiny staircase and flung herself against the door, barring his way.

'Don't go,' she said. 'If you go, you can't come back. I mean it, Dougie.' She saw that this wasn't working. Her lip began to tremble.

He looked at her as she stood there, her long T shirt failing to cover up the cellulite on her thighs, her breasts drooping without the aid of a bra. Why did she do this to herself, to him? She was making herself undignified and unattractive. He had fancied her quite a bit once. Why did she have to throw it all away? And everything was working out so nicely too.

The trouble was that it was her house, and her money that paid the bills. This made him uncomfortable, but who could blame him if he didn't want to go back to squatting with junkies and crack heads? This was a chance to make his way out. All he had to do here was make her feel like he loved her. Why did she make it so difficult for him?

He took her by the shoulders and moved her away from the door, looking deeply and sorrowfully into her eyes.

'You need to let me be free,' he said. 'If you give someone their freedom they will come back to you, if you don't, they . . . won't.'

She ran back upstairs, defeated and tearful. He listened to her thudding away and heard the creak of the bed as she flung herself in, then he glanced at himself in the hall mirror and smoothed back his hair.

Outside, he set off into the Lewes night, not knowing where the hell he was going. Lewes had little to offer Dougie at the best of times. At 2.30 in the morning, and with no money to make it down to Brighton, the most it could provide for entertainment was a walk in the cold. And a chance to think through his options for if it all went shit-shaped at Julie's.

He found himself heading towards Shelley's hotel almost as if by automatic pilot. It was a long shot and he wasn't really reckoning on his chances. Emily Fletcher had both a husband and a kid. These could be insurmountable problems. But there was a tiny chance that they could actually work in his favour. If she had really been married for that long, she had to be a bit bored now: in need of some excitement. The middle class ones were always in need of some excitement. A sixteen year old kid wasn't too much of a problem either. He would soon be out of the way. Anyway, it was worth investigating. It was worth, at the very least, checking out what sort of house she had and whether she would be worth the effort. Property was where the money was, these days.

At Shelley's hotel, he turned off the high street into Lancaster Road and began to check off the roads one by one. He wasn't sure which Pelham Street was, but he would find it eventually, if Emily had been telling the truth. He thought that she probably had been. She hadn't had time to make up a lie.

The second turning on the right showed a short street of Victorian houses and he caught his breath until he saw the sign illuminated by a street lamp. Large, three story, bow fronted. The houses were uncommon, on a slightly grander scale than most of the tiny cottages in the area. They were the kind of houses that had those huge basement kitchens where you always saw people having dinner parties, the sorts of dinner parties that he was never invited to. His heart began to thud. This was exactly what he had always wanted and could never get. Why shouldn't he have this life? Why was it always someone else?

He tried to walk as slowly and as casually as possible. There was no one about that he could see, but it was best to be careful. Then he tried to work out which one was Emily's. He decided that he would first walk down one side of the street, and then, maybe later, walk back and look at the other. The street lamps were just about bright enough to pick out some clues.

The first house on the right-hand side had a child's toy on the living room window seat, one of those plastic things with bells and whistles on it, too young for a sixteen year old. The second house was a possibility. In the third he could actually see someone sitting in the basement. This gave him a bit of a shock and he moved on quickly. She had not seen him though, it was a woman, but not Emily. She was feeding a baby and crying at the same time.

At that point, someone else rounded the street corner: a young boy, skinny, mousy-blonde hair, riding a bicycle with a blue carrier bag swinging from its handlebars. The boy dismounted and then walked straight up to the house at the end of the road and let himself in. He gave Dougie a quick glance but it didn't matter. Luckily for Dougie, the breastfeeding woman had scared him into movement, and he looked just like anyone on their way home after a night out.

Dougie walked on, trying to contain his excitement, but making sure that he got a good look as passed the house. It was perfect - even bigger than the rest of the houses on the street. And it was her kid that he'd just seen, he was positive. She'd done all right for herself, then. Emily Fletcher had just gone to the top of his list.

9. SUNDAY LUNCH

'Well, he's not on dope. We'd smell it.' Mark took a sip of his beer. It made him feel a little bit queasy, but he persevered. He needed a hair of the dog after last night. He'd drunk much more than usual.

'But what about the smiley face then? Why did he draw a smiley face on the note? That's all about drugs isn't it? I bet he's on Es. That's what they all take these days.'

Sally smiled. 'You're so behind the times Em. Smiley faces were years ago. It doesn't mean anything. And if he was on Es he wouldn't be all alone up in his bedroom. He'd be out clubbing. It makes you more sociable.' Sally's face became wistful, but she forced herself to concentrate. 'I think he was just trying not to be rude. You know, Sam likes me. We always . . .' she clasped her hands together. 'There's a connection. Anyway, what does he do for money? He can't have money for drugs, can he?'

'Oh he's got money all right.' Emily was bitter. 'Bloody Auntie Ruby. He comes into a lot when he's twenty one, but she also left him some that he can get at now. Supposed to help him through his education. Stop him from dropping out. Well done Auntie Ruby.'

Clare and Tim appeared with a flurry of apologies for their lateness. Tamsin was with them. Emily's heart sank.

'Hi Tamsin,' she said. 'Come and sit down. Do you know Sally? She's a friend of mine from London.'

Tamsin cast her eyes quickly over Sally and said ''Lo.' Then her gaze shifted round the pub, registering the middle-aged, lunchtime crowd with evident disappointment.

They took their seats and began ordering. The Pelham served a great Sunday lunch and they were lucky to get a table, so Emily was prepared to overlook having to clear it themselves. The man and woman on the next table were both smoking and the smoke wafted towards them in a yellow cloud.

'How's it going at school Tam?' said Emily.

'Alright.'

'What are you doing at the moment?'

'GCSEs.'

'Of course. What are your best subjects?'

'Maths, Physics and Chemistry.'

'Goodness!' said Sally. 'I was always hopeless at them.'

Tamsin's gaze said that she had no doubt about this.

Emily gave up. She'd done her bit but the girl was impossible. 'So how are you guys?' she turned to Tim and Clare. 'Haven't seen you for ages. Only just managed to get the bathroom sorted. Builders coming in next week.'

Clare smiled sympathetically. 'How is Sam? Is he OK? We've been a bit worried about him. Haven't we Tim?'

'Oh he's OK.' Emily said quickly. She looked at Tamsin. 'He just needs to grow up a bit.' She struggled for something to change the subject, hoping that someone would chip in to help, but Sally had fallen into a sulk. She'd met Clare and Tim several times before and it had never gone well. They were from totally different ends of Emily's life.

'Car still playing up?' said Tim. The men turned to each other, relieved.

'How long are you here for Sally?' said Clare.

'Not sure really. Depends.'

'Are you not working at the moment?'

'No. Having a bit of a break,' she smiled.

Clare shook her head. 'You are lucky. Having such a flexible career, I mean.'

'Well, it's hardly a career is it?' She looked up at Clare. 'I was working for the council in the bins department. I did the bit where if people dump their rubbish in the street, they open the bag and find something that proves who dumped it, like a letter or something, then I'd have

53

write to them and say 'what are you doing dumping your bins?' and include a photo of the bin.'

'Good god!' said Emily. 'Do they actually do that? Is that what council tax payments go on?'

'Yeah well, you know.' Sally raised her eyebrows.

Clare persevered. 'I'm just so busy at the moment. I really envy you, being able to take a break like that . . .'

'Yes, Sal,' said Emily, 'you're lucky really you know.' Now Emily was getting fed up too. Clare didn't envy Sally at all. She was just being smug. 'Anyway Clare, how are Jenny and James getting on? I've bumped into her, but I never seem to have time to chat these days.'

'Oh, great. She's lovely, isn't she? We went to yoga yesterday. She's not terribly experienced, but she seemed to enjoy it. She's more into sport. Competitive stuff.' She paused. 'She seems to be fitting in really well. Made a lot of friends down here already.'

Lunch arrived and they began to eat.

'You know,' said Clare, chewing in a way that made Emily think of a hamster. 'I think that they're going to do something really special with their house.' Her eyes darted to Emily. 'She seems to be quite secretive about it.'

'What do you mean?' said Emily.

'Well, I was round at hers, you know, just popping in for a cup of tea, and I spotted these plans on the kitchen table, like architect sort of drawings, and I was just saying 'Ooh, what's this then?' and having a look, and she went all flustered and put them away.'

Emily raised her eyes. 'Oh, let her have her secrets. It's not as if I'm likely to be jealous of her logs or pebbles or whatever it is.'

Clare drew herself up, a little smile at the corner of her mouth. 'Oh, I think it's a bit more than that,' she said.

Emily wasn't about to let herself be drawn. She was beginning to pick up on the conversation between Tim and Mark, and something in Mark's voice was making her want to listen.

'So what about your department? Are you sure it's OK? The papers said . . .'

'It's fine. Really. Lot of fuss about nothing. God, there's a lot of potatoes here, aren't there?'

'What's this?' said Emily.

'Potatoes. Do you want some of mine?'

'Something about Direct Credit?'

'Oh, they're shutting down one of the departments. It's nothing to worry about, honestly Em.' Mark looked miserable. Now everyone was staring at him, apart from Sally and Tamsin who were staring at a young man in a tight T shirt who had just entered the pub.

'What department?' said Emily.

Mark felt his face redden. He felt simultaneously cold and sweaty. She would have to know in the end. He had just wanted to get another job sorted out first. Now her curiosity was aroused she would be relentless. If he lied, she would find out anyway. He couldn't keep hiding the Argus from her. They had been running features on it all week. It was big news for a town like Brighton, Direct Credit was a huge employer and the closure of the Neal Street site would have repercussions throughout the town.

He was becoming aware that he had been silent too long. Now everyone, including Sally and Tamsin, the young man in the tight T shirt, and the couple at the next table were staring at him.

He said, 'Can I talk to you about this later Em?'

Emily was white. 'No, you can talk to me now. You're scaring me, Mark. What is it?'

Mark didn't say anything.

Emily said 'Oh, God.'

Mark put down his knife and fork, arranging them on his plate. He took his mobile phone from the table and put it in his jacket pocket. Then he put his jacket on, got up and left the pub.

Emily closed her eyes and squeezed the edge of the table. She stayed this way for a few long seconds while the others stared at their plates, then she got up and followed her husband.

***

Sally gave them a good hour before she went back to the house. Tim, Clare and Tamsin left not long after Mark and Emily. The conversation before they left had been strained. Clare obviously would have liked a post mortem, but Sally wasn't going to discuss her friend and they soon ran out of other things to say. Then the young man in the T shirt had come over and she had spent a pleasant half an hour flirting with him.

When she arrived at the house, all was quiet. She rang and waited for a long time until she heard footsteps in the hall, someone running upstairs and a door slamming, then there were more footsteps and Mark let her in. He looked miserable.

They both made their way down to the basement kitchen and Sally put the kettle on.

'So what are you going to do?' she said at last.

'Get another job, I suppose.'

'Do you get a pay off?'

'Yes, but it won't be much. They've seen to that alright.'

'But you'll be OK, won't you? With all your experience and everything. You'll get another job, no problem.' She placed the tea in front of him and he put both hands around it, feeling the heat of the mug but not drinking.

'There aren't any jobs in Brighton. All there is in Brighton is Direct Credit and American Express. American Express rejected me years ago. It'll mean commuting again, perhaps for years. And I'm not at a good age any more. I should have got further. I'll be competing against people who are ten years younger.'

Sally tried cheerfulness, 'There must be something else in Brighton.'

'Well of course I could have a career change and become a care assistant or sell candy floss on the pier. But

56

the money I'd make wouldn't even pay back the loan on the kitchen, let alone the mortgage.'

Sally was beginning to feel awkward. She was out of her depth. For the first time she was glad that she'd never got it together to buy her flat off the council. The rent was derisory. Even with her intermittent wages she had a good lifestyle. They sat in silence while she tried to think of something comforting to say.

'What about Emily?' she said at last. 'She's told me loads of times that she could earn more if she worked in London.'

Mark groaned and buried his head in his hands. Things couldn't possibly get worse.

10. NEW STARTS

Jenny applied her lipstick and then grimaced at the mirror, checking her teeth.

'Can you be back on time tonight?' she said.

'Boys' night,' said James. 'Sorry. We're going for a curry. Told you last week.'

'Oh damn,' she said. 'Do you have to? Dad said the notices were sent out on Friday, so the neighbours should get it today.'

James continued buttoning his shirt.

Jenny felt herself beginning to whine. 'You know what'll happen. They'll be round here as soon as I get back from work.'

He considered for a moment. He really didn't want to give up his night out. What with the move and everything he hadn't seen the guys for a couple of weeks. It was important to keep up with your mates. He needed to make a stand.

'You'll be all right.' He held his wrists out for Jenny to put on his cufflinks. They were his favourites, little gold rugby balls, worn especially because it was boys' night. 'Look, if they come round, just invite them for a drink or something on Tuesday. Tell them we'll go through the plans with them then.'

Jenny bit back a complaint. She was glad James had nights out with the boys. She didn't want them to be one of those couples who spent all their time together. It wasn't healthy. She thought she might work late. There would be plenty to catch up on after her break. She really didn't want to be at home on her own. The husband, Mark, would probably be OK, but Emily was going to be a nuisance, Jenny just knew it.

'Whatever we do they're not going to like it, so there's not much we can tell them,' she said. She checked her watch. 'If we don't go now, we'll miss the train.'

Emily and Sally sat at the kitchen table in silence, drinking their tea. Emily was still in her dressing gown and the kitchen was unusually messy, washing up piled in the sink, smears on the granite worktop and crumbs on the oak table.

'I'm sure he'll get something,' said Sally. 'Look, don't worry. There's always jobs, you know.'

Emily wished that Sally would shut up. She just had no idea. Sure, there were always jobs for temporary secretaries in London. Mark's case was a little bit different. For a start, they didn't live in London. The Sussex job market was a standing joke. And the thing was that his landing a permanent job had lulled them into state of stupidity. He was too old for most people to want to employ now at his level. Why should they, when they could get younger people much cheaper? Plus he was no good for freelance work either. The technology they used at Direct Credit was ancient by modern standards. No one used it any more. To get a contract Mark would need to have a whole raft of new skills and the time and money to acquire them. They were well and truly stuffed.

'It's not that simple, Sal,' she said.

There was a warning note in her voice that irritated her friend. Emily was always so gloomy about everything. Everything was always doom and gloom. Sally wouldn't have come down to visit if she'd known this was going to happen.

They finished breakfast in silence, both thinking the same thing: how to cut short Sally's visit. Emily wanted her friend out of the way at least by tonight. She and Mark needed to sit down and talk through the money situation. Work out exactly what they were going to do.

They heard the squeak of the letterbox being opened upstairs and the thud of mail falling on the mat.

'Postman,' said Sally.

'I'll get it on the way up,' said Emily. 'It won't be anything exciting.'

'Are you going to have it done, then?' Sally was talking about the hair appointment they had made on Saturday. She had talked Emily into having blonde streaks put into her hair. It had seemed a good idea after a glass of wine in the Basketmakers.

'Oh, I don't know, Sally. It seems a bit stupid now. It's expensive, isn't it? And then you have to keep on having it done or it looks a mess and it's more money every time.'

'Well, why bother to get out of bed at all? The sky might fall in or you may get hit by a bus crossing the street.'

They sat in silence, biting their tongues. Sally looked up at Emily's miserable face and felt a little bit guilty.

'You know, you should still go. It'll make you feel better. More positive. The trouble with you, Em . . . Don't get mad ok? The trouble with you is that you let things get you down. Have your bloody hair done. When's the last time you thought about your looks? It's good for you. Put you in fighting spirit. Always works for me.'

Emily smiled. Sally was a silly cow, but actually, she might have a point.

'OK,' she said. 'Let's do it.'

'And after that, I'm going home,' said Sally.

Emily said 'OK.'

They both got up and started up the stairs to go and get ready. As they reached the ground floor, Emily went to pick up the mail, but Sally took hold of her arm.

'No. You're not looking at any bank statements or anything today. I see it as my moral duty to stop you.'

Emily laughed and they continued up the stairs.

***

Dougie was getting fed up. It was unusually quiet in his spot outside Infinity Foods. Normally the shop was thronged with well-meaning organic-food-eating hippies who were an easy target for the Big Issue. Today, the weather was letting him down. It was that sort of endless drizzle that only seaside towns seem to produce, and people scurried past, hidden by their umbrellas and hooded parkas. He stood, umbrellaless, trying to keep dry under the shop's canopy, but the rain got him regardless. It seemed to move horizontally, showering fine clouds of spray in all directions, so that he was constantly having to wipe his face, and he could feel his leather jacket becoming clammy as it soaked up the moisture.

In the end he was too miserable to do a good job of it and went to the café for a warming cup of tea. Inside, everything steamed. He took off his jacket and hung it near to the radiator, and then he took a seat at the window bar, wiped a small porthole in the condensation and watched the weather with resignation. It didn't look as if it was ever going to let up. It would be like this until spring.

So what was he going to do? Julie was starting to pester him about getting a job and he was running out of excuses to give her. She was even trying to set him up with some decorating work. Julie was a teacher, and this was the sort of bossy, patronising attitude he should have expected.

He did need to do something, though. Her wages weren't as bad as she made out. He'd had a look at her bank statement. But she obviously didn't want to go on supporting him forever. Not now the first flush of passion was over. She wanted him to sort himself out. And this was something he was keen to do, too. He needed a sideline. The only question was, what should it be? He needed some new contacts, or he needed to rekindle some old ones.

Just at that moment, he saw Emily. She walked out of Kensington Gardens and crossed the road, umbrella held high and a small smile on her face. She looked a vision with blonde, styled hair. Ten years younger than the last time he'd seen her. Beautiful. Well, if not exactly beautiful, she had something, a presence that he always knew was there, that hadn't been buried completely.

He didn't get up and go after her. He remembered that he didn't look too good himself. No, he would wait and do things properly. He felt content to wait and plan now. She'd dyed her hair. That was enough. He had told her that she should do it, and she had. There could be no more obvious sign of her interest. Now he needed a plan that would jolt her the rest of the way into his arms.

**

Emily, of course, had forgotten discussing her hair with Dougie at all. It was Sally who had persuaded her to do it and Sally was right. It made her feel much better and she was already seeing the future more positively. Mark would get another job. Even if it took a while. They still had the house, after all, and it was worth so much now, she could hardly believe it. If necessary, they could re mortgage a little bit. Not too much though.

The house was their retirement plan. They'd given up on pensions. Instead, they'd decided to do everything they could to the house, improve it and keep it nice. And then one day they'd use it to fund their retirement. Emily was sentimental about the house, but was enough of a realist to know that it wasn't just a home, it was their major investment.

And she'd had an idea about Sam. It was an idea of such amazing simplicity that she was astounded at her previous stupidity. She would write him a letter and pop it under the door. Once he knew that she wasn't going to tell him off, that everything would be all right, he would come out, she was sure of it. She just had to say that he didn't have to go back to school or do anything else that he didn't want to do. And that she loved him.

She decided to make her way straight home and write the letter. There wasn't much on at the moment and the work she'd planned on doing could wait until tomorrow. Now she'd thought of the idea she wanted to do it straight away.

It would make up for everything if Sam just came out of the attic. Everything. They would be a family again and nothing could affect them.

11. DEALING WITH THE MAIL

Jenny hadn't really enjoyed her first day back at work after the move. It all seemed different these days. It wasn't as if she disliked the people she was working with. They were all perfectly fine. It was just that she felt kind of out of things. One by one her old friends had left to have babies and the new girls were just that bit younger. They hung around together.

She had sixty-three emails waiting for her on her return. This annoyed her a bit. She remembered when they had gone skiing, was it only a year ago? She'd had over 150 then. Now she was out of the loop. It didn't matter that the emails were generally rubbish that she binned straight away. She was still out of the loop.

James was all right. She saw him in the corridor and then again on his way to lunch with the boys. He was laughing and joking. Glad to be back. She had a sandwich at her desk. They didn't tend to mix much at work. That would have been too much. Sometime she was a bit annoyed to find out that the younger girls had joined the boys at the pub. Then she realised that she used to do exactly the same thing.

It was about time she got pregnant. She didn't want to be one of those women who were pushing forty when they started. And she wanted at least two. Maybe they shouldn't wait until all the work had been done on the house like they'd planned. Maybe they should start a bit sooner.

In the end she dealt with the urgent stuff and then put her laptop in her bag. She'd either finish off on the train or back at the house. James wouldn't arrive until the last train. It seemed to be a point of honour with him to come back as late as possible after a boys' night, so she'd be sure of a free evening.

She was trudging over London Bridge, cursing the weight of her laptop, when she remembered about the planning application. It was too late to avoid it now, she'd have to go back to the house. There was nowhere else to go.

***

Emily spent all afternoon on the letter. The first draft was three pages long, full of her concern and worry, speculation about what had gone on at school, criticisms of the friends who didn't phone him anymore.

She sat and read it through a few times. Then she tore it up and wrote:

Darling Sam
I'm so sorry that you won't come downstairs. Please come down. If you do, I promise that there won't be any arguments and no one will shout at you. If you want us to help you decide what to do about school, we will do, but it will be up to you.
I know that you must feel that we haven't been very good parents, and we have clearly gone wrong somewhere, but I guarantee that things will be better in the future.
Love from
Mum

She thought that this was probably the best she could do, but she wondered whether she should run it past Mark first. She made two cups of tea, put on the dishwasher and separated the laundry while she thought about it, but eventually decided that Mark would probably start adding things and changing it and they would be back to square one.

Feeling nervous, she trudged up the stairs to the first floor landing, then she read the letter through again whilst climbing the steps to the attic. Outside the door, she took a deep breath and posted it through. Then she went straight back downstairs. She didn't want him to think she was hanging around to hear if he read it.

Sam froze when he heard his mother climbing the stairs. He saw the note slide under the door and heard her footsteps retreating but remained frozen, still holding the magazine he was reading.

He stared at the letter for a long time, as if it was some kind of booby trap or a Trojan horse that his mother would shortly spring out of, berating him or giving him orders. Sending that note to Sally had been stupid. It had given her the idea. Now, if he read the letter, it would be putting the ball back in her court. He would be listening to her again. She would be inside his head, pulling all those little strings that she knew how to pull so well. The only answer with her was to deny her any access at all.

The trouble was, the letter itself was a little string, and it was pulling at him already. He just couldn't help himself. He had to see what it said.

He read it through twice in disbelief. It was a nice letter. He felt his eyes stinging a bit and blinked very hard. He remembered some of the good things that his Mum had done. He tried to push them out of his mind, but couldn't. There was the time, for instance, when his friends went bowling without him and talked about it all the next day at school. She had just put her arms around him and let him cry. She hadn't even suggested that it was his fault, like she normally did. Alright, that was nearly six years ago, but she had been nice. And then, when he was ill with glandular fever and she had brought him all his favourite foods and let him sit on the sofa with his feet up and watch cartoons. She had always been mad, with her rages and incomprehensible rules and regulations: her coaster hierarchy and colour coded cloths for different types of cleaning. But it was only recently that things had started to go really wrong.

Perhaps this was his way out. If he could come downstairs with no arguments, no shrieking and pushing and pulling, maybe he should. He couldn't stay up there forever, after all. He looked at the time. Six o'clock. His Dad would be home in half an hour. If he was going to do it he might as well wait. His Dad would be added protection, just in case.

***

The morning's mail still lay on the hall table where Emily had left it. Now she picked it up and carried it downstairs to the kitchen.

She made yet another cup of tea and tried not to listen for noises from upstairs. Dealing with the mail would be a distraction. Anyway, she could see that their bank statement was at the top of the pile, and she did need to go through it.

She scanned the row of figures, frowning with annoyance at some of the items. Had she really spent so much on the new wine glasses? They were supposed to be an investment but one of them was broken already. Then there were the figures for the mortgage and the loan that they had taken out to pay for the kitchen. It was bad, but when she thought about the house's value, it was also money well spent. Perhaps they could restructure. Add the amount of the loan to the mortgage or something. She should suggest it to Mark.

The next letter was a circular for the historical society. This irritated her. Why the hell didn't they use email?

Then there was an application form for a new credit card with a free pen. She removed the pen and screwed the application into a ball, hurling it towards the bin.

Finally, there was one from the council. Emily sighed. Did they want more council tax or something? As she removed the letter from the envelope her interest awakened. 'Planning application No. 5552424: 8 Pelham Street, Lewes'. 'Ah ha,' she thought. 'So this is what next door is up to.' She took the letter over to the sofa so that she could study the details in comfort.

She read aloud '. . .writing to let you know that blah blah blah. The proposal may affect you or your neighbourhood . . . invite you to comment, blah blah blah.' She scanned down the page until she found what she wanted. 'The proposed work: Construction of a two story extension and roof terrace.'

She stopped. Her first feeling was one of jealousy. Here she was, cutting back on things, the future looking pretty bleak, and there they were, building a huge bloody extension. And they were younger too. Just because they had rich parents. It was bloody typical. Next she thought of the mess and noise it was all going to cause. It would be hell for months. She had to work upstairs. She thought about moving her desk into the bedroom at the front of the house. There was room enough, but she would miss her view.

Her stomach contracted. If they built a two story extension, there would be no view. Not ever again. She would be looking out into a tunnel, boxed in by their extension. She thought of her beautiful patio garden, the roses, the camellia, the new palm tree in its massive terracotta pot. She had been able to plant the garden as she had because it had strong sunlight from the South West. Sometimes in the summer they could sit out in the garden until around nine, still getting sunburnt. That would all go. Her stomach clenched again and she thought she might be sick. What would happen to the kitchen? The basement kitchen only had one real window. They got some daylight from the lightwell at the front of the house but they relied on the light streaming in through the patio doors to the garden. The kitchen would become a dungeon and the garden the bottom of a lift shaft.

She sat up straight, holding the letter. Her skin seemed to be behaving oddly. It felt waxy, greasy, and yet somehow dry. She took some deep breaths and then went to look in the mirror. She had forgotten about the hair. It sat, perfect and helmet-like on the top of her head, completely at odds with the distressed face that it surrounded. She looked weird, but couldn't put her finger on why. There wasn't anything noticeably wrong. Except for her eyes. Her eyes didn't look right.

Hardly trusting herself to perform such a simple action, she unbolted the kitchen door and walked out into the back garden. Even now, six o'clock on an October evening, the concrete patio was warm and the plants along the eastern wall were lit by the sun.

She gazed up at the house next door. Its windows were dark but she noticed that they had put a new light fitting in the back bedroom. It was from one of the new ranges at Habitat. Really expensive and totally unsuitable for the house. And that was when she lost her temper.

12. VARIOUS APPROACHES

Sam heard the front door slam. He was waiting for his Dad to come in, but the sound was jarring, abnormal. It didn't sound like his Dad. He never slammed the door.

The next thing he heard was hammering on a door somewhere nearby. Next door, probably. He went over to the Velux window and looked out but the angle was wrong. He wouldn't be able to see anything unless he stuck his head right out of the window, and he wasn't going to do that.

The hammering persisted. It wasn't as if someone was knocking the door. It was more the sound you would get if you used the side of your fist to bash it. Then he heard his mother's voice. She was shouting 'I know you're in there. Open the bloody door.'

***

Actually, Emily had just realised that Jenny probably wasn't in there. Also her hands were beginning to hurt, so she gave the door a frustrated kick. She needed to see Jenny, to make her say that she wasn't going to do it. That she'd changed her mind. That this was just a nightmare and everything would go back to normal. Her mind could not countenance any other possibility. If she could just see Jenny and make her realise . . .

Then Mark was hurrying up the street towards her, looking around to make sure that none of the neighbours were watching. He grabbed her arm and hustled her back into the house.

She started shouting before he could close the door. 'Do you know what the fucking bitch has done?'

He pushed her down the stairs to the basement and she stumbled downwards, shouting as she went. 'Get OFF me. The fucking, fucking bitch. Fucking get off me Mark.'

He grabbed hold of her arms and turned her so that they were facing each other. Then he shouted 'SHUT UP' into her face.

She slumped and was silent. He let go of her arms, watching her face as he did so. She shot him a look that was full of loathing and then walked over to the table, picked up the letter and handed it to him.

He sat down and looked through it. Then he read it again, tapping his fingers on the table. Eventually, he looked up at her. 'It'll be alright,' he said. But he wouldn't meet her eyes.

'No it fucking won't be alright.' She started shouting again. 'Don't you understand, you fucking dick. There'll be no light. Not down here. Not in the garden. No view. It will be totally shit.'

He was silent.

'Do you have any fucking idea,' she enunciated the words, 'any fucking idea how much this will reduce the value of the house. Do you? Do you?' She sat down on the sofa and hid her head in her hands.

They were silent for a few minutes and then Mark got up and went out into the back garden. He spent a few minutes looking around, looking at the sun, looking at the backs of the houses. Then he went back into the kitchen. Emily was still sitting in the same position. He picked up the letter again.

'It says we can object,' he said. 'Look Em,' he waved the letter in front of her but she did not look up. 'We can object,' he said again.

They sat in silence for some time.

***

Sam was beside himself. Throughout the shouting he had pressed his ear to the door but he couldn't make out any of the words. He just knew that his mother had totally flipped. Now he was pacing back and forth in the attic. He felt very nervous. Very edgy. Would they come upstairs? Was she shouting about him? Given that she had just sent him the note he had to think so. But what was all that about next door?

He heard the back door go, and went over to the window that looked out onto the garden. His father appeared and walked to the back wall. He seemed to look up, and Sam tucked himself out of view, but his father didn't actually seem to be looking at the attic.

He couldn't believe that he had nearly gone downstairs. He was stupid, stupid, stupid. This was a mad house. He wasn't going to go down and be part of their madness ever again. No. He was going to work out a way to escape.

***

Mark and Emily came to an agreement. They decided that he should go, alone, to speak to Jenny and James. Emily had agreed because she knew he was right. If she went round there she would probably punch Jenny, or at least lose her temper, whereas Mark might have a slight chance of getting them to see reason.

Of course, Mark didn't want to do this at all. He was good at bringing people together, solving problems, reaching consensus, which was why, incidentally, Direct Credit were really stupid to get rid of him. But now, while he took his time tying his shoe laces (although he hadn't even taken off his shoes), he knew that his conciliatory skills were going to be useless. People didn't put in planning applications without thinking through the consequences. They only did it if they really wanted to build something. Mark didn't want to remind Emily about it, but now his mind flashed back to the dinner party and that business about her father. He would have advised her on this. They knew what they were doing and they were going to do it.

Still, he had to go round there. He could tell from the look on Emily's face that if he didn't, she would. She would only make the situation worse. She always did: her history of upsetting people and putting their backs up reached way back through their relationship. She never seemed to grasp the fact that it didn't matter who was right. The only thing that mattered was what pressure you could bring to bear on people.

***

Clare would have understood. That morning, when she received her copy of the application, she opened it straight away. Then she sat at her kitchen table for several minutes and calmly thought things through. After a few minutes she had made up her mind. She called in sick at work, turned the answering machine on and pressed the OFF button on her mobile. If people tried to phone her, she would say she had gone back to sleep.

She made herself a cup of coffee and took it to her armchair in the living room, adjusting the chair a little so that it faced the window to the street. Then she waited.

Soon, she saw Emily and Sally heading off towards town, they were glum looking, but, Clare was sure, Emily had not yet seen the application. Clare was not entirely certain what Emily would do when she had seen it, but she wouldn't be going out with Sally. And she would certainly have phoned or come round. Surely Emily would want to sound her out as soon as she knew about it?

So she assumed that Emily had not read her mail, and was setting off for a day out with Sally, probably to Brighton. This was exactly what Clare wanted. She finished her coffee and put on her coat, then set off to the planning office. She would have a little time to work out how all this would affect her, and what she wanted to do.

By the evening, she had decided. It was going to be a nuisance. The roof garden would overlook her patio, that was the worst thing, but it was on Emily's side of the garden, not hers, so provided that she could get Jenny to put up a decent amount of fencing it wouldn't be so bad. It certainly wouldn't be as bad as for Emily. It would be absolutely dreadful for Emily. If it had been on the other side, that would have been a different matter, but the Kimptons had just had a child and weren't in the position to lay out money for expensive extensions. Besides, they had a new conservatory, put in at the same time as Clare's. They certainly weren't about to pull that down.

All in all, it might not be so bad. If she supported Jenny and James she would put them in her debt. She wasn't quite sure how she could use this, but it might come in handy at some point. It was one of the guiding principles in her life, sort of like karma: that doing stuff for other people, where possible, was a good idea. The universe was based on such principles. Yin and yang and all that stuff. What goes around comes around. To Clare, what that meant was that if people owed you, you could get them to do things. It would obviously be better if the development didn't happen at all, so at the same time she could subtly encourage Emily to object. It was a shame about Emily. It would quite ruin her house. And after all the work she'd done too.

Clare counted the hours until she knew Jenny was due home. Then she set off on a slow walk down the High Street, scanning the returning commuters until she spotted a red faced Jenny, lugging a large bag up the hill.

When Mark knocked on James and Jenny's door a few minutes later, Clare and Jenny were already deep in conversation in the bar of the Shelley's hotel.

13. LOSS OF LIGHT

The next day, Emily was waiting outside the planning office when it opened at nine o'clock. She was third in the queue. It seemed that everyone was planning something these days.

Once inside she joined another queue for Enquiries, who told her to join another queue to get copies of the plans. Once she had them, she could join another queue to talk to a planning officer about them.

She sat outside the planning officer's cubicle, looking through the drawings, which were not really meaningful to her, and the application form, which she understood a little better. 'Two story extension with roof terrace.' There it was again, in black and white.

She worked her way through the plans, and then, for want of anything better to do, she began to study the planning officer, wondering how best to approach him. He was a small man, with a white, pinched face and round glasses. He didn't look like he'd respond to charm or flirtation, even if she'd been very good at that sort of thing. It was probably best to be businesslike: calm and professional.

Several minutes passed before he looked up from his papers and gestured her into the cubicle.

She sat down. 'It's about the application on 8 Pelham Street,' she said.

There was a pause.

'How can I help you,' he said.

'Well, can they do it?' The plans felt sweaty in her hands. Surely he would need to look at them.

'Do you have the details? Yes, you do.'

She passed him the plans and he laid them out on the table. Then he looked through the application form. Emily was getting annoyed. Why wasn't he saying anything? He didn't really seem to be taking anything in. There was something about the way he was looking at the plans that made her feel like he wasn't really studying them at all. Not like the way she had poured over them, flipping between drawings, trying to work out scales.

'So you see, I live next door, and this wall here,' she half rose in her chair so that she could point to the appropriate line on the diagram, 'this wall is right up against my garden.'

'You'll be Number 6 then.'

'That's right. Number 6.'

'We wrote to you. We wrote to number 6 and number 10. Look, it says so here. Number 6 and number 10. So you can object if you want.' He looked up, as if this should end the conversation.

'But can they do it? It'll ruin our house.'

'Well if you think it will ruin your house you can say so in your objection.' He was folding the plans up now.

'But will they listen to me?'

'Of course they'll listen to you. They'll listen to everyone and work out what is best for the neighbourhood. Is there a precedent? Has anyone else built anything like it in the road?'

Emily thought for a moment. 'Well, one house on the other side has an extension, but he's on the end of the road, so it doesn't affect anyone else.'

He sucked his teeth. 'That's a precedent. If there's a precedent they usually allow it.'

Emily felt her head drooping. All she wanted to do now was go home and wrap herself in her duvet.

He shuffled the papers together and handed them to her, watching her with interest. He coughed, and then said 'How will it ruin your house?'

'It's the view,' she said. 'We've got this view of the castle. And the Downs. It'll take the view away.'

'Views aren't permissible. You can't object on grounds of a view.'

'Why the hell not?' Her plan to stay calm and persuasive was unravelling. 'It's why we bought the house. It'll totally devalue it.'

'House values aren't permissible either. Let me show you something.' He took back the pile of paperwork and rifled through it, then he pointed to a bulleted list on the back of one of the pages. 'Here's what you can object to.'

She took the list and scanned it. Nothing seemed useful. She couldn't object because of parking problems or cooking vents. 'Loss of light,' she said at last. 'We'll lose the light out of our basement. Look, it says we can object for loss of light.' She felt hopeful for the first time since she had seen the application.

He did not seem to share her relief. 'There you go then,' he said. 'You can give that a try.' He passed the sheet of paper back to her and stood up. 'Good luck.' He tried to smile, but wasn't very good at it. 'Some things aren't worth upsetting yourself about. If I were you, I'd go home and look at the plans thoroughly. Have a chat with your neighbours.' He looked at her, holding her eyes for a fraction of a second, 'and then make up your mind to live with it. You could do the same thing yourself. Might add to the value of your house.'

She kept her voice steady. 'I don't want to do the same thing. We'd just got the house perfect. It's perfect. We couldn't afford it anyway. And it wouldn't give us back our light.'

She picked up her bag and walked out before he could see that she was starting to cry.

She couldn't bear to go home straight away: to sit in her study and think of her disappearing view, or in the kitchen, dwelling on how dark and gloomy it would become, or anywhere in the house, thinking of the ghost in the attic. So in the end she took a detour to the Grange Gardens, the park where she used to take Sam when they had just moved to Lewes. He was six then, a lovely little boy, blonde and skinny. So enthusiastic and friendly. She would sit on the bench and watch anxiously while he kicked a ball around or played with his friends.

She sat down and stared at the huge ancient tree in front of the Grange. It looked like it had been struck by lightning, its massive trunk and short thick branches were grey and ancient looking, but still, hopelessly, it continued to produce little shoots of life.

Last night had screwed things up with Sam. She couldn't be certain that he would have come downstairs but it was the most hope she'd had in months. Flipping her lid like that was the worst possible thing that she could have done, but she couldn't help it. It was all for Sam's benefit really, even if he wouldn't understand that right now. The house was his home too for Christ's sake.

She thought about Jenny with her smug little face and her swinging pony tail. Emily didn't really consider James in all of this. Everyone knew that women decided these sorts of things. She'd just walked into a town, where she didn't belong, and decided to screw up Emily's life. She was just a total bitch.

It was a miserable day. Not cold, but with a sky of woollen grey interspersed with small black clouds. Every few minutes the clouds would block the sun almost completely and wash the park in a thick shadow. The park's only other occupants, a woman with a buggy and a toddler on its buggy board, moved down the path to the exit. The woman was checking the sky and answering her little girl's chatter in monosyllables.

Then Emily was alone. She let her face crease into an agony of misery and hatred, but no tears came. She no longer wanted to cry, she wanted to hit out, to take Jenny's smiling, perky face and drag it through one of the muddy puddles by the flowerbeds. She wanted to do something to this woman who was ruining her home, taking away her hard won financial security and stopping her son from coming back to her. She wanted to take her and punch her until . . . she didn't know what.

The blackest cloud had now almost eclipsed the sun, but Emily stayed, transfixed by the movement of the trees and unable to move into the future.

'Emily.'

She heard her name and sat up straight. A hand touched her shoulder.

'Emily Fletcher! I thought it was you! What are you doing here, luv, all on your own?' It was Dougie Tate.

It wasn't an accident that Dougie had appeared in the park at exactly that moment. He'd seen her leave the planning office and couldn't believe his luck. Then he'd followed her, stopping only to check his reflection in the window of Lewes Collectables, and had actually been in the park for as long as Emily, keeping out of sight until the moment was right.

'What's up luv? You look dead miserable.'

She tried to pull herself together, annoyed that he'd caught her looking like this.

'Oh, you know, life. Nothing much. How are you Dougie?'

'I'm good, really.' He sat down beside her and looked straight ahead at the trees. 'You're not alright. Are you, luv?'

He turned towards her and she looked away. It was the first time anyone had seemed concerned about her since . . . she couldn't remember.

'You know, sometimes it helps to talk about stuff, to people who are outside your situation . . . Assists in the clarification process. Know what I mean?'

She smiled a little, wondering where he had picked up some of his new expressions.

'It's just a planning issue. The people who live next door to us want to build something that's not going to be good for our house. She explained a little about the extension, knowing that this would probably bore him, but glad anyway of the excuse to talk about it.

Dougie didn't seem to be getting bored though. He was looking at her as if he really cared about what she had to say. For a moment she forgot that this was someone that she really should keep at arms' length. It was good to talk to someone who had known her when she was young and feisty, before the world had kicked in and happened to her. She felt more like her old self.

'So this will devalue your property?'

Once again she was shocked to hear adult sounding phrases coming out of Dougie's mouth. But then, they were all older, weren't they?

'It'll kill it. You know how they say houses need to have a 'wow' factor? Well we had the view and the lovely basement kitchen. It'll take thousands off, plus we'd spent a lot of money on the place. We'd wanted to stay there for ages. It was perfect. We'd just got it perfect.'

She told him about the meeting at the planning office and how there didn't seem to be much hope that she could fight the application.

'Her Dad's a builder. I get the feeling they know what they're doing. Oh God, I've just realised something . . . her Dad owns a big building firm. Probably knows all sorts of people. I bet he's fixed it.'

Dougie sat in silence for a while. Emily started to get up but he put a hand on her arm.

'Wait a sec. There's more than one way to skin a cat.' He paused. 'What about if I warn them off?'

'What do you mean?' Emily's mind was ticking fast.

'Just tell them that their proposal isn't such a good idea.'

'What do you mean?' she said again.

'Look, if I was to go up to him one day, or her, and just say 'I don't think you should be doing that, mate. It might not be an advisable course of action.' What do you think they'd do?'

'Well, they'd ignore you. Or you might get into trouble for threatening them.'

'Number one, I wouldn't say anything threatening. Number two, I'd make sure there were no witnesses.'

They continued to sit, Emily staring ahead, watching shards of rain bounce with increasing frequency into a puddle.

'Why would you?' she said. 'Why would you bother?'

He shifted round on the bench so that he was facing her. 'I just don't like it that some people get away with shitting over everyone else. I don't like it when bad things happen to good people.'

Emily blushed a little. 'It's raining properly now,' she said. 'I'd better go.' She gathered herself together and then glanced at him. 'Look Dougie, if you were to do anything like that, I wouldn't know anything about it, would I?'

He smiled at her and raised his finger to his lips.

***

Emily walked home feeling lighter on her feet, more buoyant, and besides, she was in a hurry to get down to work. The rain came harder and thunder was grumbling somewhere nearby, but she just pushed up the hood on her parka and ploughed on.

What Dougie had said, what she had not told him not to do, kept repeating in her mind. It was nothing though, she thought, was it, really? Nothing. Just a five minute conversation in a park. If she moved really quickly she could just pretend it hadn't happened. The faster she went, the more it would disappear behind her.

Besides she hadn't asked him to do anything. He might have decided to do it all by himself. And not said a word to her about it. There was nothing to connect her to Dougie Tate anyway. He probably wouldn't do anything. It was probably all talk.

She was shocked to realise how disappointed this made her feel. Because if it worked, if he got them, or, say, James on his own, alone somewhere quiet, say going up Pipe Passage on the way back from work, and he stopped him and said it in that menacing Dougie Tate way, it would be bound to work. Who would risk annoying Dougie Tate? Even without knowing his reputation he looked scary. He looks like he doesn't care, and there's nothing scarier than that. She felt a little frisson of power. They'd respect her a little more after that. She wasn't the middle-aged nobody they took her for. She had a past. She had connections in the underworld.

They'd be angry, but what could they do? Go ahead and risk Dougie? Call the police and risk Dougie?

Climbing up Keere Street slowed her. The road was so steep she had to concentrate so she didn't fall on the wet cobbles.

If they did call the police, that would be the worst thing. She would look guilty, give herself away. This thought sobered her until she reached the top of the hill.

The best thing to do would be to wipe the last few minutes from her memory. It never happened. It was all just getting on top of her. That was all. It wasn't as if Mark was any use. Everything was always left up to her. Nevertheless, Mark didn't need to know anything about it. She would just keep quiet, wait and watch.

14. MOVING ON

'There's a job in Horsham. SunAlliance. Look.' Mark handed her the middle section of The Guardian.

Emily scanned through the details. 'That's two grand less than what you're getting now.'

Mark huffed. 'Well it's better than nothing, isn't it? I'd be bloody lucky to get it. Bloody hell, Em.'

Emily shrugged and continued to read. 'Do you have all this then, 'ERP, ITIL, CRM, COBIT'? God, how does anyone understand anything these days? Even I don't understand all of them. What's ERP anyway?'

'That's all right. I've got that. It's more the COBIT that's a problem. Is it OK if I go upstairs and get my CV together? I'll put it in the Mark directory.'

He got up to leave, then turned back, remembering. 'Oh, you wanted me to go and see next door, didn't you?'

Emily felt flustered. 'You know what,' she said, 'I don't think we should talk to them until we've decided exactly what our position is.'

'What do you mean? We know what our position is. You were ready to crucify them yesterday.'

Since her conversation with Dougie, Emily had been trying to work out what best to do. If Dougie were to come through it would be better if they kept their distance from the whole thing. If Dougie did say anything it would have to look like someone else had put him up to it. If they started weighing in with objections it would be too obvious that it was them. Before Emily did anything she wanted a chance to think through the possible scenarios.

'No,' she said. 'You apply for the job. That's more important really.' Mark was still looking at her in confusion. 'Look, I don't know . . . I just want to think about the best way to go about it. I've got a feeling we've missed something. I need to go through the plans. We've got 21 days to object.'

Mark was just starting up the stairs when Emily shouted after him.

'Don't pick up the phone up,' she said 'I don't want to talk to Clare.'

Mark went into the bedroom first, to change out of his suit. He reached for a T-shirt at the bottom of the pile. They weren't going anywhere. No point in wearing anything good. The one he pulled out had a picture of a deranged cartoon rabbit on the front and bore the slogan 'Life in Hell'. It had been bought as a joke during one far off journey to the States. He stared at it for a moment before putting it back. Emily would go mad if he put that on. It would be like he was making some sort of statement.

But actually, it summed things up. Only the joke was on him. His life was hell. Wasn't hell supposed to be a spiral? Well that was how his life was: an endless spiral of misery leading to further misery. And he still hadn't told Emily about the car yet. It made a terrible noise on the way back from work. She was going to flip.

Mark had a favourite fantasy, one that he was indulging in more frequently these days. He was living on his own in a flat. The flat was in Brighton or London. He had girlfriends and a Lotus Elise. At the weekends he would go to Paris or Rome or Amsterdam. Sam was not in the fantasy, which was the most guilt-inducing thing of all. Sometimes he tried to work him in, an older Sam, who didn't need him anymore. They were more like mates. But it didn't really work because the adult Sam wasn't recognisable.

Leaving Emily was, of course, impossible. They were tied together in every way. He couldn't work out if he still loved her, but that seemed to be irrelevant. It was Sam mostly, he couldn't even think about leaving while Sam was behaving like this. Then there was the house and the combined mess of their finances and his job, and now this new pressure with the people next door. The trouble was that they were a team. That sounded like a good thing, but he wasn't so sure any more. They seemed to be slaves to the goals of the MarkandEmily team. It wasn't making them happy, but happiness seemed always to be very low down the list of things to do.

He put on a surfer T-shirt and went through to Emily's study.

**

Sam heard the chair creak in the room below. This was unusual. His mum had strict rules about working in the evenings. There were all sorts of things going on in the house that Sam didn't understand these days. He turned back to the screen and typed in his username to enter the MerryPranxsters' site.

There were a few messages about the last stunt on the board. Most people had been able to get down there and have a look. Sam hadn't got to Brighton, but he'd seen an article about it in the Argus and there were some photos attached to the site. It was an addition to the exhibits in the Brighton Museum. NobleArson had put a fake entry in the Local History section, supposed to be a recollection by some old Brightonian. It was quite funny and smutty but all this stuff was getting old now.

Then the word 'Lewes' caught his eye. He double-clicked the heading. It was from Tizer.

Look out for something 'SPECTACULER' at Lewes Bonfire this year. Be around the De Montfort fireworks at 9.00. Check this space for further instructions. B there or b square.

The next post was also from Tizer, and was headed 'Room'.

Anyone out there need a place in Bton? Room in shared house, 20 Hastings Street, Elm Grove. Rent is 50 a week. DIRT CHEEP to fellow Pranxsters.

Sam stared at the screen for ages, his eyes becoming completely round. This was exactly what he wanted. Fifty quid a week was really cheap. He could pay with the money from Auntie Ruby. Best of all it would be with other Pranxsters. Now he had to think of something to post on the site. And he had to do it quickly, so that he could be a 'fellow Pranxster' before someone else grabbed the room.

Also, there was going to be a stunt at the fireworks. That was it. He had to see it. It was in Lewes. Somehow, he would find a way to sneak out early on November 5th, if he hadn't already left by then. His parents usually went to the bonfire party at Tamsin's house. This year the 5th fell on a Saturday too. It would be manic in town. It would be a good day to do it.

**

Dougie could see the light in the attic. It was weird. It must be the kid's room or something. It was always on. He shifted a little in his seat. Julie's Austin Metro was uncomfortable. He'd moved the seat back as far as he could but it was still all wrong. And it was smelly. It smelt of Julie and food and of the bits and pieces of teacher crap that she left lying around all over the place: mouldy old books and photocopier paper. God knows why she was so funny about lending the piece of shit to him. He looked up and down the road at the cars parked there, wondering which one was Emily's. Probably the Citroen, he thought. Perhaps he would be driving it soon.

He had only realised after Emily had gone that he hadn't asked her for the number of her house, or which neighbour it was. She'd told him the name of her road when they were in the Basketmakers that day, but he wasn't supposed to know her house number. Still, he'd think of a way to explain it away later, when she was all grateful and pleased.

The fact was that once he'd found out where she lived, it was easy to work out who the extension people were.

Emily's house was at the end of the road and she only had one next door neighbour, so it had to be them, number 8. The one with the Audi A4 parked outside.

Tonight was just a reccy, though. He wanted to see what their habits were, so that he could work out a good way of doing the job. Getting them when they were vulnerable, that would be the best thing. Where they couldn't call out. So it had to be somewhere quiet.

Dougie's luck was in. He was just starting to tidy the car a little, putting a banana peel and a sandwich wrapper into an old plastic bag, when Jenny and James appeared on the doorstep. He watched with curiosity as they began their stretching exercises and then set off down Pelham Street. Joggers. That was perfect. People didn't have anything on them when they jogged. It would have been better to get one of them on their own, but there was nothing like having a woman around to make a man behave sensibly. She looked like a nice girl too. He was momentarily distracted, watching her bottom as it bounced down the street. But the bloke didn't look like too much bother. A bit soft round the middle ... out jogging with his wife. A pussy.

He let them get ahead and then he started up the car, following them at a distance as they headed through the town.

***

Emily pressed the button at the top of her alarm clock. It was three o'clock. She didn't know what had woken her. It could have been Sam, but she didn't think so. She had been having a really terrible dream. She was back in the Steine, and Dougie Tate was cheerfully kicking at the body on the ground. He waved at her to come closer, but as she did she realised that she recognised the body. It was someone small and slim and blonde. It was Sam.

She shuddered. If she could, she would have run upstairs to check that Sam was sleeping soundly in bed. Instead, she listened, hardly allowing herself to breathe,

87

until she heard a noise from upstairs. It sounded like a magazine dropping on the floor. Then she leaned back and breathed out.

It was a stupid idea. She needed to get hold of Dougie and tell him not to do it. Dougie Tate was a nutter, he always had been. She had to keep him as far away from her family as possible. She would find him tomorrow. He lived somewhere in Welsh Passage, so she could go and look for him there. And, if not, she'd go to all the Big Issue spots in Brighton. She'd find him and tell him.

She tried to relax again but couldn't, so she went through the conversation in the park again and again until a thought struck her. He didn't know her house number. She had never told him it, so he wouldn't know where she lived and wouldn't know who her neighbours were. He'd have to find her again and ask her before he did anything.

She slid back into sleep with relief.

15. A DAY OUT

There was nothing Dougie liked more than a nice drive in the Sussex countryside. Particularly on a day like this, with the bright chalky blue sky, the trees still full of red and yellow leaves, and the occasional glimpse of a twinkling blue sea.

The car he was in was a lot more like it too: A VW golf, nice, one of the new ones. He wasn't driving though. In the driving seat was Marty Burgess, an acquaintance, not what you might call a friend, or even a mate. More of a business contact. They had known each other for a period of three months, a year ago, and hadn't really got on even then. Dougie could tell that Marty thought he was a bit thick, which he naturally resented. In return, he thought that Marty was a floppy-haired, middle-class cunt.

They both knew though, that at some point they might find each other useful. Marty was from Brighton too. Dougie hadn't known him before they met in the prison laundry, but it was odds on that they would run into each other when they were both back home.

Marty was in the antiques trade and knew a lot of people. Before his incarceration he had quite a successful stall at the Kemp Town indoor market. Then people had let him down (he knew who), and there he was, working in the laundry with Dougie for a couple of quid a week. After that, Marty didn't have a stall any more. He provided more of a personal service, obtaining items to order and then passing them on to contacts around town. That was why Dougie had bumped into him coming out of Snoopers' Paradise.

This was the break that Dougie had wanted. He'd always fancied the antiques trade. It seemed like money for old rope. His ambition was to become a 'knocker boy'. He saw himself charming his way in to old biddies' houses, and then cunningly persuading them into parting with their bits and pieces for a couple of quid. The main thing was just to stay there, drinking their tea and looking a bit menacing, until they cracked and gave you something to get rid of you. It was a job he would be great at.

For some reason Marty hadn't wanted him as a knocker boy, though. This put him out a bit really. It was as if Marty didn't think that Dougie could get invited in to these homes. But maybe he would let him do that later on, when he'd proved himself. Today's job was a little more risky.

Today, Marty had something specific in mind. There was a clock. Someone had seen this clock and they wanted it, but the owner wouldn't sell, or else they wanted too much for it or something. Dougie had to go and get the clock.

They drove out past Rottingdean and over the downs. Below them, they could see a small village called Cursey. It was no more than a pub with about ten houses around it. The house weren't even on proper roads, just chalky tracks leading to large detached properties, all of them different. Each one would have been over the million mark. Dougie saw the blue flash of a swimming pool in a back garden and his stomach twisted in envy.

Marty headed down the hill and began to talk fast. 'OK, let's go over it again. You'll need to move quickly. Climb over the back wall and look for a kitchen door. It'll be unlocked and the alarm should be off. Go through to the living room. The clock'll be on the mantelpiece. You can't miss it. It's right in the middle. The house should be empty, but if anything does happen just run for it, but don't leave the clock. I'll park up. If I see anyone I'll text you. Just get out of there.'

'You'll wait if anyone comes, won't you?' Dougie wondered how the hell he would get home again, imagining wandering over the downs with a large clock. In an area like this he'd be picked up before he'd gone a couple of miles.

'Of course I will, mate,' said Marty. 'OK, here we are.'

They drew up at the back of a large, old-looking house in grey stone. Dougie could see that the upper floors had fancy pointed arch windows but the ground floor level was hidden by a high stone wall.

Marty turned the engine off and Dougie got out, embarrassment taking over from fear as he looked up and down the wall. He leapt up and grabbed the top and then scrabbled uselessly, his feet failing to gain a purchase. After a few long seconds he let himself fall back to the ground and rubbed his grazed hands.

Marty wound down the window and leaned out, hissing 'what the fuck are you doing?'

Dougie forced himself not to lose his temper. 'I can't get up the fucking wall, can I,' he said.

'There's a fucking log over there. Use the fucking log,' Marty hissed back.

Furious with himself for not having spotted it, Dougie pulled the log nearer to the wall. It wobbled a little as he stood on it, but this time he was able to hoist himself over the top. This was where it paid to be muscular. No wonder the floppy haired cunt couldn't do the job himself.

He dropped down into the garden, then crossed to the other side, keeping to the outside edges and away from the windows. He could see the back door, which was apparently unlocked, but he wanted to check at the windows first, make sure that there was no one about before he went inside.

The first window looked into a room that seemed to be some kind of study. It was nice. A proper study, with a leather top desk and walls lined with bookshelves. Nothing interesting in it, though. Marty had said to get the clock and anything small that looked like it was old.

The next room seemed to take up the whole of the rest of the back of the house. It had three huge pointed arch windows all to itself and they seemed to open up, like doors, onto the patio. Dougie looked in the first of these windows, standing with his back flat against the wall and leaning over from the side. It was a beautiful room. All the furniture was antiques. There was a cabinet in light polished wood that ran down nearly the whole of one wall. There were two brown leather sofas, facing each other (very classy), but there didn't seem to be a TV. Next to the sofas were little side tables, also in carved wood. The only thing Dougie didn't like was the rug. It looked a bit old and smelly.

On the top of the mantelpiece, under a painting of woman with a toy dog, there was a large, gold-coloured clock, its pendulum swinging.

He walked, more confident now, to the door at the side of the house. Through its glass panels he could see a coat rack and a pile of shoes and boots, and past them, through another open door, to what seemed to be the kitchen. He felt a rush of adrenaline. He always liked this bit. It was the point of no return. He tried the handle and it opened, so he slipped inside.

It was dead quiet. He made it to the kitchen, which was empty but had a confusing array of closed doors. He opened one and found a utility room. The spin dryer clicked into action, making Dougie jump and feel stupid. He tried the next door: the larder, and then the next, which lead onto a massive hallway, bigger than the whole downstairs of Julie's house, with a large round table in its centre. A staircase swept upwards, circling around until it became a kind of gallery.

Dougie chose the doorway that seemed to lead in the direction of the back of the house. This time he was lucky. The door opened onto the room he had seen from the garden.

Three large window-shaped blocks of sunlight lit the floor. Then the sun went behind a cloud and the room darkened. Dougie focussed on the job. He stopped at the leather sofa and picked up an embroidered cushion, he pulled out the inside filling and dropped it to the floor, taking the cover with him. At the mantelpiece he first took the clock and shoved it into the cushion cover and then, after a moment's thought, picked up the candlesticks and shoved them in too. They weren't even silver, but you never knew.

He found a little silver dish on one of the side tables, and a funny looking statuette on the bookcase. It looked a bit odd, a bit out of proportion, but sometimes people liked stuff like that. There was nothing much else really.

After a final check he left the room. He was half way round the huge table in the hallway when he heard a noise from upstairs. He froze for a millisecond, then he heard a small, shaky voice.

'Is that you, Janet?'

Dougie hurried to the kitchen door, looking back only at the last second.

An old man, ghostly with his grey hair and pale striped pyjamas, was looking out from the gallery. He eyed Dougie with confusion.

'Are you the man about the toilet?' he said.

Dougie bolted.

Out in the garden, he held the cushion cover over the wall and felt someone else take its weight before he let go. Then he flung himself over.

Marty was already back in the car and starting the engine. He began moving off while Dougie threw himself inside. They drove on in silence until they were well clear of the village.

'OK?' said Marty.

'Got it,' said Dougie.

'Show me.'

Dougie reached inside the cushion cover and pulled out the clock.

'Here you go,' he said.

Marty flicked his eyes towards it.

'Oh you fucking . . .,' he said. 'That's not the fucking clock.'

'Bollocks,' said Dougie. 'I did exactly what you said. On the mantelpiece in the living room. It's a fucking carriage clock.'

'Yeah, it's a fucking carriage clock. It's also a piece of shit that goes for about a tenner. You see them fucking everywhere. It's about twenty years old. The one I wanted was about two hundred years old. You went in the front room, like I told you, right?'

'The lounge, yeah. The room at the back of the house. The big room.'

'The front room is at the front. Fucking hell, Dougie, how can you not tell the difference? How can you not know that for a piece of shit? What a waste of fucking time.'

They sat in silence until they reached the outskirts of Brighton. If Dougie hadn't been desperate, if Julie wasn't being such a silly bitch, there were all sorts of things that he would like to do to Marty. All sorts. And he thought about each one while he twisted the cushion cover in his hands.

As they neared the North Laine, where Dougie was to be dropped off, Marty began to regret having said so much.

'What else did you get,' he said, pulling the car up into the relative quiet of Foundry Street.

Dougie showed him the rest of the things and Marty brightened up a bit.

'The figurine isn't bad,' he said. 'OK, I'll let you know what I get.'

'Like hell,' thought Dougie.

'At least you weren't seen,' said Marty, trying to smile.

'Yeah, right,' said Dougie. 'At least I didn't get seen.'

16. BY THE RIVERBANK

Alex Wheeler didn't try to hide the smirk as he looked at his son in law. It wasn't as if, like Emily, he had any real objection to jogging, he just didn't need to do it himself. And in his ongoing competition with the younger man, it was one of the areas where he always came out on top.

'Going for a run then?' he said.

'Yup,' said James. 'Why? Do you want to come?'

'No. You're all right.' He patted his hard stomach. 'You should go though mate. You're looking a bit prosperous there. I thought they had you playing rugby at this office of yours.'

'They do.' He turned to his wife. 'Jen?'

She looked between her two men. 'I'll stay here. Dad's going back soon. You don't mind do you?'

James had already known what her answer would be. Jenny was a good girl. Sensible. Not a whiner or teary like some of his friends wives. She never told him he couldn't go out, or tried to stop him doing what he wanted. Her one fault was that she was a bit of a Daddy's girl. No, not a bit. A lot.

He didn't hold it against her. Her mother was dead and she didn't have anyone else. There were two half brothers from her dad's second marriage, but the new wife wasn't that friendly so she didn't get to see much of them.

He did hold it against Alex, though. Alex used it. Knew what was going on, and enjoyed having Jenny run around after him. Then there was the house. If it had been up to James, he would have chosen a sensible house, one that they could afford and one that they didn't need to do any work on. Left to himself he would probably have bought a house very similar to one of the ones that Alex developed. Nice and new and on one of those executive estates. No work to do and no problems to deal with when he came home after a hard day and a hard commute.

Alex wouldn't hear of it though. Not good enough for his daughter. There was no money in it, for a start. Also, according to Alex, all of these houses, including his own, were built so that they virtually collapsed after the new build guarantee gave out. What he suggested was that they buy an old house and that he helped them to improve it. And, of course, what he had suggested, they had done. It was certainly cheaper for Alex that way.

Now everything was a worry and a problem and his house never felt like his own. Alex was always there, in conference with Jenny or measuring something or making him make decisions about taps or tiles or other rubbish. This was a hard year for him at work too. It was all getting him down.

As he closed the front door he heard Alex say 'You should put him on a diet, Jennifer.' And Jenny laughed.

***

Dougie was also having women trouble: Julie wouldn't let him use the car. There was no reason for it. She wasn't going anywhere. She was just being a bitch. Sometimes Dougie didn't understand women. Why would anyone want another person to stay in for a cosy evening in front of the TV if they didn't want to be there? She could watch TV quite easily by herself. After a day like he'd had, he could do with some light relief.

Marty had slipped him his 'drink': fifty quid. Fifty quid was actually pretty crap for the work he'd done, especially as Marty had cocked up and the house had been occupied after all. Dougie wasn't expecting much more from the sale of the other items either. Still, it would just about pay for a night out and he was feeling a bit claustrophobic at the moment.

He thought about catching the bus to Brighton, but that would eat into the money and it was also a pain in the arse. Then he thought about going to the Crown or the Dorset, but he owed several rounds at both places, and he'd have to get them in.

In the end, he gave up on the idea of going out and wandered down towards the riverbank. He wasn't expecting to do the Emily job, as he termed it. Nobody went out jogging two nights running. What he thought he'd do was scope the place out. He didn't want this job to be another cock up, like today.

He had an idea of where it would be best to do it. When he'd followed them he'd gone as far as the Phoenix Causeway, then he'd parked the car and watched as they jogged along the riverbank. Surely that would be the ideal place.

At first anywhere along the river had seemed promising, especially on an autumn evening like this when it was already dark and people weren't using the park for football or strolls or whatever they did down there. It wasn't though. The main thing was the Tesco's. The supermarket was right on the bank. God knows why, but it was. He'd thought it would be closed by now, but as he walked past he could see that it was still too busy.

The other side of the river wasn't a worry. It didn't have a pathway and was lined with crumbling warehouses, most of which seemed to be disused. At any rate, there didn't seem to be any windows that would be a problem. Just in case it did have to get a bit physical.

But despite this, the whole of this stretch of the riverbank was too public. If he had been able to watch Emily's neighbours jogging along while he stood on the Causeway, anyone could see him too. The lighting along the path was fairly minimal, but it had still been enough for him to pick out the bloke's striped rugby shirt from at least 500 yards away. And the trees, a couple of willows leaning towards the water and some other ones that he didn't recognise, were too sparse to provide much cover.

He walked further down the path, past the football pitch. There were no games being played, but there was a dog walker with two dogs. The dogs were chasing each other around in endless figures of eight and the man smiled at Dougie as he passed. Dougie pretended interest in the river. Two ducks took fright and paddled away through the dark water.

Then the pathway ended in thick shrubs and bushes. The only way onwards was via a small metal bridge that crossed the Ouse and led in the direction of the castle. Surely this was where Emily's neighbours had gone last night. He hadn't seen them come back along the river. This must be the quickest way to Pelham Street.

He crossed the bridge. It made a metallic clacking sound as he passed, otherwise there was absolute silence: even the river seemed to slip past soundlessly. On the other side, he took stock. This was more like it. No houses with a decent view. No more dog walkers, no more people getting their shopping. On the left, there was a high wall. On the other side: nothing. A grassy bank tailed down to the river and all around there was just trees and grass and silence. This would be the best place to do it.

He followed the path along to make sure. Further up, there was the empty outdoor swimming pool, then a swing park on one side and a sort of short canal, probably an offshoot of the river, on the other. Further still, there were a few houses, but too far away to worry about. He climbed over the wall into the park and sat on one of the swings. If it was summer, if it was warmer, there might have been teenagers hanging around, but not now. He swung himself back and forth in the dark, enjoying the quiet and the sensation of the movement. Then started back the way he had come until he heard a noise, a clunk, clunk, clunk, of someone running over the bridge.

Dougie slipped into the shadows with his back to the warehouse. Yes, it was him: Mr Rugby shirt. He couldn't believe his luck. And he was all on his own too. Dougie looked around one more time and then stepped out and blocked his path.

'Got a light?' he said.

'No I don't,' said James. He continued jogging up and down on the spot. 'Excuse me.'

'That's not very friendly,' said Dougie.

James stopped jogging. 'Look, I don't have anything, alright?' He raised his open, empty hands.

'You what?' said Dougie. 'Are you accusing me of something, pal?'

'Whatever you want, pal, I haven't got it.'

'I think you're accusing me of something. I think that's out of order. I think that you're a bit of a cunt.'

'Oh, fuck off,' said James. And he pushed Dougie.

Dougie stood his ground, a smile appearing on first one side, and then the other side, of his face.

'You like pushing people around, don't you? You cunt.'

James looked around, hoping for some sign of life. There was none.

'Look, I just want to go home, OK?'

'You like pushing people around. I know all about you, mate. You want to build something on your house, don't you?'

James looked back at Dougie. 'What are you talking about? That's got nothing to do with you.'

'You're pissing off your neighbours. That's not sensible, pal. If I was you I'd be looking out for your nice little blonde wifey.'

James was confused, but didn't think that now was the time to work out what this psycho meant. He knew that he had to make a choice. Back down or stand up for himself. What he would have told anyone else to do was to back down. Get out of there. It wasn't worth it. But today he had had enough. He was angry - with Alex, with people at work, even with the new house and with Jenny. He was sick and tired of everything and he wouldn't mind giving this bloke a good kicking. His heart was punching at the inside of his chest. The bloke was small. Surely he could take him?

Dougie could see that James was making up his mind. This annoyed him. Usually people were too scared to even think about taking him on. His reputation and his manner did the job for him. He hadn't actually been in a fight for years. He hadn't needed to. He certainly hadn't been expecting any trouble from this middle class office boy.

James darted to the left. Dougie blocked his path. He tried the right, but Dougie was there too. Dougie smiled, and James punched him on the jaw.

The pain was intense. Dougie reeled, astonished and furious. He pulled himself upright and headbutted James, catching him on his nose, which cracked with a pleasingly loud crunch. Blood poured down from James' nostril and into his mouth. The taste was bitter and he spat, aiming for Dougie's face.

Dougie turned away, but the bloody spit landed, dripping, on his ear. He wiped it off, disgusted. 'Not fucking sensible, pal,' he said. He grabbed James who twisted out of his reach. Dougie tripped, falling and bringing James over on top of him.

They rolled on the ground until Dougie managed to get his hand under James' throat, pushing his head backwards until James had to let go. Then Dougie was on top, holding him by the hair.

Dougie paused, breathing hard. The sleeve of his leather jacket flapped, exposing his bare arm, and this made him angrier than anything. 'You tore my fucking jacket, you fat fucking cunt.' He bashed James' head on the ground, emphasising each expletive. James moaned and then fell silent.

This was enough. Dougie got up, leaving James lying on the ground. He gave him a last kick and started walking unsteadily away.

James rolled over, groaning, and pulled himself up. He staggered towards Dougie and punched him as hard as he could in the kidneys. Dougie toppled to the ground. He turned painfully and tried to get up but James sank down on top of him.

'People like you make me sick. You fucking low life scum.' James was surprised to hear that his voice sounded slurred. He dragged up the last of his energy and brought his fist down onto Dougie's shocked face.

Dougie saw the fist connect with his cheekbone, and then felt the impact. His brain seemed to jolt inside his head and his vision blurred, as though his eyeballs had been smeared with Vaseline. James raised his fist again, but he was dizzy and moved too slowly. Dougie's hand clasped something on the floor. It was a half brick. He smashed it, full force, into the back of James' head.

The pain shot through James, obliterating everything except for the colours that flashed and burned inside his head. Then the colours evaporated and there was nothing. Nothing at all. He keeled over, coming to rest at right angles to Dougie, his leg still stretched over the other man.

Dougie waited for a couple of seconds, then he took hold of the leg, and moved it away. He tried to look at James' face, hoping that he had passed out. They had rolled too far away from any streetlights to see properly, so he took his zippo from his pocket and flicked it alight. James' eyes were open. They shone in the light of the zippo, but it was the glutinous shine of cold, set jelly.

Dougie stood up quickly, which made his head throb. He couldn't understand what had happened. His first impulse was to run as fast as possible, anywhere, away from those eyes. But his legs felt weak, unreliable. It wasn't supposed to happen. But it had, and he had to do something about it. He had to pull himself together, right now. He had to sort this out. Otherwise . . .

He heard a plop as something fell into the river, something small, like an animal. That was it: he would drag rugby bloke to the river. Get rid of him. He picked him up by the ankles and dragged him down the bank. This was fairly easy, the incline was steep and the momentum nearly had Dougie in the river as well. He was just about ready to move around and start pushing him in from the other side when he realised that he should find something to weigh him down. Didn't bodies pop back up to the surface otherwise? He had heard that. Something to do with gases. Dougie winced.

He looked around for anything useful. There were a few more bricks and stones around and he picked them up wondering what to do with them. He stuffed a few in James' tracksuit pockets, which made him feel nauseous. Then he cast around again, wondering what else to use. Then he thought, perhaps he shouldn't. Perhaps it would be better if it looked like he fell off the bridge and banged his head, so he reached into James' pockets again, and took the stones out.

Then he remembered the stone he had hit James with. That would be vital evidence. It must have had blood on it, and in the daylight that would be visible. He had to get rid of that too. He went back up the bank and looked around for it, flicking on the zippo and then turning it off in case he was seen, but he couldn't find it.

This was stupid, he realised. The priority was to get the body into the water. So he turned back to James and rolled him down the last bit of the bank. He watched as James slid into the blackness and disappeared, and stayed watching until the water was still again. Then he turned back up the bank and was sick all over his shoes.

He wiped his mouth and looked at the sick in dismay. The first thing was to get it off his shoes, so he returned to the bank and dipped his feet in the water. Then he realised that he had just left his DNA all over the scene. So he ran up the bank, scooped up the warm, sweet smelling vomit and ran back to the river, with it. He did this several times before he realised that he would never get rid of all of it. So he cupped his hands in the water and ran back to the spot, which was now almost bare of grass from his

102

exertions. He let the trickle of water fall on the ground, hoping to dilute what was left of the sick.

There was a noise. Not someone running, but the soft, clicking sound of a bicycle. Dougie stood up, his mind blank. The cyclist, a thin, bearded man in a cycling helmet, sounded his bell as he came off the bridge. He saw Dougie and nodded.

'Nice night for it,' he said.

Dougie smiled back, his eyes a counterpoint of horror.

17. WAITING

Emily knew that she couldn't wait any longer. She had spent the day in an agony of indecision, telling herself that Dougie didn't know her address and that everything was fine. There was the pressure of work, too. She had forgotten that one of her biggest projects, an estate agency site, was going live. She still wanted to find Dougie and call him off, but it could wait until tomorrow. If she wasn't at her computer today to deal with any problems, it could be a disaster. Especially now, because of Mark's job, it was important that she didn't drop the ball. She simply didn't have the time to try and find Dougie.

But however hard she convinced herself that it was all talk, and that without her address it could come to nothing, she couldn't stop thinking about that night in the Steine. Then stories from those days began to re-emerge into her memory. It was a time when casual violence was the norm, in the way that young people can be thoughtlessly violent. There were a lot of fights: between Teddy boys and punks, then soul boys and punks, then mods and punks, and always between punks and punks, but Dougie Tate was a Brighton legend. No one messed with him. This had been reassuring in a way. As long as Dougie Tate was about, you knew where any trouble would be. As long as you kept on the right side of him you were fine. He had an odd kind of loyalty about him.

And if Emily was being honest, part of her wanted Dougie to do something. Not much, just scare the bejesus out of them. Maybe even beat James up a little bit. Just a little bit. She even quite wanted them to suspect that it was something to do with her. That would show them a thing or two.

But the stories . . . You never knew if they were true, but there were so many of them, enough of them to make most people think that at least some of it must be real. She remembered one in particular. Dougie had supposedly beaten up his girlfriend outside one of the pubs. It was closing time and there were a lot of people about, but they had just walked around them while she lay on the floor and he kicked her. Nobody dared to do anything else.

That was the trouble, Emily realised. The whole idea had been dependent on Dougie being able to act with self control. And the reason why he was so feared was that he didn't appear to have any.

In the meantime, Clare kept phoning, and Emily knew that she would have to do something about it. At first Clare's voice was bright and cheerful.

'Hi Em, it's me. Phone me back.'

Then it had moved up a gear to gentle concern:

'Are you OK? Call me back.'

And then she had gone all out for mournful commiseration:

'Emily, please call me. I'm very worried about you.'

Emily had to do something. She had to talk to Clare but she didn't want to give her hand away. She would have to call off Dougie, but in case, just in case, something happened before she could get to him, she would have to be careful.

She decided that the best option was to go round to Clare's. That way she could leave when she wanted. If she invited Clare round to the house she would never get rid of her. She would be digging and poking until she found something.

**

Clare opened the door, beaming.

'Oh, thank goodness,' she said, and then did a double take. 'Look at your hair! It's very . . . It's very young, isn't it?'

Emily let herself be taken downstairs, passing Tim and Tamsin who were watching TV in the living room.

She sat on the wicker sofa in the conservatory while Clare made the tea. She already felt at a disadvantage, as if she was waiting to see the headmistress on one of the few occasions when Sam had been really naughty.

Clare appeared with a tray. There was a teapot and biscuits on it. This really was annoying. Patronising. She never normally got this kind of treatment.

'So how are you?' Clare set the tray down and sat opposite Emily.

'Fine. Well, you know, not fine, but dealing with it. Sorry I haven't called you back but it's been so busy. The Walker Palmer site just went live and . . .'

Clare was trying to gaze into her eyes with a look of sympathy. Emily wasn't having it.

'Mark's started applying for jobs.'

'Is he? Good. I'm sure he'll get something.'

'So am I.'

Their eyes met, for a second.

'But what about this bombshell of Jenny's. Have you had a chance to see the plans?'

Emily had already decided not to lie about this. The best approach was always to keep things as close to the truth as possible.

'Yes, I got a copy but I haven't had much of a chance to have a look. The Walker Palmer site went live, and it's been so busy.'

Clare was dumbfounded. Eight years of friendship had led her to expect several possible reactions, but this wasn't one of them.

Emily pursued her advantage. 'What do you think?' she said.

She watched Clare struggle to recover herself. 'Well I don't know really. We'll both be a little overlooked.' What could she say? She couldn't say that Emily really ought to be concerned, that it would be dreadful, ruin her house. It would make her sound like a bitch. Plus then Emily would expect her to object, out of friendship, and she didn't want to do that. Jenny's dad was sending someone round to sort out the damp in the back wall. For free.

'Well, I'll have to have a look and let you know. Are you going to object?'

'No, I don't think so.' Clare looked down at the biscuits. They were the expensive ones and Emily had already eaten three. She wished she hadn't put them out. 'So anyway,' she said, 'did I tell you that Tamsin came top in Maths?'

***

Jenny watched her father drive away and then went back down to the basement. James wouldn't be back for at least twenty minutes so she decided to start on the dinner. She put on the water for the vegetables and crushed the garlic, but it was still too early, so she took out the ironing board and began on James' shirts.

When he didn't appear she left the vegetables in the pan and carried on ironing. The radio was playing songs that she liked, songs from the mid nineties, and she let herself drift off into reminiscences. The next thing she noticed, all of the shirts were hanging, neatly pressed, on the door frame.

She glanced at her watch. It was 9.30. That meant that James must have been gone for over an hour. An hour and a half probably. That was too long. Maybe he had stopped off at the supermarket, or the pub. This was unlikely though. He wasn't likely to go to a pub by himself. He wasn't that sort. Unless he was annoyed with her.

She tried his mobile. As expected, it rang upstairs, in his jacket. She went upstairs and got the jacket, and went through the pockets. His wallet was in there too. She looked through it and found all of his credit cards and £40 cash. So he had nothing with him.

Jenny sat down, her face creased into a frown as she concentrated, puzzling at the problem. She wasn't going to be silly about this, but perhaps it was time to get a bit concerned.

***

A few streets away, Julie was also becoming concerned. Or perhaps concerned is not quite the right word. Julie was becoming angry.

After all that she'd done for him, and everything he had said about trust and honesty and walking life's pathway together, he was bloody staying out late again. He was treating her like an idiot, like a silly little girl. And she was a woman. She deserved more than this, surely?

She tried to work out how things had gone wrong. Their relationship had started so beautifully, like a fairy tale. The attraction between them had been immediate. She had felt her whole body respond as soon as he walked into the room. Who knew what it was that had this affect? Some people just belong together physically. As if their very molecules cry out for each other. Her mother had said 'Of course he took a fancy to you. What other women did he get to see?' But that was Mum for you: always negative, always picking holes and doubting her. One thing that therapy had taught her was to rely on her own judgement and not to keep going back to her mother for approval that would never come.

So when she saw Dougie she knew that for once she had to rely on her body and what it was telling her. Her body knew the truth. Its reaction wasn't distorted by their relationship: teacher and pupil, prisoner and authority figure. They were just two beings who felt the irresistible draw of passion.

Everything had to be secret, of course. She saw him during class, and then he began to stay behind afterwards to talk about the books they were studying. She recommended more books for him to read, and lent him her own copy of Sons and Lovers. He had returned it with a note.

She had to help him in any way that she could, and the best way to do this was by filing favourable reports and giving evidence at his parole hearing. It was the way the world worked. She'd had to be strong for both of them.

She could feel his fear, his doubts. He didn't want to harm her career, and sometimes she had felt him pulling away, as if afraid of the consequences of their love.

But it had worked out. And then, after all of the waiting and the agony of desire, they had met for the first time outside the prison walls and she had driven him home, to start their new life together. They were both ecstatically happy.

So what had happened? Why was he messing it all up? It wasn't that she wanted gratitude. Of course she didn't. She just wanted some kind of recognition of their love. She didn't expect him to be endlessly thanking her for everything that she'd done, for helping to get an early release date, for risking her job, for giving him a home, money and the rest. That's what lovers did for one another. It was just that, increasingly these days, Dougie wasn't being very lover-like.

Julie put on the kettle and turned up the music. It was Billie Holiday, her favourite. When Dougie came home, they would have to sort it all out, once and for all.

***

Emily decided that it was time to leave. She'd done what she came to do and now Clare was starting on Sam again. Firing questions like nobody's business. Emily knew that she was going to have to deal with this sooner or later. Lewes is a small town. Tamsin went to a different school, a private one in Burgess Hill, but it didn't make much difference. Sooner or later Sam's behaviour, at the very least his dropping out of school, would make its way through the teenage grapevine back to Pelham Street. Emily was already formulating various spins on this: he had decided to go to a sixth form in Brighton, he was suffering from some unspecified illness. But all this could wait. One problem at a time.

They were on the doorstep saying goodbye when Jenny appeared.

'Hiya, Jenny,' said Emily. It came out a bit too loud.

'Hiya. You haven't seen James anywhere around have you?'

Clare and Emily shook their heads.

'Hasn't he come back from work?' Clare had her concerned look on again.

'Yes, he's just gone out for a jog. But it was quite a while ago.' Jenny beeped the car and opened the door. 'I've left him a note, but if you see him, will you just tell him I've gone for a drive round?'

'Of course,' said Clare. 'Let me know when you find him.'

Jenny smiled and pulled away.

'Well,' said Clare, turning back to Emily. 'Someone's going to be in big trouble.'

Emily became very aware of her facial expressions. She was unable to decide which expression was appropriate and her face twisted back and forth between a smile and a frown. 'I've got to go now,' she said.

Luckily, Clare was too absorbed in this latest drama to notice that anything was wrong.

***

When she returned to the house Mark was watching the telly. He said 'How was Clare?' but didn't even bother to look round for the answer, so Emily slipped away up to the bedroom.

She sat on the bed and waited. If Mark came up she would say that she had a headache. But he didn't. She lay in the dark, listening to the sounds of the street. A door closed, far away: not Clare or Jenny's. A car drove past, too fast. Upstairs, she could hear the faint sound of Sam's music. He never played his music too loud.

She stayed like this for some time, then she heard another car, going slower and then pulling up outside. She jumped up and went to the window in time to see Jenny rush into her house, and then a few seconds later, rush out again.

Then there was the sound of a door being knocked. Emily heard the low murmur of women's voices, which was then joined by the deeper tones of a man. There was silence for a few seconds, and then Jenny appeared again with Tim and they both got into the car.

The phone was ringing even before the car had left the street. Emily picked up the extension by the bed.

'It's me,' said Clare. 'You'll never guess. Jenny's just come round. She's taken Tim to go and walk down the river.'

'He's not back then?'

'No. It's getting ever so late, isn't it?'

'What does she think has happened?'

'I don't know. Do you think they've had a row? I bet he's in the pub. I'd be going round all the pubs if I was her. I think she's worried that he's fallen in the river or been mugged or something. But this is Lewes.'

'Well, they're from London, aren't they? They probably worry about that sort of thing.'

'I'm sure he's in the pub. I'd wait until they close and then start worrying.'

'Well, I'm sure you're right.' Emily had to get off the phone.

'Okay then. Bit of excitement, isn't it?'

'Isn't it.'

Emily went back to her vigil. She was still awake, three hours later, when the police car arrived.

18. WHAT DOUGIE DID NEXT

Dougie stayed, frozen, watching the cyclist until he disappeared, then he took off. He didn't know quite where he was going, just as far away as possible.

He took the road down the side of the swing park. The river was too public. So was the road that led up towards the castle. The road he chose led through the back of some of the warehouses. Hopefully not many people would be about and he would be able to find somewhere to hide for a while. He needed to get himself together.

In the end, he found a doorway with a van parked in front of it and he sank down onto the step. His heart was still pumping too hard and he still felt sick, so he waited, doing the breathing exercises that Julie had taught him until he was a little calmer.

What he really wanted was to go home, back to Welsh Passage. To slip into bed with Julie, cuddle up to her nice big arse and have her look after him. Make him a cup of tea with lots of sugar in. That's what they did for shock, wasn't it? He was in shock.

He got up and had a look at his face in the van's wing mirror. She would go mad. He was going to have a massive bruise on his cheekbone and he seemed to have all sorts of other injuries that he hadn't noticed happening at the time. There were going to be marks all over his body. She would accuse him of fighting and there would be weeping and wailing and all sorts of crap.

The main thing though, was that if they found rugby bloke, she might put two and two together, with him coming home beaten up on the same night. They could work out exactly when people had died now. He'd seen it on the telly. She said that she loved him and all that, but if it came down to it he didn't know which way she would fall. She's seen his police records. She knew all about him. Well, not all . . . but in Dougie's experience people's upbringing usually came through in the end. Their loyalties were to their own class and type. And her mum was a bloody Tory councillor for Christ's sake. He just couldn't risk it.

So Julie was out, and he only had one other option. He looked at his watch. If he hurried he could make the last train down to Brighton. He checked himself in the mirror again, smoothing down his hair and trying to make himself look respectable. His leather jacket was in a terrible state and he knew that he'd have to get rid of it. This made him feel sad. It would be like losing an old friend. But thinking about it, it probably had Rugby bloke's blood and spit on it anyway. He took the jacket off. His T-shirt was dark, and didn't show too much damage, but he would have to find somewhere to get rid of the leather jacket.

He set off in what he hoped was the direction of the station, avoiding anywhere that looked well lit or busy. At the back of one of the shops there was a skip that was nearly full of old bits of kitchen and rubble. He dug around into the rubble until he'd made a kind of well, then he buried his leather jacket in it, covering it up afterwards and arranging bits of cupboard doors on top. Now he was really cold, and he began to shake in peculiar jerky movements, which surprised and alarmed him.

From the next corner, he spied on the high street, waiting for the right moment to cross. There was no escape; he had to cross it to get to the station. He waited, checking his watch, while a woman closed the off licence, pulling down the shutters and chatting on her mobile until a car drew up and drove her away. Then he spotted something on the other side of the street.

Outside the charity shop he could see a large black bin bag. A woman's shoe had become dislodged and lay on the floor beside it. Something knitted and purple exploded from its top. He glanced around then rushed over the road and tipped contents of the bag onto the floor. A lot of rubbish poured out. Mostly women's stuff. But there was something, a hoody, in a nice dark blue. It was a bit small but he managed to get it on. It would warm him up and, with the hood pulled up, it would help to hide the mark on his cheek.

Then he slipped away, down towards Southover, making his way to the station via the back streets. Once outside, he loitered again, waiting for stragglers from the London train to leave the station. When they had all disappeared over the bridge he pulled the hoody up, and bought a single to Brighton from the machine.

He walked as far as he could up the platform, hoping to find an empty carriage. The wind was picking up, and even in the hoody he was shaking again. He had to stop this. He would look like a junkie. Everyone would look at him.

He saw the orange lights of the train approaching. He scanned the carriages as they passed and then got in the last one. The only other occupant was a sleeping office worker. The man's briefcase lay unattended on the seat beside him and Dougie cursed his luck that he would not be able to take it. He couldn't risk the possibility of drawing attention to himself. A plan was formulating in his mind. If it ever came down to it, he would say that he had been in Brighton for the whole evening. When he got to Brighton he'd be OK.

By the time they reached Brighton station, Dougie had cleaned himself up in the train toilet and was feeling a little better. At least the shaking had stopped. Navigating the station was a problem. The train pulled in at the last platform, which Dougie knew from experience was where the police hung out, and where they kept their vans full of dogs. It wasn't as if he had anything on him that would interest a sniffer dog, but if they pulled him over there would be a record that he had been at the station at this time.

He walked, head down, towards the far exit and took the turning down Trafalgar Street, then he carried on moving eastwards to the scruffier end of town, Elm Grove. The streets became quieter; the pubs had already let out and this was not a part of town where anyone went for their social life. The Grove was an area that estate agents always promised was on its way up, and where hopeful young couples would buy dilapidated looking houses, hoping to renovate and make a profit, only to move out, perplexed and scared by the old neighbourhood families. Some roads were worse than others and it was into one of these that Dougie turned.

He knocked at the door of the most disreputable house of all. Dougie tutted when he saw that they still had sheets hung in the window, as if they had only just moved in. He happened to know that they'd been there for a year.

The door opened, still on the chain, and a young redheaded man of about twenty-seven, pale faced and saggy eyed, looked at him through the gap.

'Hiya Dougie,' he said.

'Hiya. Jimmy about, is he?'

'Nah, mate. He's gone. Couple of weeks ago.'

This was awful. Dougie was momentarily stumped. 'Where'd he go?'

'Up North. Back up North.'

Dougie thought fast, then he smiled in his most charming manner. 'Aren't you going to let us in then?'

The man behind the door considered his options, but only for a millisecond. Then he opened the door and let Dougie inside.

In the living room a scruffy mongrel dog looked up and then laid his head back on the knee of the hippyish girl on the sofa.

'Alright,' said Dougie.

'Alright,' she said.

She reached down onto the floor and picked up a magazine, careful that the cigarettes, Rizlas and small lump of hash stayed balanced on its top. Then she began to roll a joint. The telly blared on in the background. The young man went over to the set and turned the volume down.

'Where is everyone?' said Dougie.

'The Freebutt. Be back in a minute,' he said. 'You know Janice, right?'

'Is it all right if I crash?' Dougie pulled the hood of his top down. 'Got a bit of woman trouble.'

'What happened to your face?' said Janice, leaning right over to stare at it.

The young man shot her a look that she was too stoned to appreciate. 'I don't know,' he said. 'I suppose, for tonight. It's up to everyone else.'

Dougie leaned back in the chair. He felt very tired. 'I can have Jimmy's room, can't I?' he said.

Janice passed the joint to her boyfriend. She drew her legs up onto the sofa, adjusting the dog and making him whine.

'Make us a cup of tea Tizer,' she said.

19. THE MORNING AFTER

'How about another cup of tea?' PC Roberts was getting a bit fed up. There was nothing more to do here really. It was a ninety-nine percent certain to just be an ordinary domestic: the type of job that she was always sent on, and even worse, she was missing her breakfast. The Station did lovely bacon rolls. She thought about the way the butter melted on contact with the warm roll, and her stomach growled. 'Or some food?' she said.

Jenny shook her head. When the police first arrived she had been grateful. She doubted whether they would even have bothered to come out in London. Now, though, she was starting to resent the invasion. The woman had been there for ages and had made Jenny two cups of tea already. She wasn't disabled. Her husband had just gone missing. She was quite capable of making her own tea in her own kitchen. Also, PC Roberts had a disconcerting habit of drifting off, as though she was thinking of something else, and then snapping back into a concerned act, her head on one side, her eyes staring too far into Jenny's. And she was really getting pissed off about the way she kept trying to make her say stuff. Putting words in her mouth.

'So, even though, as you say, it wasn't exactly a row, you didn't really part on the best of terms, did you?' Her eyes fixed on the photo of them at her 30th birthday party, obviously drunk.

'Well it wasn't like that really, as I said, we just . . .'

'And this problem between your husband and your father, this had been going on for a while?'

'Not really, they weren't that close that's all. Look, we didn't have a row; he didn't row with my Dad. He just went jogging.'

PC Roberts felt irritated. What she wanted to say was 'Oh come on love. Why's he done a bunk then? Open your eyes and smell the coffee.' The trouble with the

117

punters was that they never seemed to realise that she'd seen it all before. Yes, even in Lewes. Especially in Lewes.

Her radio crackled and she took it out into the hall.

***

Ffion Jennings was much too early for school but she wanted to get a head start in setting up her project. It was important that she came first this time. It always was important that she came first, but this time she needed to get higher marks than Tristan Piggot. She wanted him to look really stupid and then to laugh in his face. It would serve him right.

First of all though, she had to go to Tesco and get some more tin foil. Mum had given her the money and she was to bring the rest of it home. She just needed a bit extra for the backdrop. It would make it look more dramatic. The project she had chosen was Movement of The Planets and the tin foil backdrop would hopefully look like space while hiding the bits of string that she needed to manipulate the tennis and ping pong balls to make it all work.

It was difficult to carry, though, especially over the bridge. The wind was blowing the balls this way and that and they were getting all tangled up. She tried to walk backwards for a while to shelter it from the wind. It didn't help much and she felt stupid. Then she tripped. She managed to right herself before she fell, but somehow Jupiter had worked its way free. It dropped with a bounce onto the tin foil surface and then shot off sideways. Ffion watched helplessly as she held fast to rest of the contraption and the orange ball lodged itself in the marshy area of the river bank below. She peered downwards. It didn't seem to be too badly damaged. She could find somewhere to put the rest of the project and then go down and get it.

It was quite wet so she grabbed a bit of branch lying on the bank and tried to nudge the ball back towards her. It rolled in the wrong direction. She bent down, and stopped.

She took a step backwards, stumbling on the bank, then edged nearer again. She took hold of the stick and poked the stripy thing in the water. It bobbed and then, released from whatever was holding it, James' body turned, its eyeless face looking back at Ffion.

'Oh Christ Almighty. Oh totally gross.' She scrambled backwards as fast as she could and then ran towards Tesco trying to shout but unable to do so. Her eyes, though, shone brightly with excitement. She had just seen a dead body. Tristan Piggot would be jealous as anything.

***

Mark was going to be late, but he didn't care. He bounded down the stairs with more energy than he'd felt in weeks.

'That was ComputaJobs,' he said. 'SunAlliance want an interview.'

Emily had her back to him, cleaning the sink. 'That's good,' she said. She didn't turn around.

Mark's face fell. She could have been more enthusiastic.

'I know it's Horsham, but it's a job. At least it's not London. I just hope I get it.'

She turned towards him. 'I know' she said. 'I know. I hope you get it too.'

Mark eyed his wife guiltily as she took the basket out of the cupboard and began to unload the washing. She looked awful. She'd taken all this even worse than he'd thought. He would have preferred the usual: the shouting and the grief. She didn't even seem to be taking an interest. He wondered if she was becoming what people meant when they talked about 'depressed'.

A car pulled up outside and he watched her eyes drift away towards the lightwell. There were two clicks and two thunks as doors opened and closed, and then low voices.

'It'd be a good company to get into,' he said.

She looked at him blankly and then her eyes slid back to the lightwell. He gave up.

Once outside, his good mood returned. He noticed the police car parked outside. Of course he did. It was Lewes after all. You hardly ever saw the police except at bonfire night. But it didn't really register. Something to do with the student house opposite, he thought. That was good. A bit of street gossip would be bound to cheer Emily up.

***

Something was wrong. Sam was so attuned to his mother's rhythms and daily routines he would have noticed any departure from the usual, so now he struggled to work out what it was that seemed different. She had gone downstairs at roughly the normal time and then he could hear the sound of the dishwasher starting up, then the sound of the washing machine. His father left for work and there had been no more of the shouting of the other night. So what was it?

He had once heard that when a large predator passes by in the jungle, the atmosphere changes suddenly to an unnatural stillness, as if every animal in the vicinity is motionless and holding its breath until the danger has passed. It made him think of that. Of course he wasn't expecting to bump into a tiger on the stairs or anything, but something was wrong.

The door of Emily's study clicked shut and he relaxed slightly, only slightly, just enough to start thinking straight. Recently he spent most of the time tensed up into small ball of nerves, wondering if the moment had come when she would march upstairs and break the door down. He had replayed the scene to himself many times. She would get Dad to do it and she would stand there, issuing directives. 'Watch the paintwork' and 'Please be careful, remember we had the door specially made.'

It was time to start making preparations. Tomorrow was the day he had been waiting for, November the 5th. It was the ideal time for his plans. The town would be full, his parents would be busy with the party down the road, and there would be enough confusion for him to disappear. He felt a bit scared, mostly in a good way, but it was time and he was ready at last.

The plan had taken him a long while to think up. The trouble was that Lewes people were so very 'right on'. There was nothing much that could shock them, and there was no point in doing something that wouldn't cause any kind of controversy. And anyway, they liked controversy. As every schoolchild in Lewes knew, the town was the home of Tom Paine and the Protestant Martyrs. Every year the various bonfire societies marched through the town with flaming crosses shouting 'Burn the Pope!' much to the horror of unsuspecting Catholic visitors who took them seriously. Then they would march to their respective bonfire sites where they would burn effigies of just about every authority figure they could think of. What can you do to shock a town like that?

But eventually Sam realised their weak point, the one thing that would really upset the nice people of Lewes. The Peace Statue is sacred, untouchable. On bonfire night, before they go off to burn the Pope and whoever else had offended them that year, the societies march, one by one, to the Peace Statue in the high street to lay wreaths and show their respect for the war dead. Or, as Sam liked to call them, the war criminals, who were currently killing innocent Afghans and Iraqis for oil.

His plan, after much consideration, was to crucify an effigy of a Guantanamo prisoner from the top of the Peace Statue. Of course they would remove it, but not before photos had been taken which could be sent to the Evening Argus and maybe even The Guardian, and obviously, loaded onto the Pranxsters' web site. Also, the whole thing would be covered in fake blood. Hopefully that would take a bit longer to get rid of.

The lack of red paint held him up for a long time. Even with the remains of a fairly substantial Airfix collection, he couldn't imagine there would be enough red for his purposes. Then there were his father's acrylics, used once only, to paint a bowl of unappetising, unhealthily-hued fruit. He could mix some of them together, he supposed, to make a sort of reddy-brown. This, too, he had deemed hopeless. Whatever you mixed together always just seemed to come out sludge coloured, and it just wouldn't be enough. What he needed was gallons of real blood red, enough to make a real statement. Having it delivered was not an option. He could just about assume that his parents would leave ordinary boxes and packages on the hall table for him to pick up, but a tin of paint? Never.

A sound made him concentrate again. It sounded like a police radio, and now he remembered a similar noise that had become mixed with his dreams. He went over to the Velux at the front of the house and peered out. He couldn't quite see what was parked directly outside, but he could just catch a glimpse of something white outside next door. The voice came again, slightly too loud to be from a person, and ending in a crunching noise.

It had to be coming from next door. He went to the back window and looked out at their garden. Then he opened the window and craned his head outside. The new woman next door had been painting the shed. He had watched her for quite a while. She was lovely looking, for an older woman, with her track suit on and her blonde hair up. He was disappointed when she stopped half way through, as if she meant to go back to it later. But now there was the can of paint: rust red, waiting for him in next door's garden.

He reached under the mattress and pulled out a brown paper packet. It was already open and he slid the contents out onto the bed and then unfolded it: a neon orange jumpsuit, slightly crumpled from having been slept on.

Next he felt around underneath the bed and pulled out a box. The blow up man was not anatomically correct, Sam was pleased to see. He didn't want there to be anything whack about this. He'd had a few anxious moments, wondering whether his parents would decide to open it and what they would make of it, especially if instead of the 'ideal car companion' advertised on the internet as 'helping ladies to safely enjoy their independence', it would actually turn out to be some sort of gay sex aid.

It was going to be difficult enough anyway. He had spent a lot of time trying to think of the best way of doing things. At first he thought that he would blow up the dummy and dress it at home. The problem would then be trying to get it to the war memorial. It would never work. Lewes was quiet, but there would always be someone around. The second option: blowing it up and getting it ready somewhere nearer to the memorial, would be difficult, and possibly really embarrassing if he did get caught. He imagined standing there bike pump in one hand, naked blow-up man in the other.

He thought through the area street by street. Nowhere was perfect, but in his nocturnal ramblings he had noticed some building work going on at the back of Tilsey Street and a couple of skips that he could hide between.

It was nearly time, just one more thing to do. He went over to his computer and opened up the draft email that he'd been working on for days. It said:

> *Hi*
> *I am interested in the room you said about on the Pranxsters site. I can pay the money.*
> *I am very interested in the work of the Pranxsters and would like to do more. I have a prank organised for Lewes bonfire and will need the room after I have done it so I will come tomorrow. I hope this is OK.*
> *Fletch*

He read it through once more, feeling pleased with his new nickname. He wasn't going to be 'Sam' anymore.

He pressed 'Send' and then shivered a little, feeling scared, but pleasantly so. It was all coming together. All he had to do was to wait until night time. It never even occurred to him that he wouldn't be able to have the room.

***

Emily sat at her desk for about ten minutes, staring at the black computer screen. Eventually some kind of automatic impulse kicked in and she turned it on, but then she resumed staring as it spun through its start-up procedures. After a couple of minutes it resolved itself into a photograph of herself, Mark and Sam two years ago in Wales. You could see a craggy blue inlet behind them and they were all smiling with suntanned, happy faces. Emily looked into each of their eyes, first Sam's, then Mark's then her own. Then she focused on the indigo sea in the background.

She carried on looking when the phone rang, merely holding the receiver up to her ear while she stared. She almost didn't recognise Clare's voice.

'Emily' she whispered. 'It's me. Have you heard?'

'Have I heard what?' she said.

'It's James, next door. There's been some sort of incident, the police said. They want me to go round and sit with Jenny until her Dad gets here.'

'What kind of incident?'

'I don't know. It must have happened while he was out jogging. Tim was out looking for him for ages last night.'

'What happened to James?' Emily could hear her voice becoming strange, high pitched.

'Oh, god, didn't I say? He's dead, Emily. Isn't it awful? It's made me feel really terrible. I feel really sick. When they first told me I thought I was going to faint. Luckily the policewoman got hold of my arm. Now I've got to go round there. I won't know what to say. Look, I'll phone you later, OK? Better go.'

Clare put the phone down, and, some time later, so did Emily. After a few more minutes she got up and went downstairs. She put on her jacket and then, catching sight

124

of herself in the hall mirror went back upstairs to the bathroom and brushed her hair. She grabbed her bag and set off down the road. A passing woman looked at her feet and smirked. Emily looked down at her pink towelling slippers and walked quickly back to the house. She changed into her shoes and then set off again.

She was heading towards Welsh Passage but she didn't have a plan in mind. She didn't know Dougie's house number for a start. It was a short street, so she could knock on a few doors. Someone would be bound to recognise his description. But she couldn't do that. She couldn't have anything that connected him with her. Then what would she do? Hope to bump into him and ask him if he'd killed James? The more she thought about it the crazier a plan it seemed. Still, she couldn't stop walking in the direction of Welsh Passage. It was as if her now correctly clad feet had nothing to do with her.

Emily knew that what she ought to do was to go straight to the Police and tell them of her suspicions. But she couldn't bear it. She couldn't bear the thought of anyone else in the world knowing that she'd done such a thing. She felt so ashamed and horrified she didn't know how she was going to live with herself if any of it had anything to do with her. And it would all come out: the whole thing. She might even be prosecuted, for procuring something or other. She could say that she didn't think he was serious, but would that help? The fact that she even knew such a person, that she was telling him her deepest worries. How would everyone look at her after that? And how was she already looking at herself?

If it was not true, she did not have to think about any of it again. She would not even have to confront herself. The whole thing might be some kind of bizarre, dreadful coincidence, and if she told anyone she would make a fool of herself, and worse, for nothing. She just had to see Dougie's face, and then she'd know for sure. Then she'd think about what to do for the best.

Welsh Passage is just off the high street. It is a quaint, one sided alley, that you get to by walking through a narrow tunnel between two shops. The cottages are all on the right-hand side, about six of them. None has more than two bedrooms and each of the rooms, including the tiny living rooms, would not comfortably hold more than three people.

Emily walked past the entrance to the alley. There was no one around. She walked past again and pretended interest in the display of the adjacent antique shop. The woman inside the shop looked up hopefully and then pretended interest in her newspaper. The two women carried on in this way for several minutes. Then the shopkeeper gave up and turned around to reorganise the display shelves.

Emily realised she'd made a mistake. This woman could be a witness. Emily wasn't sure to what, but all the same. She moved off and turned decisively into Welsh Passage.

The momentum carried her down the small street too quickly. At the end she paused, wondering what on earth to do; the end of the street tapered into an alley that came out in the brewery car park. If she kept on walking she would have to make a complete circuit and then come back along the high street and past the antique shop. She looked around quickly and then doubled back, this time, walking more slowly.

She scanned each house for signs of Dougie. She didn't know what they might be, but she knew that if she saw one, she'd recognise it. Eventually she stopped outside a house that, annoyingly, did have nets at the living room window. A black rubbish sack lay ripped and leaking outside it and next to that there was a large, empty and dissected Rizla packet. She looked back at the living room window and then up at the bedroom.

The door opened and Julie appeared. She did not look good. In her distress at Dougie's disappearance she had not gone to work or bothered to dress or even comb her hair. Aware that her breasts drooped badly without a bra, she crossed her arms over her chest. This gave her the aspect of an aggressive washerwoman.

'Can I help you?' she said. A cat appeared and twisted its way around her ankles.

'Oh, no, that's all right. Thanks.' Emily tried to move off.

'Are you looking for someone?'

'No. No. Not at all. Lovely street, this. Isn't it?'

'I know you, don't I?' a vague recollection was beginning to form in Julie's mind.

'No. You can't do. I'm not from Lewes. Thanks.' Emily took a couple of steps onward.

'Yes I do. The historical society. You gave a talk. What was it . . . ?'

Emily marched firmly onwards.

Julie called out after her. 'Sympathetic Refurbishment! That was it!'

Emily reached the end of the alley and, head down, joined the High Street.

She knew that she'd made a mistake. The woman had to be something to do with Dougie. She was the right age and class. Dougie had always liked the middle class ones. And that had to be the house. It wasn't just the Rizla packet. None of the other houses were remotely suitable. They were too tidy looking and respectable.

It was all just getting worse and worse. How would she ever explain that one away? Being seen hanging around Dougie's house? If any of this was connected to Dougie, she was finished now. She felt in total limbo, hardly able to breath with anticipation: either her life was finished, or it wasn't. The more she thought about it, the less she could stand not knowing. If it was all going to blow up, and if she was going to feel guilty for the rest of her life, she had to know now.

She turned off the High Street onto Station Street. She would go to Brighton and try to find him there. Her mobile sounded loudly and made her jump. She looked at the screen and saw that there were seven missed calls, all from Copperfield Estates. There was obviously some problem with the Web site. If she was sensible, she would answer the phone and make some sort of excuse. All she needed to do was say she was sick. Then she would just have to make sure she didn't bump into any of their staff while she was in Brighton. Their office was in the North Laine too, which made things difficult. Somehow though, she just couldn't press the green button on her mobile. She couldn't have a conversation with anyone about anything.

She stood on the bridge overlooking the railway tracks. A train came in to the station and disgorged its passengers: two elderly ladies with a black Labrador and a young man with a bicycle. Emily watched them blankly until they disappeared inside the station, and then she tried to organise her thoughts. Not being at work today was a mistake. If she was right about everything it could look very suspicious. Added to the incident in Welsh Passage . . . and if she was seen lurking around Dougie's pitch in Brighton . . . She was starting to look at her behaviour as it would appear to the police or even a jury. Maybe it would even seem as if money had changed hands. She groaned. The man with the bicycle wobbled as he passed and gave her a peculiar look. The train chugged off out of the station and reluctantly, Emily turned towards home. Tomorrow was Saturday. She could go and look for him then.

**

Dougie was in Brighton, but not anywhere that Emily was likely to bump into him. He was in Tizer's lounge, watching This Morning and teasing Sid the dog. Dougie prodded Sid with a rolled up newspaper until Sid got up and moved away, then Dougie swapped seats until he was near enough to start prodding him again. Sid eventually got up and moved so that he was sitting right in front of the closed door, desperately waiting for someone to open it.

Dougie looked around the room for something else to do. The magazine on the floor had a little bit of joint leavings on it, but not really enough to make a new one, or even a roll up worth smoking. He had the remains of the money that Marty had given him and no way of getting any more unless he went back to Julie's tomorrow to pick up his dole cheque. He didn't dare trying to sign on from Brighton yet, just in case.

He knew he would have lost his Big Issue pitch by now. You couldn't not turn up, not for days at a time. The pitches in central Brighton were too popular to fuck around. He couldn't do anything about it though. Standing there like that he'd be easy meat if anyone had made some sort of connection.

All the same, he couldn't sit around the house any more. It wasn't just the money; it was doing his head in. He needed to get out and do something to take his mind off the scene by the river. He was now quite persuaded that it was the rugby cunt's fault. He shouldn't have been a cunt in the first place and in the second place he shouldn't have answered back. But all of that didn't make it easier when Dougie remembered the flat sheen of the man's eyes in the glow of his lighter.

He changed channels on the TV. The local news would be in a few minutes and he'd make his decision after that.

Someone knocked, hard, on the front door. Dougie started and then sank back into the padded velour of the sofa. Sid sensed his imminent liberation and whined and scratched at the living room door. Dougie stayed, frozen, for a good two minutes while the person at the door continued to thump the brass knocker. It couldn't be anything good. Anyone who knew the house knew to not to knock like that.

Eventually there were footsteps on the stairs and Dougie heard Tizer shouting 'Hold on, who is it?' as he walked downstairs.

A muffled voice behind the door coughed and then said 'It's Barney. About the room.'

Dougie relaxed again as Tizer unlocked the door and brought the visitor inside. Sid sidled out as they opened the living room door.

Barney was a large chap, unkempt and a little bit ripe smelling, but he gave the other two men a big friendly smile and shook their hands. Dougie returned his hard man smile, and then focussed on the telly, leaving Tizer to deal with the formalities.

The 'riverside murder' as they called it, was the main story. Dougie tried to block out the chat from Barney and Tizer and leaned towards the television. He didn't want to turn the sound up and arouse suspicion. There was a bit about the rugby shirt. Dougie was thrilled to see that they were getting it confused with the stripy smuggler uniforms of the Lewes bonfire societies. They spent quite a few minutes discussing the rival societies and linked the shirt with Cliffe whose members wore a black and white striped shirt.

Then there was a bit of film of the wife pushing past photographers outside the house in Lewes and getting into a new BMW. Dougie felt a twinge of envy at the car. She was going to do alright for herself out of it. Those sorts of people always fell on their feet. They bounced back. It was less easy for someone like him.

Finally there was an appeal for witnesses. There was nothing about any suspect. No dodgy drawing or photofit picture. They didn't seem to know anything at all. Dougie leapt to his feet.

'Right,' he said. 'I'll see you guys later. Nice to meet you Barney.'

Tizer followed him out to the hall. 'So what do you think then?' he said.

Dougie looked confused. 'Oh, old Barney in there. Yeah whatever. Couldn't give a fuck, mate.'

'Well I need the rent, so I'm going to let him have it. You need to pay me your rent too Dougie. Can you get it today?' Tizer was sure that he wouldn't get it, today or for a long time to come.

'Sure,' said Dougie. 'No problem.'

19. EXPLANATIONS AND RATIONALISATIONS

Emily felt sick and rather wobbly as she walked back up Pelham Street, glancing manically from side to side, desperate to avoid seeing Jenny. She fumbled with the keys and let herself in as quickly as possible, breathing a huge sigh of relief as she closed the door behind her. Then she trudged straight up to the security of her study.

The problem with the Web site was the sort of thing that she could fix on autopilot, and somehow she managed to get through it, but when she had finished she could not hold herself together any longer. She took herself to bed where she curled up into a foetal ball.

It was some time before she could let herself think the situation through. It was as if the pain of thinking that she could be responsible for another person's death was too intense to last in its current form. She simply could not take the blame for this. It was too much, too great a punishment for her crime. A human life could not hang on a couple of sentences uttered on a park bench. She had done nothing, really. Nothing to be ashamed of. And anyway, it all had to be to do with something else. It was too much of a coincidence. What did she know about these people anyway? They could have enemies. Who knew why they moved to Lewes in the first place. A picture of James' slightly round and uninteresting face slid, uninvited, into her mind and she pushed it out. Actually, the whole thing was more likely to be a straightforward mugging gone wrong.

She began to uncurl. If it wasn't her fault, what then? She was very sorry for Jenny, of course. She would make a bit of effort. Pop round with stew etc. Jenny's face now appeared in her mind and she pushed this out too. Well, maybe she wouldn't pop round right away. It might be considered intrusive.

She sat up. What would be the implications for the planning permission? Surely it wouldn't go ahead? The brief, guilty, feeling of euphoria subsided. The process would continue, regardless. Whatever Jenny's future plans involved, she was unlikely to be contacting the planning office any time soon. Once the permission was granted it would be too late. The threat would always be there. Emily's only hope would be if it was denied and that was unlikely to happen.

She heard Sam moving around upstairs. Cupboard doors opened and closed. Drawers scraped open. He was being active today. She couldn't work out whether that was a good thing or a bad thing.

Now that both the pain and the euphoria had subsided, all she was left with was a low-level ache. Was there nothing good about her life? What did she have to look forward to: another miserable evening with Mark? Then she remembered that Sally was coming for the weekend and bonfire night. Sally was useless. An utter flake, who would be of no real help at all, but the thought of seeing her made Emily feel a bit better.

She heard Mark's key in the door and then his footsteps in the hall. He did not call out. She got up slowly and glanced at herself in the mirror of the dressing table. She smoothed down her hair and pulled her cardigan straight and then went down the stairs to meet him.

By the time she had reached the basement kitchen he was already pouring himself a large glass of red wine.

Emily grimaced. 'Do you have to do that' she said, ostentatiously looking at her watch. It was half past five. As a response, Mark picked up the glass and downed it in a couple of gulps.

'I've taken the car to the garage,' he said. 'It's buggered. Like everything bloody else.'

He put down his glass and turned on the television. He did not look at her the whole time.

The local news was just beginning. The riverside murder was still the lead item. Emily swallowed her internal tirade and turned away, intently preparing the evening meal.

***

Next door but one, Clare was making cakes. She was in full domestic goddess mode, wearing a flowery cotton apron. Radio 5 Live was on the kitchen radio.

Baking helped Clare to think. The methodical nature of the work, the weighing, sifting and mixing, somehow left her free to ponder. And there were a lot of things to ponder about. First of all: the murder. How awful! Lewes was going downhill fast. It was getting more like Brighton every day. She did wonder whether situations like this had to do with the growth of social housing in the area. She wouldn't say this out loud, Lewes being absolutely full of Guardian-reading bleeding heart liberals, of which she, of course, was one. It was common sense though. These people were unable to afford their own homes because they had problems of one sort or another. Problem people brought their problems with them, she reasoned. It was just a fact of life.

Mostly, however, she was pondering the news she had just received from her daughter. After Sam's dramatic intrusion into Emily's dinner party Clare had subtly, and out of Tim's earshot, asked Tamsin to find out what was going on with him. The incident had jolted her into realising that this was the first time she had seen him for ages, and Emily was being decidedly cagey. Clare had an instinct for these things. Emily had a sore spot, and Clare intended to prod it.

Tamsin did not mix in the same circles as Sam. They went to different schools and Sam was nearly two years her senior. Also, despite the age difference, which could have added interest for another kind of girl; he was, thankfully, just not her type. Her crowd hung around at parties in the big houses in the surrounding countryside.

Her friends' parents were mostly rich and sometimes Clare got the feeling that Tamsin was slightly embarrassed about the house in Pelham Street. She certainly wasn't interested in the boy who lived next door but one.

The last time that Tamsin had registered Sam's existence he had been one of the goths from the Priory school who hung around near Tesco on the riverbank. They looked stupid and ugly and were not of interest. All the same, Lewes is a small town. There was always someone who knew someone else. It didn't take the girl long to find out what the story was. In fact, she had heard the essentials before, but just hadn't associated them with Sam.

***

The outside world seemed to be beckoning Sam. From the attic window he could see the bright blueness of the sky dotted with tiny white clouds and it looked inviting. He realised that he longed to be outside. He was ready.

He looked into next door's garden. The new people didn't seem to notice that their fence paint was missing yet. It was now safely hidden under his bed after his midnight foray to their garden. The plan was coming together and he was feeling pretty happy with his progress.

Then something gave him the feeling that he was being watched. He stepped back hurriedly from the window and peered out again. There were people in Tamsin's garden. It was Tamsin and her mum, having tea at the table outside their conservatory. They were speaking in low voices, leaning towards each other. Then they both looked up towards his attic and he could see both of them smirk and whisper again.

So they knew. They definitely knew. That was that then. If they knew then his Mum would soon know too, if she didn't already. This was beyond awful. It was definitely time to get out of Lewes. Sam sat down on his bed and cradled his face in his hands trying to block out the unwanted memories.

It had been a really hot day in that really hot summer. The heatwave was getting to everyone, especially Sam and his friends, probably because they all wore black and would not give up their enormous boots with unwalkable platform soles. Someone, probably Eileen, suggested swimming. It wasn't something they would normally do. It meant taking off their clothes and virtually everyone in the group was either quite fat or unattractively skinny. (Sam saw himself in the latter category.) Appearing without make up was an issue too. Complexions were not ideal.

Still, he was willing to go because he had a thing about Eileen. She was an exception to the fat and spotty rule. She was also considered to be a bit of a sure thing, and she'd been looking at Sam a lot recently.

Pell's pool is beautiful in its simplicity, a huge turquoise rectangle with the changing rooms at one end and the kiosk/café at the other. To one side there is a large stretch of flat grass for sunbathers and a small kiddy pool. The whole thing is surrounded by trees.

Inside, Sam immediately noticed that there were several people from school. A couple of them looked up and then looked away hurriedly. He saw Fleur Peterson fail to disguise a smirk.

A cloud of thick, hormonal embarrassment enveloped the group as they advanced. Sam felt his legs become heavy and walking became something that he had to think about rather than a natural process. The pool is large and the distance to the changing rooms seemed to grow further and further in front of him. Anyone who wasn't swimming was sitting or sunbathing on the grassy area. This meant that they had to negotiate a kind of catwalk between the swimmers and the sunbathers. They were all quiet now, even Eileen. The people on the grass stopped talking too, and those who had originally been facing in another direction turned around to look. A little girl wearing knickers and nothing else seemed to be the only person who had not noticed them. She was turned in the other direction, dragging a float towards the paddling pool and Sam could hear her high, reedy voice as she talked to herself. 'And Maisie will come to tea and Amy and Aeisha.'

At last they reached the changing rooms and the whole pool seemed to heave a sigh of relief. Sam dived into a cubicle and sat on the wooden bench, listening to the others talking outside. Pete Russell was refusing to get changed. He really was quite fat and Sam couldn't blame him. Then a couple of the others said that they weren't going to go in either.

'For fuck's sake!' This was John Watkin. 'Sam, you're coming aren't you? They're really going to laugh if none of us even go swimming.'

Sam got up and started to strip. 'Yeah, I'm coming.' He was really too hot. The weather didn't agree with him, he was too pale for the heat. He felt that if he could only get in the water and cool down he'd feel better. This was actually becoming more important to him than worrying about whether a few people would laugh. He felt sure that Eileen would go in too. This might be his chance, with most of the others out of the way. He wondered what she would look like in a swimming costume and then quickly thought about George Bush. When even this didn't do the trick he tried to solve a maths problem they had been set that afternoon. The last thing he wanted was to start 'tenting' while wearing swimming shorts. He wondered if he should quickly knock one out to minimise the risk, but realised that he couldn't stay in the cubicle for much longer without arousing suspicion.

'Okay' he said as he emerged, 'Let's go.' He looked at the two other boys wearing trunks. They were not an attractive group, he had to admit. John was not really overweight but his shoulders seemed narrow when compared with his hips and he was hairless and pink. The other boy, Saul, was extremely hairy despite the fact that he had still not reached five foot four without his platforms. 'Let's jump straight in,' said Sam.

After the initial sniggers as they got into the water everyone settled back down again. Sam would have enjoyed himself but he seemed to be developing a headache. His neck was very hot and even leaning back in the water did not help. He swam away from the shallow end and the screaming children, and then put his whole head under water. This helped briefly, but only briefly.

Then Eileen appeared. She really was very fine in her bikini: slim with curves, pale but not pasty like him. She appeared to know how good she looked and glanced over at a group of girls from school to make sure that they had checked her out. They had, and their faces were sour.

She climbed in and swam towards Sam. He felt himself become hard again and swam away so that it would not be visible.

'Sam!' she called out, 'race you to the side.'

It was the last thing he felt like, but how could he refuse? The sun hit the back of his neck all the way there and she beat him effortlessly. She swam over and grabbed him by the shoulders, playing at dunking him.

'You let me win!' she said.

He tried to smile, amazed and mystified to find that despite feeling quite ill, he had an erection again. She shook his shoulders and her small breasts jiggled.

'You are such a cheater! I'm going to get your trunks for that!'

She lunged towards him and he backed away, terrified. Her hand had nearly made contact. He found himself trapped in the corner of the pool where the sun hit him squarely on the back of the neck. He looked up at Eileen. Her breath smelt of tuna and onions.

Then his stomach did a strange sort of double flip. His hands were still holding fast to his trunks and he could not move them quickly enough. He vomited straight into her laughing face. At the same time, he felt his shorts become warm and heavy.

***

Tamsin's eyes shone. 'They had to get everyone out of the pool and everything,' she said. 'It was awful.'

Clare almost managed to control her features. 'Oh dear! Poor Sam' she said.

'Yes' said Tamsin. 'They got him out and took him into the kiosk and then they must have got his clothes and taken him home. Anyway, nobody's seen him since.'

Clare wandered back to the kitchen, still thinking. She checked that the oven was hot enough and then poured the mixture into a greased dish. An idea had occurred to her. She ran her finger around the mixing bowl and then licked it, closing her eyes. 'Lovely,' she said.

21. ESCAPE

At three o'clock in the morning, nothing happens in Lewes. The streets have lost their bustle and its cutesy country town feel has disappeared. It takes on another air, which is slightly different. It's closer, tighter, and strangely unpleasant. Such an ancient town is made up of corners and turnings. There could always be something around the next corner or the next. Narrow bending streets rise up towards the castle ruins and then dip down, meandering to the slow depths of the river. The River Ouse, black, syrupy and reflectionless, slides out of town towards the shadows of the South Downs.

Everyone is asleep. Well, almost everyone. On this particular night there were at least two people who were awake. One was Sam. He was still in his room, re packing, stuffing socks and underpants into his rucksack. He remembered his toothbrush and toothpaste as an afterthought and put them in too. He spent a lot of time thinking about what clothes he should take, putting one thing into his rucksack and then taking it out again as he thought of something better. He was done with being a goth. Anything black now just reminded him of the day at the swimming pool.

He was aware that he was putting off the final decisive moment. He really should get going. He had packed the important things hours ago, the doll and the orange jumpsuit. The can of paint could swing from his handlebars. Now he had a last look around and took a deep breath, then slowly and quietly, he turned the handle on the door and stepped outside.

Once in the street he found the keys in his pocket and, with a rush of adrenalin, posted them through the door. He heard them clank, too loudly, as they hit the doormat and quickly manoeuvred the bike into position. He took one last look at the house, which seemed to gaze emptily back at him, and then jumped on the bike and let it roll him quickly down the hill. It carried him down the backstreets that ran parallel with the high street and towards the war memorial. He began to peddle in earnest when he got near to it. If he was going to do this he had to do it quickly.

***

At least one other person was out and about in Lewes: PC Roberts. The station was in an uproar about the body in the river. Everyone had to do a double shift and the police station was still alive with lights and the self-important noise of her colleagues. The murder was the most exciting thing that had happened in years.

She got into the car and turned on the engine. There was a Mars bar in the glove compartment. If she parked up in one of the side streets she could eat it in peace. There hadn't been time to eat anything for ages. Besides, there was really no point in dashing about at this time of night. One murder was unusual enough. There was hardly going to be another one tonight. She let her anticipation build, thinking the different layers of the sweet; the chocolaty bit merging into the toffee and then melting into the soft nougat. Who had thought up that combination? It just wouldn't have worked as well the other way up. That was why Mars bars had a top side. The thought struck her as very profound.

***

Sam stopped round the corner from the war memorial. He had found the same building works and skip that Dougie had used to bury his jacket in only a few days earlier. This would have to do. He needed somewhere to blow up the doll. Somewhere that he couldn't be seen. He was aware of what he would look like, blowing up a plastic doll. It would be alright once he'd put on the orange jumpsuit and the fake blood. Then people would understand what he was getting at. Until then he would just look like some sort of pervert.

He crouched down beside the skip and removed the doll from its packaging. It didn't take as long to blow up as he thought. Soon its body was filling out and its legs and torso looked less flaccid. He took a quick break to loosen the lid of the paint. It was a little painted on and his hands were cold, but, with the help of a two p piece, he managed to prise it open. Then he put it back on top of the tin and resumed blowing up the doll.

PC Roberts looked around quickly, split open the empty wrapper and licked the remaining traces of chocolate. She folded the wrapper neatly and placed it in the glove compartment. She supposed that she should move off: make another circuit of the town, but now she felt a little bit lazy, so she turned the radio down as far as it would go and dozed for a few minutes. Her eyes were just drooping closed when she saw some kind of movement behind the skip. She paused and turned around. There was nothing. She waited for a few moments and then turned to start the car. Then she saw it again. It was over in a flash but she was sure that she had seen an arm: a pale, stiff and naked arm.

Slowly at first, and then with increasing frenzy, Sam pulled everything out of the rucksack. The brown packet containing the orange jumpsuit was not there. He had left it at home. 'Crap! Crap! Crap!' he hissed. He would have to go back and get it. It was then that he remembered his grand gesture: he had posted the keys through the door.

He stared at this rucksack in disbelief, willing it to yield the orange jumpsuit. Without it, what had he got? No one would know what he meant. The jumpsuit was the thing that spelt Guantanamo. Without it he just had a blow up doll and some fence paint.

The doll was now deflating slightly, which made it even more grotesque. Its face was made of stronger plastic than the rest and stayed relatively firm but flat, whilst the body took on a decayed and shrunken look. He thought about throwing it in the skip. The whole thing was such a let down, he just wanted to give up and crawl into a corner to hide. He couldn't bring himself to do it though. It had cost quite a bit. Maybe he could think of something to do with it later. The paint could stay there. He'd never intended to carry that as far as Brighton.

Meanwhile, PC Roberts was frozen with fear. She supposed that she should get out of the car and investigate but she had no intention of doing that. The doors of the Astra were locked and would stay that way. She would sit and wait until she was sure and then call for backup. She sat quite still, willing nothing to happen. A leg, slightly flaccid this time, fell out from behind the skip and was dragged back behind it as Sam tried to squash the doll into his rucksack.

That was enough. She grabbed at the radio controls and, at the same time, switched on the lights.

Mercifully from Sam's point of view, the lights faced the wrong direction and only illuminated a white transit van to the right of the skip. He leapt up, kicking over the open can of fence paint. It rolled away under the van, leaving a trail of rusty-coloured gloop behind it. He picked up his bike and pedalled off as hard as he could, still holding the rucksack in his hands. PC Roberts, momentarily disoriented by the lights, did not even see him go.

Sam pedalled hard in the first direction that came to him, careering down Rotten Row and down towards Southover. Two minutes later he found himself outside Southover Grange. This was probably the best route he could have chosen, the area around the Grange and its gardens are quiet even during the daytime at that time of year. That night, there was absolutely no one to wonder what he was up to. He locked the bike to a lamp post and surveyed the wall surrounding the Grange gardens. A couple of metres away some of the stones were loose and had left small holes in the surface. Shifting his bag to his back he scrabbled up and over the wall.

The garden was a black grotto. Shadows caused variations in the blackness from blue to black to kohl. He walked towards the darker shadows, smelling the autumn smells of damp leaves and soil. Soon the warmth of the bike ride would wear off and it would be cold. There was nothing he could do for now though. If he was seen by the police they would take him home. He would have to hide for the rest of the night and then cycle to Brighton where there were more people about.

Meanwhile PC Roberts had called for backup. She waited until she heard the patrol car approaching and only then left the safety of the Astra. She shone her torch around to make sure that no one was hiding in the shadows and then concentrated on the skip. The wet trail of fence paint caught her eye at once. Under the artificial light of the torch virtually all colour was drained from the scene, but the paint still showed a faint copper tint.

'Sarge' she said as her superior officer approached. 'Look at this.'

By the time they had found the can of paint and realised their mistake the dogs had caught the scent of something interesting in the skip. Dougie's black leather jacket was soon in a large plastic evidence bag.

22. BONFIRE MORNING

By the morning of the fifth of November most of the preparations for bonfire night have already been made and there is an air of anticipation in the town.

The work had been going on all year. The tableaux had been discussed, argued over and painstakingly made. Fireworks had been bought and stored in warehouses on the edge of town. Working bees had spent Sundays sitting outside pubs in the October cold, fashioning a seemingly endless supply of wooden torches and crucifixes.

Costumes were also ready. Some of the bonfire boys stuck to the smuggler outfits: the stripy jumpers and long hats in the colours of their society, originally, and sometimes still, chosen so that the police would be unable to identify wrongdoers. Others dressed in their particular society's 'First Pioneer' costume: As Clare walked back from Waitrose laden with party supplies she spotted several Vikings and three monks smoking outside Threshers. Being in the catchment area for the De Montfort society, quite a few people normally turned up at her party in their medieval costumes. It was all jolly good fun.

Police were already evident, preparing to herd the crowds off trains from London and Brighton like so many football hooligans. Later in the evening they would herd them back on again. Even people who live in Lewes have found themselves unable to escape once caught up in the crowds and have ended up on the train to Brighton.

But the best part happens when all the last trains have gone. Then, the Bonfire societies have the town to themselves to do what they want. Attempts at following fire regulations are thrown off. Burning barrels of tar litter the high street and the red Indians and Vikings throw fireworks at them, filling the air with explosions and coloured smoke. Trying to get from one side of town to another can be the closest feeling that the nice middle class people of Lewes get to visiting a war zone.

This year, though, no one knew quite what to do about Clare's party. Was it quite right to hold it so soon after the murder, and in the house next door to Jenny? The phone rang in Clare's house every few minutes. The conversation was virtually the same each time.

'Oh I know . . . Yes, absolutely awful . . . No, the police don't seem to know a thing . . . Poor Jenny . . . No, she's away, with her father apparently . . . I don't know if she'll come back at all to be honest . . . absolutely . . . no, I'll pass that on . . . such a shame, they were such a nice couple . . . oh I know . . . well, I did think about cancelling, but the children would be so disappointed . . . I think so . . . as she isn't here . . . Oh good, have you? Oh lovely, I always look forward to that . . . no, really . . . delicious . . . see you later then.'

And so preparations for the party went on in much the same way as always, as Clare had always known that they would.

**

Emily had been one of the first to phone. She was up early to meet Sally in Brighton. Sally had said that she wanted to go shopping in the North Laine. When she first suggested this, Emily had been glad; it meant that she had an excuse for being in the areas that might bring her into contact with Dougie. Now she had decided that she didn't want to see him. She had convinced herself that it all had nothing to do with her. It was probably best to leave well alone. She didn't really want to see anyone, but she knew that she had to attend Clare's party. Anything else would look odd.

Mark was up before her. He was sitting in the kitchen stirring Coco Pops into a bowl of milk. He did this every morning. He couldn't eat the things until the milk was brown and the cereal was mushy. It annoyed Emily so much that she couldn't even look.

'What are you up to today?' she said. There was no assumption that they would spend the day together any more.

'Thought I'd look for jobs on your PC. If that's ok. I can't count on SunAlliance.'

'No, fine. Good idea.' Emily made coffee and took it over to the sofa. 'I expect we'll come back for Clare's party. You going to it?'

'I expect so. It seems a bit wrong. What with next door and everything.' He paused, waiting for Emily to agree, but she wasn't really listening. 'Tim's got this new video game: You steal cars and stuff. It's supposed to be really amazing.'

'How adult.' She bit her tongue. He was making an effort. 'Ok. I'll see you later then.'

She took her coffee and trudged up the stairs. There was nothing holding them together now. How long it had been getting like this? They had been so busy with their jobs and with the house and with Sam, and then, without warning, there had been nothing left between them but those things.

The post pushed through the letter box, getting stuck before it hit the floor. She tutted and went over to remove it. Then she saw Sam's keys lying on the mat, glinting in the light from the door glass. She picked them up and held them in both hands. She didn't need to go upstairs to look, but she went anyway. His door was open and the room was tidy, as much as a room that hadn't been vacuumed for three months could be. This was oddly touching. He hadn't wanted her to break the door down or to leave a mess.

Everything was there. There were no clues. She went to the desk ran her fingers over the computer keyboard. She toyed with the idea of giving him his privacy, but soon, she knew, she would log on and do whatever she could to break his passwords and read his mail. He was just too young. He was sixteen; he was just too young to decide to leave. She would have to call the police.

At this thought she sat down on Sam's bed and groaned. Why now, she thought. And she would have the added worry of him being out in the world when there was a murderer on the loose.

She looked up and saw Mark standing in the doorway.

'So he's gone,' he said. His voice sounded strained, miserable. She had never seen another human being look so wretched. Without even realising that she was doing it, she held out her hand, and then they were holding each other, uncomfortably, but tightly. Their failure with their son was the last thing that they shared.

***

Sam had been awake for a long time. In fact he had only managed a couple of hours sleep before his sleeping bag had become clammy with dew and the cold seemed to seep into his bones, numbing his fingers and toes. Then he had to get up and move around. He felt as if he might actually die of cold if he didn't. It was still too early to go, though, and he didn't dare move around too much in case he was seen, so he wrapped the damp sleeping bag around his shoulders and shivered. He had to wait until at least the start of the morning traffic before he could leave.

His plan hadn't changed in spite of the previous night's failure. There was no alternative. He had to go to the address Tizer had given and beg for the room. He would no longer be able to impress them with his Guantanamo 'prank', but they had to let him stay. He had nowhere else to go.

It was seven o'clock before the traffic noises began to pick up outside. The gates were still locked so he looked around quickly and then climbed back over the wall. His bike was where he had left it. He gave a sigh of relief and set off towards the A27 to Brighton. He reckoned that he had two hours before his parents woke up, realised that he was missing and then called the police. It would be better to be in the crowds of a Brighton Saturday by then.

***

His timing was about right. Emily let Mark phone round Sam's friends, only to hear what they had expected, that Sam hadn't been in contact with any of them for months. Sometimes it was even longer than that. They hadn't really know who Sam was hanging around with for some time. A couple of boys had to be reminded of who Sam was and one of them sniggered when he was reminded. John Watkin sounded worried. He had known Sam since primary school and had phoned the house several times when he first disappeared. He couldn't suggest anything.

Mark then phoned the police. The constable invited him to the station to fill in some forms but was not enthusiastic until Mark suggested that a missing person should perhaps be a course of worry in a town where a murder had just taken place. The thought of another murder victim seemed to cheer the policeman briefly, but he could see that this was unlikely given the circumstances.

'He left his keys, you say. Sixteen, not getting on with parents, and left his keys. If I was you I'd have a look round Brighton. That's where they go. The excitement . . . nightclubs, girls, drugs,' he said wistfully, 'it's all down there.'

Mark missed out the last piece of information when he relayed the conversation to Emily, but agreed about Brighton. 'He's right, you know. One of us should go.'

'Oh God!' Emily looked at her watch. 'I said I'd meet Sally. She'll be on her way by now.'

'That's all right. You go. Look for him with Sal. I'll try the pier and the sea front. You could do the North Laine. Where else do kids hang out? He doesn't look old enough to get into pubs. Mind you, three months . . . he might have grown a couple of inches.'

149

'What about London?' said Emily, hardly daring to say the word out loud. The thought that Sam had gone to London was unspeakable.

They stared at the floor.

Eventually Emily roused herself. 'What's the point? If he's gone there we've had it. We wouldn't know where to start. We just have to hope that it's Brighton.' They sat in silence, staring at the mysterious orange jump suit. 'What's the point of looking for him anyway. We can't make him come back.'

'No,' Mark took hold of her hand. 'We can just ask him to. We can make him see that we care that he's gone.'

'He hates me the most, you know. You should be the one out looking for him.'

Mark didn't attempt to deny it. 'We both need to go' he said. 'We can cover more ground that way.'

'First' said Emily 'let's try the computer. He has to have somewhere to stay and he must have arranged it via his computer. He has to have made other friends somehow. There's no other way.'

***

Tim watched Clare with amusement as she stirred the saucepan. He knew his wife and he could see that she was sporting what he called her 'bad twinkle'. She was going to do something naughty. An extra firework for the party, he imagined. Probably something to do with what she had told him about Sam.

'Possum,' he said, 'are you up to something?'

She looked back at him, her face a model of pained innocence. 'What do you mean? Of course not.' She dropped a slither of black toffee into a glass of water where it formed a string question mark. 'Just looking forward to the party, that's all. Toffee's ready.'

Tim shrugged. Emily could look after herself. Girls would be girls, after all. Anyway, he often found Clare's antics quite amusing. The party would be fun.

23. SATURDAY IN BRIGHTON (AND SURREY)

Saturday in Brighton; the hustle and bustle; the crowds of young and not so young, everyone looking for bargains, looking at each other, eating, drinking. To some people, nothing could be more fun. Others would pay good money to avoid it.

Emily and Mark found themselves being emptied from the Lewes train and forced by the tide of people out of the station. They were part way down the Queen's Road before they could find a place to stand and say goodbye.

'I'll phone Sally. I can't go back in that station. I'll meet her somewhere else. Where are you going first?'

'I thought I'd head straight for the pier. Have a look along the sea front on the way. Then double back and go out towards King Alfred. I could come back along Western Road and meet you.

'Ok' she kissed him lightly on the cheek. 'Phone me, won't you. If there's anything.'

'Of course.'

They turned in their different directions. Not hopeful, but less desperate than they had been a couple of hours earlier. After the phone call with John Watkin they had both been conscious of a new fear, which neither of them had expressed out loud. Would Sam kill himself? They had had plenty of arguments over the past few months about whether they should bring in a doctor to try to talk to him. Emily had wavered, sometimes in favour, but Mark was against, feeling that this would humiliate the boy and end up being counter-productive. What eventually swung the decision is that there was no cosy relationship with a local doctor who knew the family. The practice had become one of these modern affairs where you never knew who you were going to get when you turned up, and where you never seemed to get the same person twice. Neither of them could face the thought of going into their family difficulties with a complete stranger.

The search of Sam's room had allayed their fears to a certain extent. The computer had not yielded much information. Sam's computer skills had improved sufficiently that he had been able to remove evidence of his emails and internet search history, but there had been a couple of clues that gave them hope.

Although he had deleted all his messages, he had kept a record of his Hotmail password in a Word file named 'Keep Out' which they found in the Recycle Bin. He had also forgotten to delete his contact list. Most of the names were familiar from before his seclusion: the friends from school that they had called that morning, but there were also some interesting addresses, in particular tizer42@hotmail.co.uk.

They debated for some time about what to do with these addresses. If they emailed them and pleaded for information about their son, Sam would no doubt be told and would probably be humiliated. He would also know that they had searched his computer. On the other hand he had to know that they would search his computer, and they had absolutely no other leads.

Eventually they settled on sending Sam a message to his Hotmail account telling him how much they loved him and wanted to have him back, and if he wouldn't come back would he please just let them know he was alright. Then they emailed the 'Tizer' address asking for whoever it was to ask Sam to get in contact and signing the email 'Mark'. That way it would hopefully just sound like a friend was looking for him and would be more likely to result in a reply while not embarrassing Sam.

Next they searched the room. The supply of porn under the mattress was expected and quickly returned to its hiding place. It was difficult to work out what exactly he had taken with him, but his sleeping bag was definitely missing. This was great news. Someone who plans to kill themselves does not need a sleeping bag. On the down side, they couldn't find his passport.

The orange jump suit had completely foxed them. It was still in its packet on the bed where Sam had left it. They laid the suit out on the bed, unable to know what to make of it. If he had been an ordinary boy with a social life they might have seen it as a fancy dress outfit, but as things stood this seemed unlikely. And then there was the fact that he had left it, unopened, on his bed. They couldn't help but feel that this was some sort of clue, but they didn't know to what.

By the time they arrived in Brighton, they knew that looking for him there was pretty pointless. It was just something to do to keep busy. Emily found a seat outside the café on the corner of Kensington Place. It was cold but sunny and most of the seats were already taken. Brightonians need a howling gale before they will give up on sitting outside and pretending that they have a Mediterranean climate. She saw a group of kids of around Sam's age pass by but by the time she thought of showing them his photo they had merged into the crowds. Then, further down Gloucester Road she thought she saw a familiar leather jacket and greying quiff. She sank back into her chair and put her head down. Was it Dougie? She had almost succeeded in blanking him from her mind.

***

In fact, Dougie was still at home in Elm Grove. Unusually, he was up before everyone else. This was because he had woken up feeling incredibly hungry. He went straight to the kitchen and raided the fridge. He knew that this wouldn't make him popular, but he didn't care. He finished the last of the bacon and the bread and most of the cheese. Then he had a bowl of cereal, leaving enough milk for his own coffee. Might as well be hung for a sheep.

After that he felt a little better, but he knew that something had to be done quickly. He had to go to Lewes and pick up his dole cheque. Julie would have gone to her mum's in Surrey with the cats by now. She hated bonfire night.

In the meantime, he had to get a little bit of money, just to survive until he could cash his giro. He had to conserve what he had left. The bus was the cheapest way to get to Lewes, but he wasn't sure if they ran on bonfire day. Normally he would try bunking the train, but he couldn't risk that at the moment.

One possibility was Marty. If he could get hold of Marty there might be some work he could do. Also, he could try and get something for the china shepherd and the rest of the stuff from the Cursey job. Marty wasn't picking up his phone though, so he'd have to try to find him. It was Saturday so there were a few places where Marty would normally be: Snoopers' Paradise, or any of the little antique shops around the centre of town, or the Basketmakers. That probably wouldn't be until later. Marty tended to be in the Basketmakers at the end of a day of wheeling and dealing so that he could prance around looking important with his chums. Not for the first time Dougie felt bitter that the Martys of this world ended up with all the money while he had to scratch around for a living.

No, he thought, he was best off getting up to Lewes and getting his dole cheque, but he couldn't turn up too early in case Julie hadn't left yet. He turned the telly on, loud. It was time that everyone woke up. There would be trouble when his housemates realised that he had eaten all of the food, but so what? He would persuade them that if they lent him some money to get to Lewes he would be able to replace it all.

He sat down with his coffee feeling better than he had in days. He would get the dole cheque and do some work for Marty and everything would be alright again. He'd forget about the other business, just forget it ever happened. Maybe he'd even go back to Julie eventually. He was sure she could be persuaded. He smiled at the prospect of getting his life back.

Then he heard the words 'Lewes murder'.

He looked up at the telly, the smile congealing on his face. Someone was holding up his ripped leather jacket which was encased in a clear plastic bag. A policeman was pointing to the blood stains.

**

Julie was actually already sitting in her bedroom at her mother's house. Archie was on her knee, Bubbles was by her side and Henry was mewing to be let out. Julie didn't notice, however. She had been watching TV pretty constantly since she arrived and had enjoyed every moment from Midsomer Murders to Jeremy Kyle.

This was completely different, though. The program was the news, and she appeared to be looking at a photo of Dougie's leather jacket. She counted back to the day that Dougie had disappeared. It was the same day that the 'bonfire murder' had happened.

Henry continued to mew, and the news carried on to a story about a skateboarding goose, but Julie remained quite still, propped up on her old single bed, staring blankly at the poster of Boy George on the wall. So Dougie had got involved in another fight. She didn't believe for a moment that he had killed anyone on purpose. Deep in her heart, in a place that she did not consciously ever look, she knew Dougie pretty well.

So that was what had happened. He was too frightened to come home. Now she felt guilty for doubting his love at the very moment he needed it most. The silly, childlike man. The trouble was that he couldn't be trusted. He had no sense of restraint. He needed looking after.

She got up and got her handbag from the chair, letting Henry out of the door as she did so. She sat down again and pulled out her purse, flipping it open to display a photo of Dougie in the plastic window. The photo showed Dougie sneering into the camera, the birthday cake she had made for him in the foreground. She kissed the photo and sighed. It honestly wasn't that she preferred their relationship when he was safely in prison, she told herself. It was just that he needed more help than she could give.

Then she picked up her mobile and called 999.

***

Sam was sitting in a cafe at the bottom of Elm Grove. It was busy and he didn't like it. He hadn't been anywhere like this for months. People pushed past to get to a seat, talked loudly, scraped chairs and plates. They were all a bit rough, too, if he was honest. The trouble was that he was really, really hungry. It seemed such a long time since he had eaten and cycling to Brighton had only made his hunger worse. He ordered the full English and watched the door to the kitchen intently, almost crazed by the smell of bacon and toast and jealous of any diner who received food before him.

At last it arrived and he set upon it, not looking up until he had mopped up the last of the bean juice with bread and margarine. He looked at his watch; it was still a little bit too early, he thought. He picked up a copy of the Evening Argus from the pile of newspapers by the counter, ordered another tea and, as an afterthought, another round of toast, and settled back to wait. The murder in Lewes held his attention for a few minutes, as long as it took him to feel a pleasant thrill that he had been wandering around alone at night while a murderer might have been watching him. After that, he forgot about it, as most sixteen year olds do forget anything that isn't directly related to them. He was in Brighton now. It was a bit rough, and he wasn't sure that he liked this part of town, but it was exciting. Lewes was the past. He was moving forward.

With that thought he got up and shunted his rucksack before him through the crowded cafe and out of the door onto a chilly Elm Grove. He couldn't wait any longer. It was time to meet Tizer.

***

Dougie turned the volume right down while he watched the rest of the news item. They still had nothing else, but they had the jacket. This was really bad. His mind seemed to go blank and he struggled to process the new information except to realise that it was really bad news. The next story was about preparations for bonfire night and the happy-looking newsreader and small children in their costumes seemed to Dougie like an unbelievable affront. He turned the telly off so he could think.

They had the jacket, which had to have his DNA on it. He wasn't quite sure what DNA was but he knew that the jacket would have both his and rugby cunt's blood on it and that blood would be bound to contain DNA. All they had to do was connect him with the jacket. It was a fairly common design: classic was how he liked to look at it. It was an expensive one. He'd got it from a pub, the King and Queen; just put it on and walked out. For a moment he was cheered by the thought that it would have the original owner's DNA on it too, but on reflection he realised that this wouldn't help him much. People associated him with that jacket. There might be loads of other people with the same one, but if you showed that one to the regulars at The Crown or the Dorset, they would think of him.

He thought for a moment of Julie. Would she grass on him? Even if she made the connection, she was crazy about him so surely not. Anyway she was far away in Surrey, wherever that was, and it probably wouldn't even make the news there.

Still, he needed to get out. Right out. His dole cheque was no longer a possibility. Julie was no longer a possibility. Finding Marty was the only thing he could do. He'd need to do another job. The thought of going it alone crossed his mind. He needed more money than

Marty would be likely to give him, but Marty knew where to go, and he had the contacts for selling the stuff afterwards. This time though, he needed a better job. He at least had to get away, but abroad would be best, Spain or something. What he really needed was a large enough sum to get out of the country.

He paced the room and realised that he was panicking. His thoughts raced away from him and he couldn't seem to hang on to them.

Then there was a knock at the door.

24. LOOKING FOR PEOPLE

To Sally's credit, she did listen to Emily and tried to understand her worries about Sam. It was all rather beyond her though. Firstly she didn't have children of her own, and secondly Sam was sixteen. She didn't want to remind Emily of what they used to get up to at that age, but she did know that whatever their parents had thought about it wouldn't have made a tiniest bit of difference.

Another thing was that she had come to Brighton to go shopping. She had some money now that she had a new job and she'd been looking forward to a day going round the shops. Brighton was a lovely place to go shopping. All this was very frustrating. She always seemed to pick the wrong time to come down.

'So we should have a look round the North Laines then?' Most of the shops she wanted to look at were in the North Laine.

'Yes, I suppose that we should. I've brought a photo of Sam. I thought we could show it to people who look around his age.'

Sally grimaced. 'I wouldn't do that. It would be really embarrassing. I mean, for Sam. You know what sixteen-year-olds are like.'

Emily recognised the truth in this and groaned. 'I suppose so. Well, what shall we do then? Let's start at Trafalgar Street and work our way through the main streets.

'Can we go down Gloucester Road though? I just wanted to look in Voodoo. We don't have to. I'm just saying. You could have a look around for Sam while I go in. I just wanted to look at the skirts. I need a new skirt for work.'

Emily glanced at her friend. Her spirits sank lower as she realised the reality of the situation: she was going to look for Sam; Sally was going to go clothes shopping.

Mark wasn't getting on much better. He trudged along the sea front scanning faces and distant figures so hard that his eyes began to hurt. It was cold but bright which meant that the promenade was almost as crowded as a summer day. He realised that even if he did see Sam there would be little he could do to stop him from backing off and losing himself in the crowd. He didn't like to admit it but the only point in his favour was that Emily wasn't there. He might just persuade Sam to talk, man to man.

The pier was crowded too. The seagulls whirled and dived, forcing people to duck as they swooped on lost chips or dropped ice cream cones. Then they sat on the rail, screeching and ignoring the sea, waiting for the next chip.

Mark pushed through the crowd and into the arcade. Here it was darker, the crowds were thicker and the noise was oppressive. Families and groups of youths stood next to beeping machines feeding them with money; occasionally there was a jingle as someone won a little back. Two boys shot zombies, fiercely concentrating on their task, and next to them two little girls tried to follow the steps on the dance machine. All around there were boys of Sam's age, but no Sam.

Mark walked on, towards the rides at the end of the pier. Sam had loved the dodgems when he was little. Now it would be more likely to be the waltzer or the roller coaster. He stopped to watch the waltzer, checking off each face that was not his son.

The operator, a thin man with pale eyes, leaned off the slowing ride and jumped to the ground.

'Two tokens' he said to Mark.

'No, I'm not riding' He rummaged for his wallet and then flipped it open. 'Have you seen this boy at all? I'm looking for him.'

'Your kid is it?'

'Yes.'

The man took in the misery on Mark's face and shook his head sadly. 'Sorry mate.'

Mark started to walk away but then heard a familiar laugh. He turned around to see Ted Harris, his arm around the shoulders of a sassy looking blonde who Mark recognised as the new girl from Human Resources. Two other couples joined them, smirking. This was not the first time that Mark had bumped into Ted since that Saturday in the empty office, but they hadn't had to speak much. Mark guessed that, as far as Ted Harris was concerned, he wasn't really worth speaking to any more.

'Hello there Mark! All by yourself?' Ted boomed as the group walked towards him. The girl from Human Resources had a sheepish but sly grin and Mark realised that he had just been the subject of a joke.

'Going on the waltzer? We are, well us lads anyway. The girls are a little nervous, aren't you, Luce?'

The ride slowed to a stop and began to fill up with new customers. The operator made his way from car to car, removing rubbish and checking the safety guards. The three men climbed onto one of the cars and Ted shouted over at Mark.

'You coming Mark? Or are you staying with the girls?' All six of them laughed, the girls pretending not to. 'By the way, forgot to ask, got a new job yet? Or is that what you're doing round here. Making a career change?' He nodded towards the operator to make his meaning clear. 'Going up in the world?' The men laughed loudly. Mark was unable to think of a reply but was aware that his face gave him away. 'Only joking, mate!' said Ted. 'Don't cry!' The six laughed even more loudly now. Even the girls didn't pretend not to.

The ride started up and for a brief moment the operator's faded blue eyes looked directly at Mark. He gave Mark a flicker of a smile, then he jumped up onto one of the cars and was whirled away.

The cars increased in speed, spinning and swooping past. Ted and his friends laughed and took their hands from the rail to wave in the air. The girls kept half an eye on them while they chatted. It was near to the top speed now, and Mark just got glimpses of Ted as the car whipped past in streaks of red and green.

Mark couldn't tear his gaze away. Normally it would stay at this speed for a couple of turns before it slowed again. This time it didn't seem to be slowing. Again and again the car swooped past. The men had stopped whooping and were holding on tight.

The operator jumped off the internal podium and onto the back of a moving car. He leaped from one car to the next with easy grace until he reached Ted. The three men now looked rather uncomfortable. Mark realised that they had probably been drinking. The operator grabbed hold of the car and spun it. He waited until it had almost stopped and then he spun it again, then again and again and again. Ted and his friends stopped even pretending to enjoy themselves.

'That's enough, mate' Ted called out. The spinning didn't stop. 'I said, that's enough!' The operator appeared to be deaf. Elvis's Burning Love boomed out over the speakers. The girls stopped chatting and stared with embarrassment at their men, who all now looked quite terrified.

Eventually the operator jumped back through the cars and on to the podium. The ride slowed and Mark could see more clearly. Ted and the man sitting next to him looked white and furious. The third man was green and was holding his hands over his mouth.

Mark smiled at the operator and walked slowly away. There was hope in the world, after all.

**

Dougie thought that his heart had stopped. He had to make a conscious effort to breathe. Meanwhile, he was frozen, standing in the middle of the living room, waiting for another knock. Then it came. It was a hesitant, polite sort of knock. It did not sound like the police. They would knock loudly, not caring if they woke anyone up. He moved a little over towards the window. Whoever it was could not be seen. They must be right inside the door alcove.

He heard the dog give a small token 'woof' from upstairs, not concerned enough to come down and have a look. Dougie edged out into the corridor and crept towards the door, leaning in to the spy hole.

The person on the other side knew he was there and coughed, embarrassed.

'It's Barney,' he said. 'I'm moving in today.'

Dougie was so relieved he flung open the door with a welcoming smile.

'Good to see you, mate. Come in, come in.'

Barney looked at him warily. He hadn't really taken to Dougie when they had met before, and didn't understand the display of effusiveness.

'I've got the van just round the corner. Looking for somewhere to park up. Don't suppose you'd give us a hand?'

Dougie had no intention of helping the fat cunt. He had things to do. 'Sorry mate. Got to go. Just on my way out now.' He turned back to the living room, leaving Barney to get on with it. He collected his hoodie and had a look for anything else he'd left around. Then he'd have to go to his room and pack. He was just feeling down the side of the sofa when he heard another cough.

'Sorry mate, can't help you. In a bit of a hurry.'

A small voice replied 'I've come about the room.'

Dougie spun around. 'What the fuck . . .' he begun. A slim blonde boy stood in the doorway. A very familiar looking blonde boy.

'Are you Tizer? I've got the money' he said.

Dougie realised immediately whose son this was. Sam looked so exactly like Emily that he would have made the connection even if he hadn't seen the boy outside Emily's house that night. The kid had money too . . . This was fate giving him a helping hand. It would be rude not to take it. He felt elated with his luck and cunning.

'You've come about the room?' He paused, working out how to play this. Barney would be back at any moment so he had to think quickly. It would be good to have the boy start by feeling some gratitude towards him. It would start things off nicely.

'The room's gone, mate. You should've come earlier.'

Sam looked utterly crestfallen. This was the one possibility that he hadn't been able to countenance.

'Oh,' he said. 'Ok. Thanks.' He turned to leave.

'Hold on a moment there,' said Dougie. 'Are you alright, kiddo. Got somewhere else to go?'

Sam turned back to Dougie, blinking. 'No, I haven't. D'you know anywhere? I can pay. I need somewhere straight away though.'

Dougie pretended to think. 'You know what?' he said eventually. 'I think you should have the room. The bloke who was going to have it, he doesn't really need it, y'see. A young lad like you though . . . I don't want to think about what would happen to a lad like you, out on the streets, no one to look out for you. Brighton, well, it's a shithole, isn't it? Full of creeps. Paedos and that. Not that you're a little kid, but you know what I mean.'

Sam looked suitably worried.

'I don't think my conscience would let me . . .' Dougie was getting into his stride now. He smiled at Sam in what he hoped was a beatific manner. 'It's a moral duty really, isn't it . . . to look after the young.' He sighed, as if picking up the heavy burden of responsibility. 'You remind me of myself at your age.'

Sam was nonplussed. 'Do I?' he said.

'Not in looks, obviously. Not in looks. More like, sort of, well, I was young once . . . at your age. Someone helped me too.' Dougie realised his chance. 'And I always said I'd repay that debt. I was that grateful, y'see.'

'And did you?' said Sam eagerly.

Dougie realised that it was time to end this line of questioning. 'He died,' he said, 'tragically, before I could ever really give that man his due. But now here you are. It's like karma, isn't it?'

They heard a noise in the hall and Barney appeared in the doorway, red faced and carrying a large box.

'Barney, mate,' said Dougie. 'There's been a change of plan.'

***

Emily and Sally were discussing Clare's party.

'We have to go.' Emily was not going to budge on this one. She had to be seen at the party. She always went to it.

Sally took a large sip of red. Her eyes darted to Emily and then away.

'But I don't have to, do I? Can't I just wait at yours? I'll come out to the fireworks after.'

'Oh bloody hell, Sal. I never see you. Besides, I need the moral support. There'll be loads of people. You might meet someone.' Emily had forgotten that Sally had been to Clare's parties before.

'No I won't. They're all married. All they talk about is houses and children and if I talk to a husband the wife comes up and gives me a filthy look.'

'No they don't.'

'Yes they do. And anyway, I really don't know what you see in that Clare. I don't think she likes you very much.' She looked at her friend wondering if she had gone too far, but Emily only looked pensive. From the next table a voice bawled out above the general racket and a man with curly, floppy hair said 'And it turned out to be a genuine Meissen! 17th Century!' He slapped the table and the men he was sitting with chuckled appreciatively.

Emily gave her friend a small smile. 'No, I think you're right. And I don't really like her either.' The floodgates were open now. 'All she's interested in is being queen of the Lewes scene. I ask you! And she's sly too. I never have trusted her.'

Sally was open mouthed with shocked amusement. 'Why do you hang out with her then? Bloody hell Em.'

'Because that's Lewes, isn't it. You've got to get along. It's not like London. We're stuck with each other. Besides, she's a neighbour. We have a good time sometimes. You have stuff to talk about, you know, the area and that.'

Sally knew about James. It had been on the national news after all, but so far she hadn't managed to get much out of Emily about it.

'It just seems a bit funny, that's all. Having the party just after someone next door was murdered.'

'I suppose . . . It didn't happen at the house though. And they hadn't lived there long. Anyway, she's gone away now.'

'Will she move out, do you think? It would be quite good for you, though, wouldn't it? If she did. What with the building work and everything.'

'Yeah' said Emily but without any real enthusiasm. It was beginning to strike her how radically her feelings had changed, or if not changed, had lessened from the almost hysterical peak of a few days ago. It wasn't that she didn't care about the house or the extension any more. That would be stupid. She had to admit that hadn't all been put in perspective by the murder either, or even her possible part in it, which she had now almost persuaded herself was a paranoid fantasy, or Sam's disappearance either. She couldn't claim to be that noble. It was undoubtedly good news from her point of view that the building work probably wouldn't go ahead, at least this time.

The problem was, she just knew that even if Jenny didn't build the extension, someone else might later. Whether it was actually built straight away or not didn't really matter very much. She no longer felt that the house was safe. It would always be hanging over them. For the first time since she moved in, she could contemplate moving out. She didn't feel settled any more.

They lapsed into silence, surveying the room. The Basketmakers was heaving. It was still early for the lunchtime crowd but everyone in town seemed to need a drink as much as Emily.

'D'you remember last time we were in here?' said Sally. 'We bumped into that Dougie Tate, d'you remember?' she sniggered. 'Have you seen him since? I think he quite likes you Em.'

'No' said Emily 'I haven't.' She looked quickly around the room. 'We should have gone somewhere else.'

25. DOUGIE'S PLAN

'What the fuck's going on?' Tizer was bleary eyed. Barney had cut his departure short when he spotted a certain look in Dougie's eyes, but before then there were a couple of minutes when he had made his feelings about his pre-emptive eviction loud and clear.

'Who slammed the fucking door?'

Dougie and Sam were in the kitchen where Dougie was making Sam a cup of tea.

'That was Barney,' said Dougie. 'He doesn't want the room any more. What a cunt eh? I said to him 'Thanks for letting us know, mate. Thanks for leaving us in the lurch.''

'Oh fuck,' said Tizer. 'I need the bloody rent.' He looked at Sam quizzically. Dougie didn't normally bring friends back to the house. 'I'm sorry,' he said. 'I'm being rude. I'm Tizer.' He put out his hand for Sam to shake. 'Fucking bad morning, this morning. '

'This is Sam,' said Dougie quickly. 'His mum is an old mate of mine.' He turned towards Sam and winked, as though he wanted Sam to go along with the story.

Sam didn't know what to do. He wanted to tell Tizer that he'd come about the room, but he didn't want to upset Dougie. 'Hi,' he said, and looked at Dougie for direction.

'Sam can have the room instead, can't he? He was just telling me that he needed somewhere when old Barney came round. He can pay, can't you, kiddo?'

Sam nodded vigorously, grateful but not appreciating being called 'kiddo'.

Tizer shrugged, 'Fine,' he said. 'Some other guy was interested. I've only just written back to say that the room's gone.' He thought about the strange email that had seemed to imply that this 'Fletch' could just move in without even meeting them first and added. 'He seemed a bit weird though.'

Tizer didn't feel altogether happy about giving the room to Sam either, but he was half asleep, confused and had been painted into a corner. They needed the rent. If he hadn't seen Dougie with plenty of women he would have been even more worried. The kid looked very young. He knew Dougie liked women, but this just didn't feel right. He would keep an eye on the situation. Dougie was definitely up to something.

A conversation about breakfast, where it had gone and who was responsible, took up most of Tizer's energy for the next few minutes while he made tea and then stomped off back to bed. Sam sat there, tongue tied, glad that he didn't have to join in the conversation in case he said the wrong thing. He'd already given his real name to Dougie by accident, but he was quite glad about that now. He definitely wouldn't admit to his email to Tizer after being called 'weird'. Also, he didn't know how it had happened but he was now beholden to this rather strange looking old bloke. Did he dye his hair, Sam wondered. It looked a bit odd. He was really old, as well; old enough to actually be friends with his mum. All the same, thanks to him he was now where he wanted to be. He looked around the kitchen at the stack of washing up, the unclean table with its peeling veneer, the overflowing bin. This was the life. This was real life.

Dougie waited until he heard Tizer's door shut. 'Sorry about the bit of subterfuge there kiddo. Best not to let Tizer know about Barney. He might not understand. Not everyone's on the same level about these things, know what I mean?'

Sam nodded, obviously not knowing what Dougie meant at all. 'I feel a bit bad about him, that bloke. But I really do need somewhere.'

'Course you do.' Dougie knew that he had to take things slow. He didn't want to frighten the kid off, but he had to get the conversation on to money somehow. He needed to work out how much the kid had got and how he was going to get it off him, and he had to do it quickly. What was the best way to get a kid of that age on side? He wracked his brains.

'So what kind of music are you into Sam?' he said.

'Er, The Typists, Wildlife of Costa Rica, The Fun Ideas. Lots of stuff really. I went to see the Typists at the Dome. They were really excellent.'

Dougie was horrified. He had never heard of any of these bands. 'Cool,' he said. 'What else are you into?' There had to be something. He had to make a connection somehow.

'I really like the stunt stuff. Are you involved in that? That's how I heard about the room, from the Pranxsters' web site. I saw Tizer's advert.'

'Oh you mean all that dressing up and putting up fake signs and that. Yeah, that's all good, isn't it?'

'Have you done any of it? It's really excellent. I tried to do something myself, but, well, it didn't work out.'

'I'm more of a behind the scenes type of person. Fully supportive, though.' Dougie remembered something that Tizer had said, 'Especially the bit about fighting against American cultural imperialism. Shall we go and look at the room then?'

The room was small and bare, containing only an ancient chest of drawers with two of its fake brass handles missing and an old divan that took up so much room that they hand to stand sideways. A lone sock lay on the dirty carpet under the radiator.

Dougie was kicking himself. Of course! How could he have nearly missed this opportunity?

'So it's up front, the rent money. That OK, kiddo? Do you need to get to a bank? We can go out now if you want. To secure the room. You wouldn't want someone else coming along. It's not much, but it's cheap.'

Sam felt awkward. It didn't feel right to give the money to Dougie but he didn't know why. What difference did it make whether he gave it to Tizer or Dougie?

'It's OK,' he said. 'I've got the money here.' He reached into his inside pocket, then stopped suddenly. He didn't want Dougie to see how much he had in there. He didn't know whether his Mum and Dad would be able to stop his bank account, so he'd drawn out a bit extra, to tide himself over.

He moved to the side and Dougie craned his neck. If the kid was being coy about it there had to be more than just a month's rent in there.

'And you've got the deposit? I nearly forgot about the deposit.'

Sam felt stricken. 'Deposit? How much is that?'

Dougie decided to see how far he could push it. 'Another month,' he said. 'It's quite normal.'

Sam did not know what was normal. 'I can't. I won't have anything left to live on,' he said. 'What am I going to do?'

'Can you get any more out of the bank?'

'I have to give notice on the account.'

Dougie calculated quickly. 'How much could you give? I tell you what, why don't you just tell me how much you have in there. Then we can work out a budget. We can't have you doing without food. Don't worry about the others. I'll deal with them.'

Sam felt small and mean. Dougie was only trying to help. He pulled the money out of his pocket and put it on the divan. Dougie sat down and counted it out.

'Well look,' he said, 'this is it, is it?'

Sam nodded. It seemed like a lot to him.

'Ok. Well you need to get a job straight away, but that shouldn't be a problem. I've got some contacts. We'll go out this afternoon and I'll see what I can do. If you start work on, say, Monday, you'll have your wages at the end of the week. In the meantime, what do you need to spend money on?

'Food?' volunteered Sam.

'Right!' said Dougie. 'Anything else?'

'Um, bus fares?'

'Good thinking. But, hold on a sec, you can walk just about anywhere from here. Anything else?'

'I don't know.'

'I can't think of anything, apart from the odd pint. I tell you what: I'm going to give you fifty back. That should be plenty. You can pay it back later. How does that seem?'

'I suppose so,' said Sam. 'Can you really get me a job then?'

'No problem.'

'Thanks so much Dougie. Really appreciate it.'

'No problem at all.' He knew that he would be long gone before he had to live up to that promise. 'Right, kiddo, I need to go out. I'll see a few contacts about your job. You make yourself comfortable here, OK?'

'Shouldn't I come with you?'

'Probably best not to go in mob handed, kiddo. I'll see you later on today.' He left Sam sitting on the bed and looking a bit worried and made his way quietly down the stairs. He paused at his room to gather the meagre possessions he had managed to collect during the past few days: the T shirt Tizer had lent him and some bits and pieces that the previous tenant had left behind, then he crept past Tizer's door.

The toilet flushed and Janice emerged from the bathroom.

'If you're going out, you can get some more bacon,' she said in a loud, annoyed voice.

Dougie closed his eyes, trying to blot out what he knew would happen next.

'Dougie!' As expected, Tizer was now wide awake. 'Dougie, did you get the rent money?' He flung open the bedroom door.

Sam opened the door of his bedroom. 'I gave it to Dougie,' he said.

Tizer said nothing, just held out his hand.

26. DOUGIE'S PLAN B

Dougie went back to his room and closed the door. He sat on the bed, staring at the carrier bag containing his clothes. He felt rather sick.

Then a small smile began to take over his face, starting at his mouth and then reaching his eyes. It was blindingly obvious. It was Emily's fault he was in this mess. He was trying to help her out when it happened so she should be the one who paid for it, not him. And now here was her son, like fate or something. The kid had to be useful and Dougie thought that he knew how. It wouldn't be as quick as it would have been if he'd been able to keep the rent money, but it had more potential. The only question was how exactly to do it and he had to think quickly. Time was really not on his side. He had to get out as quickly as possible and so the plan had to get moving. At the same time though, Dougie recognised that panicking could ruin everything. He had to think things through.

A short while later he knocked on Sam's door. 'Sam, kiddo? I've changed my mind. I think you should come with me. So we can get your job sorted out.' While he was making up his mind what to do he needed keep the kid with him. The kid was as good as money and Dougie planned to hold on to him as tight as he could until he was able to cash him in.

Sam didn't mind. If Dougie wanted him with him then he really must be planning to get him a job. Once he had a job he would be sorted. He'd read somewhere on the internet that if a young person of seventeen and above had a job and a flat his parents couldn't take them back home. He wasn't seventeen yet, but it wasn't too long. It might take them a while to find him.

They set off towards town. Dougie was quiet, thinking, while they walked past the junk shops, funeral parlours and broken glass that line the end of the Lewes Road. His main problem was money. He needed money desperately, and he now had a golden opportunity to get some, if he played his cards right.

'So, will your old lady be coming round to do your laundry and that? Or will you take it home so that she can do it?' he gave Sam what he hoped was a conspiratorial smile.

'Oh no!' Sam reddened. 'I don't want her coming round. I won't go back either. Anyway, I don't have the keys any more. I put them through the letter box when I went.'

'Shit,' thought Dougie. There was one possibility gone. He hadn't wanted to go to Lewes but easy entry to a nice house would have been irresistible. 'So you don't get on with your folks? That's a shame.'

They walked on in silence for a while.

'They're not always the best role models, parents, are they? You're supposed to respect them and that, but . . .'

'My mum's crazy. My dad's all right but he's under the thumb. Does whatever she says. My mum's really mental.'

'Is she?'

'Yeah, I just couldn't take it there anymore. She just doesn't get out of my face, like, ever.'

'Know what you mean, mate. You need to cut the apron strings.'

Sam looked confused.

'Need to get out from under,' Dougie elucidated. 'Women, they just don't want you to be your own man, know what I mean?'

Sam knew exactly. He smiled at Dougie, recognising someone on the same wavelength.

'She doesn't know where I've gone,' he said.

'Really?' said Dougie. He looked at Sam with admiration. 'You going to phone her? Let her know you're alright?'

'Do you think I should?'

Dougie thought for a while. 'Yeah, I do,' he said. 'You don't want the police involved, do you? You should definitely call her.' He looked around. 'Look, let's cut through the Level. It's quieter in there.'

The Level is a flat, scruffy park that divides the Lewes and London Roads; it is pretty much unloved except by skateboarders. They crossed the road and entered the park, finding a bench just inside.

'What will you say?'

Sam was looking terrified. 'I don't know. Just, I'm Ok and don't look for me.'

'Ok,' said Dougie, he waited until Sam had got his phone out, noting that it was kept in the inside pocket of Sam's jacket and then he moved discretely away, still within earshot but with his back to Sam. He heard Sam punch some keys and then there was a pause. Eventually he spoke.

'Mum, it's me. I'm Ok. I've moved out. I'm not coming back so don't look for me. Bye.'

Dougie heard Sam breathe for the first time during this communication and turned back to look at him.

'Well done, mate. That was fine.' The phone was restored to Sam's inside pocket.

***

'Was that my phone?' Emily hurriedly put the drinks on the table, spilling wine onto the beer mats. 'Sally, why didn't you tell me?'

Sally snapped back to attention. 'Oh, I didn't realise.' She felt very guilty but she had completely forgotten that Emily might want to answer it.

Emily scrabbled in her bag and retrieved the phone, all the time giving Sally a hard stare. Really, she was getting completely useless. It was Sam's number, and she had a message.

'He's says he's Ok. And he's not coming back. So that's that I suppose.' She took a large glug of red.

'He will be back, just give him some time. At least you know he's still got the phone. You can still leave him messages can't you?'

Emily was still cross about missing the call. 'Oh yes, I can leave him messages. Great.'

Sally stared at the table. Emily stared at the wall.

'Shall we go to the party then?' said Sally.

***

Dougie's plan was developing. He would provide a service: information about her son's whereabouts in exchange for a fee. To get money in any useful amount he would have to imply that her son might be in danger. Dougie didn't really feel like hurting the kid. It wasn't that he was squeamish. He'd probably beaten up other people who were just as easy, but it was different when he was all riled up: when people had pissed him off or when he'd had a drink or two. Walking along the road with Sam beside him the idea of, say, hitting him or tying him up, for example, just seemed stupid. Besides, real kidnappers needed a safe place to put someone. He had nowhere. If he tried to lock the kid up in the house Tizer would just let him out. No, his mum would just have to think that he was in danger. All Dougie needed to do was work out how to achieve this.

The first thing was to get hold of the phone so that he had Emily's number and so that Sam couldn't relent and answer her calls or leave any more messages. It was no good persuading his mum that he was kidnapped if he kept on calling her and saying that he was alright. Dougie would have to get hold of the phone and then make sure that the kid didn't go near a phone box. He tried to think about how they did kidnapping in films but all he could remember was the Mel Gibson one, which didn't really fit and where it had all gone wrong. That wasn't going to happen to him. For a start the kid was too old to give everything away by peeing himself at the wrong moment.

Secondly, as far as the kid was concerned, they were mates. He had nothing to be afraid of.

He was undecided about the finer details. Should he call her from that phone? On the plus side it would show that he was with Sam. In the films though, they could trace the call and pinpoint his whereabouts. He'd have to be stupid to give the game away like that.

The answer, he decided, was to make the first call from Sam's phone, and from then on use public call boxes if he had to call again. He wasn't quite sure why, as these calls could surely be traced too, but it seemed to be what people did. He might have to think about disguises too. And accents. He could make out like there were other people involved. He did a top West Indian accent, people had said.

He realised he was getting a bit carried away. What he wanted was to make a phone call and get the money as quickly as possible. The longer things dragged on the more chance there was for Emily to find out that Sam was ok. Also, bonfire night might keep the citizens of Lewes busy until tomorrow but it wouldn't be long until conversations at the Crown returned to the murder, the news and the leather jacket.

Dougie groaned as he realised that it was Saturday, the banks weren't open and Emily, like everyone else probably had a limit on her cash withdrawals. This would be nowhere near enough, even if she had a couple of cards. He had banked on getting at least five grand. How was he supposed to start a new life on anything less?

Sam coughed. 'Are you alright Dougie?' he asked.

Dougie turned to Sam, showing a smile that Sam found rather disturbing. For a split second Dougie was reminded of Emily again, and he remembered her in the Basketmakers, sitting there looking so composed and elegant, her hand holding her glass and that huge diamond flashing on her finger. Then he remembered the Citroen sitting at the front of their house. Money wasn't everything.

'I'm good, kiddo.' he said. 'Just thinking about that job of yours. How do you fancy the antiques trade? We should go and meet this mate of mine.'

27. PARTY PREPARATIONS

Frankly, Clare just wished that Jenny would go. She had invited her in, of course, as soon as she'd seen the car parked outside, and she had been properly concerned for quite a while. She really was genuinely concerned too. She liked Jenny and it was an awful thing to have happened to anyone. Now, though, there were things that needed to be done, cakes that needed to be got out of the oven, decorations that needed to be found and put up. The list was endless, and Tim hadn't even come back from the pub yet.

'I don't know if I should stay. The police may need to talk to me. I wanted to go to the . . . the place where they found him too. Apparently people have left floral tributes. If I stay tonight I can go and see them tomorrow. Pay my respects.'

This was terrible news. The party would have to be cancelled. They could hardly have it with her sitting there next door.

'I wouldn't do that,' Clare said quickly. 'Not just yet. You should be with your family. I'm surprised your Dad didn't come with you. You shouldn't be on your own. You poor thing.'

'Dad's very busy, and then Vero's got the twins. I'm kind of . . .'

'Of course! You have brothers, don't you! They must be such a comfort.' Clare saw a denial of this or some sort of confidence rise in Jenny's face. It needed to be averted quickly. 'I tell you what. I'll come and help you gather up some stuff.' She stood up, surreptitiously turning off the oven. 'Come on. And then I'm going to pack you straight off back to your family.' Jenny let herself be got up and was propelled in the direction of the door.

Twenty minutes later Clare was back in her kitchen working like a whirlwind. Cakes were on trays, the Guy was properly dressed and the stainless steel sink shone. After that she glanced out of the window and was pleased to see that Jenny's car had gone.

She was truly sorry about it all, but the thing was, and she could hardly say this, obviously, but everything wasn't always all about Jenny. She'd lost her husband and that was terrible, but the murder had also affected other people. It had put the whole town on edge. Clare had never felt unsafe in Lewes before and other people were saying the same thing. The murder was ruining it for everyone. A party was exactly what the community needed, if you looked at it from that point of view.

She was glad that the police seemed to be making headway. She'd seen the leather jacket on the news. It was a funny, old-fashioned sort of design, and she was sure that she knew it from somewhere. Perhaps it would suddenly pop into her mind. At the moment though, she was too busy. She was really looking forward to the party this year.

***

Dougie stopped Sam at the door of the Basketmakers. 'I'd better go on my own, he said. We don't want to crowd him.'

Marty had already spotted Dougie and was looking towards them with an air of annoyance. 'Who's the kid,' he said, as Dougie approached.

'No one.' He pulled up a stool and sat down. 'Marty, mate, I need to get some cash together. You got anything?'

'Can't help you. Nothing doing at the moment. What's up? Buying presents for your little friend?'

Dougie's eyes narrowed and Marty knew he'd gone too far. For all the contempt he had for Dougie, he didn't want to push him.

'Look, you live in Lewes. We were just talking about it' His voice lowered. 'Bonfire night, you've got all those empty houses. Nobody's going to phone the coppers if they hear a loud bang. They're all busy anyway. And you know the place! You know if people are in or out, the back ways, the alleys . . . You're sitting on a gift, Dougie.'

Dougie turned away trying to hide his frustration and desperation. Lewes was the last place he wanted to go, but everything was forcing him back there. He knew that if he got hold of Emily's jewellery Marty would help him unload it, but the risk was so high, and as usual, it would be him that would be taking it while Marty sat in the pub and mouthed off to his mates. He forced a tight smile as he thanked Marty and stepped back outside.

'What did he say,' said Sam, 'have I got the job?'

Dougie couldn't bring himself to come out with a barefaced lie.

'He's got to sort some stuff out. He'll let us know. Come on.'

They made their way down Kensington Gardens towards the town centre. Dougie didn't know quite what to do with Sam now, unless he went ahead with his plan. Now that it came to the crunch, he didn't like it. It wasn't his usual style but there didn't seem to be a way out. One way or another, everything seemed to be pulling him back to Lewes.

*****

For Emily, Clare's party was something to be endured, but normally she endured it with good grace. There were a few points in its favour, she got to keep up with what was going on in the neighbourhood without the effort of holding a party herself, and sometimes it could even be quite amusing. One year, for example, Coleen Prentiss had set her hair on fire. Once, too, Frank Marshall had been caught with Jill Watson's daughter. The girl was nineteen, but still.

The down side was having to talk to the many people she managed to avoid during the year and having to be at Clare's beck and call, working as virtually a free cater waiter. Every year she promised herself not to get roped in, but every year she somehow was.

The party was really an open house, with people popping in and out throughout the day. Some people would go to the bonfire societies' processions through the town, others would wait until the societies had split up and headed to their own displays at various spots around the outskirts of Lewes. People at Clare's party were usually from around the area and most would go to the De Montfort display at Parliament fields, this display being the nearest. Fireworks did not start until about nine thirty, which left plenty of drinking time beforehand.

Emily and Sally took their time getting ready, moving around the bathroom in a synchronised set of movements that only women who have been putting their make up on in the same bathroom since they were sixteen can achieve. Finally they stood next to each other and smiled.

'The hair's good, Em' said Sally. 'You look like your old self.' She yiked down the neckline of her top another half an inch.

The phone rang and Emily sighed. 'That'll be Clare. Ignore it. We'll have a drink first.'

What with the glass of wine in the Basketmakers and the two that Emily drank before leaving for Clare's they were already well oiled before the party had even started.

***

He was going to have to go back to Lewes. There was his dole cheque, the possibility of making some money from Emily, even the need for his passport and some clean clothes, that is, if Julie hadn't chucked all of his stuff out on to the street.

Nevertheless, he needed to be in and out as quickly as possible. Quite apart from the prospect of some clever dick putting two and two together about his jacket, he had found that being away from Lewes had made it easier not to think about rugby bloke and his blank, glutinous eyes, during the daytime at any rate.

At least the town would be crowded tonight. Like Marty had said, the police would be busy. Then an idea hit him: an idea of such beauty he was amazed that it hadn't struck him before: Tizer and that lot were going to Lewes too. They were planning one of their stupid stunt things. He could go up with them as part of a crowd. He would be less conspicuous. That was the word. He'd just be another bloke going to see the fireworks. Of course he'd have to split before they got into any of that funny business. Stupid twats, attracting attention like that.

He glanced at Sam and found the boy starting at him expectantly. How the hell was he going to persuade him to go back to Lewes? The little idiot had posted his keys back through the door, so doing Emily's house was probably out, but maybe there was something else, one of his posh friend's houses or something.

'Lewes bonfire tonight' he said, testing the waters.

'I know. So boring. Nobody ever goes.'

'Don't your folks go?'

'Oh yeah, they go. I meant people I hang around with. You know, my age.' His voice trailed away, embarrassed. Dougie was so old. 'My Mum loves it. There's this stupid party every year down the road and everyone in the street goes. It's pretty crap. They make all the kids go and there's, like, babies and everything.'

'Sounds radical.' Dougie felt considerably perked up by this bit of news. Emily would be out of the house.

'This year I was planning something. I wanted to do some stuff to the peace memorial. You know, 'cos they call it that but it's really all about war . . . I was going to dress up a dummy like a Guantanamo prisoner and pour fake blood all over it. They would have taken it down, but the paint might have stayed on. It would have made the papers.'

Dougie was feeling very clever. 'Oh yeah, you like that stuff, don't you.'

'Yeah, but it went wrong, I forgot the jumpsuit and . . .'

'Did you know, Tizer and that, they're doing something at Lewes tonight.'

183

Sam's eyes became perfectly round. 'They are, aren't they?' he said. With the failure of his own stunt, and the excitement of the move, he had completely forgotten.

'Let's go back. Maybe you can do something with them. You'd like that, wouldn't you?'

Sam didn't speak, but nodded so vigorously that he looked a little deranged. At the next corner they turned off towards the Steine.

28. PARTY GAMES

Sally was feeling slightly alarmed. Emily appeared to be getting a bit squiffy. She'd seen Emily drunk before, naturally. They had both got completely pissed on a regular basis in their teens and twenties. But now Emily was the mature one: responsible, with responsibilities. The one who gave Sally a meaningful look when she reached a certain part of the evening: if her voice got a bit loud or she got too flirty.

Not that Emily had done anything daft. Nobody else would probably even notice apart from Mark, and he wasn't at the party yet. Emily was just more animated, more flushed, than was usual. It put Sally on edge. She didn't know why. It was bad enough being there, Sally didn't fit in and she knew it. Even Emily didn't always seem to like her neighbours, often referring to Lewes residents in general as 'angry ex hippies with mortgages'. Tonight, with the murders to talk about, they seemed worse than ever: angrier, more self-righteous. Especially the women.

Emily was talking to one of them at that moment: a woman with a greying brown bush of hair, no make up, and livid red patches on her cheeks. She was dressed a bit like an ageing Maid Marion.

'I mean, most of us moved here for a reason, but now we seem to be importing all of the problems from Brighton that we're trying to get away from.'

'Brighton and Hove,' said Emily. The woman nodded, pleased that Emily seemed to be agreeing with her.

'I always wonder about that, don't you?' Emily went on. 'Now that it's the city of Brighton and Hove, are you supposed to always call it 'Brighton-and-Hove' or can you just say 'Brighton'?'

'I don't know.' The woman sounded confused.

'You know what people from Hove are like. Always saying they're from 'Hove, actually'. Ha, ha, that's it! We'll have to call it 'Brighton-and-Hove-Actually'.' Emily threw her head back and laughed.

The woman managed a few forced chuckles before turning towards the person on her other side. Emily headed towards the drinks table, Sally following behind.

'You alright Em?' She said.

'I'm fine. I'm absolutely fine. My life is just a big load of crap, that's all. My son's run away, my husband has lost his job, and there are other things.' She caught her breath in a gasp. 'There are other things. You're so lucky Sally. I wish I had your life. Forget about all this doing the right thing, careers and children and houses all that crap. You're better off as you are.'

Sally looked around hurriedly. 'You don't mean that. You're just having a bad day, that's all. Come on! Sam'll contact you. He's just being a teenage boy, that's all. Come on Em.' She dropped her voice to a whisper. 'Don't let these people see you upset.'

With a fine instinct for timing, Clare caught Sally's eye and homed in on them.

'What are you two whispering about?' She took in the look on Emily's face and her dimples twitched, just slightly. 'Could you please help with the glasses? We'll run out at this rate. Sally, could you help me too. There's a dear.'

Sally turned her face away and picked up the nearest glass. It still had something in it and a fat man wearing jeans and a suit jacket reached for her hand.

'Hold on there, gorgeous. You wouldn't deprive a man of his one solace in life would you?'

Sally winced and followed Emily downstairs to the crowded kitchen, which smelt of mulled wine and spice. A group of teenagers surrounded Tamsin at the fridge. A couple of parents sat on the sofa, keeping an eye on the teenagers and the alcohol making sure that the two did not mix. Three mothers with crawling toddlers inhabited the adjoining conservatory.

Mark and Tim were sitting at the table, both holding PlayStation controls and looking at a television in the corner of the room with quite manic interest. Another man stood near, egging them on. 'Drag him out of the car! No! No, not like that. Oh now look! You're dead, pal. You're finished. Let me have a go!'

Mark looked up at Emily. He knew that she would be annoyed that he hadn't checked in with her at the party. He'd sent a couple of texts to let her know the lack of progress of his search, but hadn't been able to face her in person.

'Emily!' he said, as if pleased to see her. 'Come and have a look. It really is amazing.'

Her eyes flicked towards the television. She could see the back of a cartoon man as he ran towards a car. He appeared to open the car door and drag the driver out before getting into the driving seat.

'Nice,' she said. Now the man seemed to have crashed the car. He got out and ran, shooting as he went. A passer by sank into a pool of blood. Emily turned away, a ghastly emptiness in the pit of her stomach.

The teenagers were getting restive. 'You should have stolen the cop's weapons' said a tall boy with moulded hair. 'I'll show you if you want.'

The men admitted defeat and turned over the controls to the boys. Tamsin curled her lip and watched, still propped up by the sink. One of the boys, shorter than her and extremely hairy, tried to engage her in conversation. Emily thought she recognised him from the days when Sam used to bring his friends home. Then she caught sight of one of the other boys. It was definitely John Watkin. What on earth was he doing here? He was one of Sam's best friends. What was he doing with Tamsin? Or rather, what was Tamsin doing with him? He wasn't her usual sort. Tamsin always acted like she was above the local boys. She did look extraordinary today, Emily had to admit. The girl was wearing bright yellow trousers that emphasised the impossible length of her legs, her trainers were filthy and she carried a tiny and ladylike quilted yellow handbag.

Clare used the spatula to move the gingerbread men onto a plate. She whispered something to her daughter who smirked and, just fleetingly, her eyes met Emily's. Outside, a single firework fizzed and then exploded, sending red sparks into the twilight. Clare beckoned to Emily.

'Nearly time for sparklers, don't you think? Would you like to hand them around or do you want to take the gingerbread men?'

Tamsin was whispering to the short, hairy boy, who looked utterly thrilled and quite drunk. The kids had obviously got booze from somewhere, Emily thought. She took the gingerbread men but had hardly turned around when people started to gather around her. She set them down on the table and picked one out for herself.

Something about Tamsin's tone of voice made Emily pay attention through the general buzz and shoving around her.

'What did you say you call him?' she said.

'Floater Fletcher, Sammy Skidmarks. There's loads of them.'

Emily turned around, biscuit in her hand. 'What are you talking about?' Her voice sounded a little thick. Tamsin looked away, towards her mother. The short hairy boy obviously didn't recognise Emily and was too drunk and elated at Tamsin's attention to spot the danger signs.

'Floater Fletcher? Oh he's just some kid at my school. He, um, went to the toilet in the Pells Pool.'

One by one, conversations in the room died, until the only sound came from Coldplay in the upstairs room. Outside in the garden, parents oohed as a little girl made patterns with her sparkler. Sally touched Emily's arm and was immediately shrugged off.

Emily put the headless biscuit down carefully on the kitchen surface and turned to walk away. Then she turned back and went towards Tamsin, stopping two inches from her face.

'You little . . .'

Mark pushed his way through the crowd and grabbed her shoulders. Emily spun around catching the edge of the table. The plate containing the remaining gingerbread men tilted and then slid to the floor crashing on the stonework. Shards of crockery and decapitated, limbless biscuits bounced on the floor. Mark pushed Emily out of the room, up the stairs and out onto the street. Sally looked round apologetically and followed them.

***

Once he was safely on the train, Dougie tried to ignore the others. The carriage was packed and there were plenty of girls to look at. He felt embarrassed to be with the rest of the crowd. Not only because they were so much younger. He was a product of his era and had an old punk's distrust of people he saw as new age, limply left wing, tofu eating hippies. This didn't preclude pretending enthusiasm to get what he wanted.

Now they were full of their little plan for the evening. Sam was pink with excitement. Not only had they asked him to join in, they had been absolutely ecstatic when they heard about the orange jumpsuit. Now he just had to find a way of getting back into the house.

At this, Dougie perked up interest.

'What about the back. Can you get in there?'

'No, it'll be locked. I could get a key from our neighbour, but my mum'll be round at hers, for that party.'

'Where do they keep the key to the back door?'

'In the door, I suppose.'

'Glass door is it?'

'Half glass. Little panes of glass.'

Dougie smiled over at Tizer. 'I'll go with him and get it.'

Tizer really didn't like the sound of this. He knew that Dougie planned to break in. He wasn't into destruction, he said, but the others overruled him. Nobody said as much but the general feeling was that Sam's parents were probably middle class and consequently deserved the inconvenience of mending their door. It would all be worth it to get hold of the orange jumpsuit.

The plan was this: The others would go to their own base of operations, a house rented by some students not far from the centre of Lewes. Sam and Dougie would go and retrieve the jumpsuit. Then they would meet up at the house to prepare the stunt.

Dougie insisted on going home with Sam. He said that he didn't want Sam to have to do it on his own. It might be difficult for him. Sam was grateful. He wanted some moral support in case he ran into his parents. He knew that they should be at the party by this time, but just in case, he'd be happier with someone else there.

'Can you think of anything else you should pick up while you're there? You don't want to be going back every two minutes, do you kiddo?' Dougie wanted Sam to be kept busy for as long as possible.

'I'll have a think' said Sam.

Tizer watched the two of them with concern. He wouldn't want Dougie going back to his own parent's house. He wanted to get Sam on his own before they split up, to warn him.

At Lewes, however, rivers of people converged and flooded towards the high street. Bonfire boys of both sexes and all ages appeared from everywhere proudly wearing stripy jerseys and long coloured caps. A group of Vikings stood outside the White Hart, their pints of Harveys being jogged from their hands. Three women dressed as pioneers pushed past in the wrong direction, their faces set in determined scowls. The river of people flowed forward through the town, pushing onwards to find a good spot, a friend they were supposed to meet, a pub that didn't have queues thirty people deep. The bitter, metallic smell of gunpowder already clouded the air, and the crack and pop of stray fireworks sounded at irregular intervals. The sky was petrol blue and Lewes seemed to sparkle in the jewel-coloured illuminations.

Sam and Dougie parted from the others at the High Street then pushed on upwards through the crowds.

'The processions will start soon,' said Sam, looking at his watch. We should go up the back way.'

He indicated to Dougie and they ducked into Pope's passage, an alleyway that ended in another alley behind the town hall. A man wearing a Zulu outfit and spectacles nodded at them as he passed by.

The backstreets were less crowded but disgorged a fairly constant stream of people heading into town. Dougie began to wish that they'd stuck to the main route where there was more going on and more out of towners. The backstreets were full of Lewes people, bonfire boys, young people on their way to the pubs, families with children going to the procession. At any moment they could turn a corner and bump into someone who knew him, someone who would see him without his trademark leather jacket and who would put two and two together. It wasn't quite dark enough yet.

They took a tangential route, eventually emerging at the top of Pelham Street on the corner with Barn Road.

'How d'you know if they're in?' said Dougie.

'They'll have the lights on. The one in the living room is on a timer, but if there's a light on anywhere else . . . My mum goes mad if you leave a light on.'

They rounded the corner then Sam stopped. Someone was emerging from Clare's house. His heart seemed to stop until the man, who he didn't know, and who was wearing a long cloak, turned left and walked away down the hill.

'You'd better go,' he said. 'Just have a look. There should be a lamp on in the living room window, but nothing anywhere else.'

Dougie nodded. This was not ideal. He didn't want to look like he was casing the joint.

He walked slowly down the road, carefully checking the house, but then carried on past so as to not look suspicious. He could hear music and people laughing further down the road. The momentum carried him forwards and he couldn't help but look. Why did no one around here use nets? He was horrified to see Sally, unmistakable with her long red hair and curvaceous profile, talking to a fat bloke who looked like Jeremy Clarkson. He turned his face away quickly and carried on, taking the first turning and walking all the way around the block back to meet Sam.

'Nothing, no lights or anything except in the front room. Nothing in the basement. Anyway . . . I think I saw your Mum. In the party down the road. With a big girl, red hair?' He looked sideways at Sam who smirked and nodded.

'OK. . . cool.' Sam looked embarrassed. 'We can get over the wall here. Can you? I mean will you be OK?'

Dougie knew what he meant and his previous humiliation was still too fresh to deny it.

'You let me in the front door,' he said. 'You gotta break in to your own house, mate. I'm not fucking doing it. Anyway, people see you climbing over they won't think anything. They'll call the cops if they see me.'

Sam looked distraught but nodded and leapt up and over the wall in a couple of quick easy movements.

'Be quick' hissed Dougie. He looked around self-consciously, agonising at the noise that Sam was making. He couldn't quite see over the wall but he heard him trip and say 'ow' quite loudly, then he heard the glass smash and he held his breath, looking around anxiously. Then he

192

heard a key turning in a lock, a door being opened and the sound of Sam wiping his feet on the mat.

Dougie returned to the front of the building, shivering in the cold until Sam let him in to the house.

The door closed and they smiled at each other in the dark, partners in crime.

'I thought we shouldn't turn the lights on,' said Sam. 'You know . . .'

Dougie nodded. 'Yeah, nice one,' he said. 'So where's this jumpsuit then?'

'Come up,' said Sam and led the way up the stairs towards the attic.

Dougie took his time, checking each room as he passed. The door to the study was open; he could see the glint of a computer screen in the gloom. He could also see the bathroom. The room he really wanted to see, Emily's bedroom, had to be through the only remaining door. Women kept their jewellery in their bedrooms.

Sam led him onwards to the attic. The dusk gave just enough light to see that there was nothing of interest. Computer games were the only things that Dougie could imagine were of any value, but they were not his speciality. He wouldn't know what to do with them. He was still cold though.

'Sam, mate,' he said. 'Can I borrow a coat or anything? Have you got anything?'

Sam opened his wardrobe. 'Help yourself,' he said.

There was a whole row of coats. Dougie suddenly felt bitter towards Sam. All this, he had all this, and the little snot nose didn't even appreciate it.

He felt his way through the coats until he found a fairly new looking black parka.

'This OK?' he said.

'Fine,' said Sam, scarcely giving it a look.

Dougie put it on immediately. It felt like a big soft cloud. He put the hood up and rubbed his cheek against the fake fur lining. Then he felt embarrassed and put the hood down again. He felt very pleased with himself. Now he would be warm and would look less like he was without his leather jacket, and more like he had gained a coat.

Sam was stuffing a packet into his rucksack. Dougie assumed that it was the jumpsuit.

'You should check while you're here. Is there anything else you should take? You don't want to have to come back.'

Sam nodded. He was already opening and closing the drawers of his desk. 'There's this book on capitalism I was telling Tizer about. I thought I put it here.'

'Tell you what,' said Dougie, 'I'll go and use your lav and meet you downstairs.'

'Ok,' said Sam without looking up.

Dougie walked straight down the stairs and into the main bedroom. The curtains were drawn and it took a little time for his eyes to adjust. He bumped into the end of the bed and cursed, then he held still and listened to see if the noise had alerted Sam.

Eventually he let out a long breath and took in his surroundings. The dressing table was in front of the window. A marquetry jewellery box sat on its top.

He crossed the room in three silent paces and opened the lid of the box. The light was too bad to see properly so he carried the box nearer to the window and twitched the curtain just slightly until a sliver of light from the streetlamp lit the box's contents.

He knew enough to be disappointed immediately: mostly silver, modern stuff. There was an emerald pendant that looked like it would get a couple of quid and a ring with three sapphires in it. Emily must have been wearing the diamond ring. He slipped the pendant and ring into his pocket and returned to the hall.

Sam was already coming down the stairs and looked anxious and wary when he saw Dougie emerge from his parents' bedroom.

'Wrong room, kiddo,' he said. 'This must be the bathroom over here.'

Sam forced a small smile. It was very dark in the house, he supposed.

Dougie closed the door and gazed at himself in the bathroom mirror, trying out 'trustworthy' faces in the gloom. 'Fuck,' he thought. 'How did the little cunt get downstairs without making a sound?' He knew he had some ground to make up now, and all for virtually nothing: the pendant and the ring would hardly get him to Gatwick, certainly not as far as Spain or Portugal. When they got back to the student house they'd all be busy. He would have to get hold of Sam's phone and move on to plan B.

***

Exactly three minutes after they left the house Emily stumbled into it followed by Mark and Sally. She went straight to the kitchen and sat on the sofa with her face in her hands, knowing that as soon as she looked up she would have two expectant faces looking back at her, like baby birds waiting for a meal.

Eventually she heard the sound of a cup being placed on the coffee table and reluctantly raised her eyes.

'Coffee,' said Mark. He sat down and put his arm round her. It felt clumsy and awkward and he soon removed it.

Sally sat on the chair opposite them looking embarrassed.

'That Tamsin, she's a little cow, isn't she?'

'She's just a kid.' Emily sighed, then she almost smiled. 'She is though, isn't she? What a little bitch. Just like her mum.'

Mark coughed. 'So that's it then. That's what happened. I can't think of anything worse to happen to a teenager. It would be bad enough anyway. God! Can you imagine? Poor Sam.'

'How did we not know? Why didn't anyone tell me? Someone must have known who he was.' Emily thought

195

back to the start of Sam's reclusiveness. A few things started to make sense now. The woman from the Historical Society who had asked her in a pitying and too soft voice 'How is Sam? Is he alright?' There were a couple of other, similar comments too. She supposed that she wasn't close enough to any of these women for them to say anything to her. Clare though, surely Clare had known. Clare would have loved to have told her. She'd obviously engineered the revelation at the party.

'You know what though,' said Emily. 'I don't think we can blame it all on that. I wish we could, in a way . . . but he wasn't a happy kid anyway. Before he stopped talking to us we hardly ever saw him.'

Nobody said anything.

'I didn't notice a sudden change, d'you know what I mean? He obviously, um, was ill in the pool and couldn't face his friends because of that, but I couldn't tell you when it happened. There was no day that was really different to any of the others.'

'I bet they sent him texts and that. 'Floater Fletcher' . . . you know.' Sally's voice faded as Emily looked at her crossly. 'Well that's what they do. It's not my fault. Cyberbullying they call it. I'm just saying.'

They sat in silence.

'Oh bloody hell,' said Emily. 'This means that they all know Sam hasn't been going to school or seeing his friends. Bloody Clare. She'll know I've been lying to her.'

'It doesn't matter now,' said Mark.

'I suppose not. Bugger.'

A rocket screeched up into the sky behind them, making them all jump. The phone rang at the same time.

'It'll be Clare,' said Emily. 'Oh shit. What'll I say?'

'Just don't give her the satisfaction,' said Mark.

Emily picked up the phone. 'Oh hi Clare,' she smirked at the others. 'No, don't worry about it. Really. No problem. Teenagers eh! No I'm sure she didn't mean to . . . No, of course you didn't know. Probably. Must have been.

Yes, of course. Later. Yup. See you up there. See you. Really. No problem. I'll talk to you later. OK. Bye.'

She put the phone down and grimaced. 'She's doing the comforting thing. In other words she wants all the details about Sam. Swears she knew nothing about it. I suppose she might have been on holiday then. Knowing Clare, she would have said something…' Emily sighed and looked at her watch. 'She wants to know if we're still going to the bonfire. I couldn't say no, could I? It's the last thing I want though. Oh God, do we have to?'

Sally did not intend to stay in all evening being miserable. 'I know what you mean,' she said, 'but you should go or she'll probably make even more of a big deal about it.'

The phone rang again.

'Oh bloody hell,' Emily let it ring. 'What the hell can she want now?' She picked up the phone.

'Clare,' she said, her tone flat.

'It's not Clare,' said the voice at the other end.

29. DOUGIE GETS DESPERATE

Dougie felt like a granddad. Everyone else in the house was screaming with laughter and running from room to room in an excitable and totally inexplicable way. More than ever he missed Julie and the quiet and relative order of her little house, but he had to think ahead, concentrate on the future, and Julie was the past. He'd have to go round there later to get his passport and clothes, and he could have a look for anything else she might have left around. Nothing of Julie's was worth that much though.

He could pick up his dole cheque too, but this was a bit of a waste of time. He'd have to wait until Monday now to cash it. Waiting that long would be stupid. Hopefully, he would be out of the country by tomorrow.

In the meantime he had to put up with the kids and their squealing. Worse, too, they had got Sam into their pathetic joke thing. He had to stay with Sam, which meant he'd have to go along with them. It was dangerous, but for once what they had planned wasn't actually illegal. It was just really stupid and would draw attention.

The original plan had been for them all to carry a part of a George Bush effigy: an extra suit, some stuffing, and so on. Once they were at the bonfire they would put the bits together and put a George Bush mask on its face, then they would put on their own masks, leap the boundaries surrounding the bonfire and throw him on. At that moment they would unfurl posters with slogans on them: 'Wanted for crimes against humanity' and so on. It made Dougie physically flinch with embarrassment. Worse, they had already notified the local papers that something would happen.

The only possible up side to this situation from Dougie's point of view, was that there were spare masks for him and Sam. He didn't intend to wear his unless really necessary, it would make him feel like a prat, but he was feeling increasingly paranoid about bumping into someone he knew. He was glad that Sam seemed thrilled with his own mask. It meant he could hide from Mummy and Daddy. This was exactly what Dougie wanted for Sam too.

Everyone disappeared up the stairs, making preparations and arrangements with their friends, leaving Dougie alone in the living room. Once again he was in the position of knowing that he was unwanted and in the wrong place, but was unable to do anything about it. He daydreamed about his new life in Spain. He would get a job in a bar or something, get his own place, or preferably he would get a woman with a bit of cash and move into her place.

He caught sight of Sam's jacket on the sofa. Moving quickly, he went to the door and peeped out. No one was in the kitchen; they were all still safely out of the way. He slid his hand into the jacket's inside pocket and retrieved Sam's mobile. He flipped it open and scrolled through the names until he found what he wanted.

Now he just needed a place to make the call.

***

Tizer was in the bedroom using the computer to make a final check on his emails. Everyone he knew was going to be at the bonfire and it was getting really exciting. Quite a few of them were bringing their own George Bush masks and banners and everyone seemed to be bringing more people. It would be quite a sight.

Scanning through the junk mail to find the emails he wanted to read, something strange caught his eye. It was titled 'Looking for Sam Fletcher'. He double-clicked it.

Hi

I'm looking for Sam Fletcher. If you know where he is can you please ask him to call me on 07800 245 555. It's urgent.

Thanks

Mark

Tizer stared at the email for a few seconds, then he called out. 'Sam, is your surname 'Fletcher'?' Sam wandered into the room looking worried.

'Why?'

'Look at this email. Do you know someone called Mark?'

Sam leaned over his shoulder and read the mail. 'Oh,' he said, 'it's OK, you can delete it. I know what it's about.'

Tizer felt unsure. He still felt that something was wrong but Sam stayed in the room, watching him. He clicked 'Delete' and smiled at Sam. 'Funny they emailed me,' he said.

Sam looked embarrassed and rather shifty. 'Yeah,' he agreed, and slunk out of the room.

Tizer glanced around to check that he had gone and then opened his Deleted Mail folder. Then he took out his phone and added Mark's number to his contacts.

***

Dougie debated with himself. He could wait until the others had gone out and insist on staying at the house and meeting them later. They wouldn't like it, though, and they'd probably arrange for someone to stay behind with him. Plus he really didn't want Sam out of his sight. The only other option was to find somewhere in the house. The toilet, he realised reluctantly, was the only place he could get some privacy. He would have to be really quiet too. It was going to be difficult to sound threatening when he was whispering. He thought about Marlon Brando in the Godfather. He didn't have to shout. He had authority. That was the way to go.

And what was he going to say? How would he put it? He considered for a moment and then decided. He would be subtle: menacing but polite and he wouldn't really say anything straight out.

The downstairs toilet was at the back of the house. He replaced the lid and sat down, took two deep breaths and dialled the number.

'Clare?' said the voice at the other end.

'It's not Clare' he said, confused. 'Is that Emily?'

'Yes,' she replied drawing out the word as if she wasn't sure that she wanted to admit to it. 'Who is this?'

He'd already thought this though. 'An old friend,' he replied.

'I've got lots of old friends. Which one are you?'

'An old friend who you asked to do you a favour.'

There was silence at the other end.

'I don't know what you mean.'

'Do you want me to draw a diagram?'

There was silence again.

'What do you want?'

'I need a favour from you now, Emily. I've got myself in a spot of bother for you. As a mate, I think you should help me out.'

'I don't know what you did. I didn't tell you to do anything. I don't know what you mean.'

'That's a pity. I need to get out of town and I need a little help with finances. I thought you could help me out.'

'I'm sorry. I'm not having this conversation. I'm going to put the phone down now.'

'How's Sam?' Dougie said quickly.

'What?'

'I said 'How's Sam?' You know Sam, don't you? Your son.'

'Yes I know who he is. What about him?'

'Well really, you know Emily, I could tell you how he is. Because he's with me right now. You didn't know that, did you?'

'I don't believe you. Why would he be with you?'

'He's a nice kid. I wouldn't want anything to upset him.'

'I don't believe you. He's not with you. You don't know him.'

'Called you earlier today, didn't he? Left a message.'

He heard her swallow. 'You don't know him,' she said.

'Tell you what: when you put the phone down, dial 1471. I think you'll find that I have Sam's phone.'

He let her hang for a moment.

'Nice house you've got there, by the way. I like your bedroom. Dark wood doesn't sell so well these days, but I like a bit of mahogany.'

This was the clinch, Dougie almost smiled, relieved that he would soon know how things stood. Then he heard someone moving around the kitchen and knew he had to hurry things up. The footsteps approached.

'Dougie, hurry up mate. I need to get in there.'

He put his hand over the receiver and hissed. 'Piss off!'

'I need to go. Tracy's in the bathroom. I really need to go, man.'

'Fuck off!'

'Come on man, this is serious. I'm fucking desperate. You're only on the phone anyway. I heard you.'

Dougie took his hand away from the receiver and hissed 'I'll call you back. You think about it.' Then he smacked open the door and stalked back into the living room. That would never have happened to Marlon Brando. These kids were fucking ignorant little cunts.

After a while he calmed down a bit. It was ok, he thought, she could spend a bit of time working out how to help him, and thinking about the consequences if she didn't.

28. CONFESSIONS AND DEMANDS

Emily walked out of the kitchen as soon as she recognised Dougie's voice. She walked up the stairs to the study, went in and shut the door. This was the place where she dealt with things. She would deal with this too.

She sat for a few minutes before she dialled 1471. It was really unnecessary. She already knew that it would be Sam's number. She pressed 3 to return the call and listened to Sam's answering machine message.

After that she sat for several more minutes listening to shrieks of laughter from the smokers in Clare's garden. Then she walked out of the study and into the bedroom. Mark, hearing her walk around, shouted up the stairs.

'Who was it, Em?'

She shouted back, 'I'll be down in a minute.'

She looked around the room at the mahogany furniture. Her eye caught the jewellery box on the dressing table and she crossed the room to open it. The pendant and the ring were missing and she was not surprised.

She felt very short of breath and sat down on the bed to concentrate on breathing in and out, in and out.

How had he done this? It must be true; he must have Sam. Sam had to be somehow in his power. She could not believe that her son would be involved in stealing jewellery. The thought would not even occur to him.

The last vestiges of her self image were crumbling away now. She could not be the person she thought she was, capable, mature, responsible. Not if she had managed to screw everything up so comprehensively. Not if she was connected to a murder and the kidnap of her own son.

For the first time in her life she did not know the way forward. There was nothing for it: those two sitting downstairs, who she often patronised and bossed around, were going to have to help her, because she was incapable of helping her son. She got slowly to her feet and started the short journey downstairs to her disgrace.

Sally liked Mark. She liked him a lot and she'd known him for years now, longer that just about anyone apart from Emily. All the same, she really didn't like being left alone with him for too long. She couldn't flirt with him; that was the trouble, and she had absolutely no idea of how to talk to a man on any other basis. They'd already covered speculations about who was on the phone and the best time to go to the bonfire. Then they stared at their coffee cups.

So when Emily eventually reappeared Sally was relieved for at least five seconds until the look on her friend's face sank in.

Mark was quicker to work out that something was wrong.

'Em, what's up?' He got up and went over to her, taking hold of her hand. Then he dropped it, panic in his face. 'Oh, God, it's not Sam is it? Emily? It's not Sam?'

Emily seemed to break out of a trance. 'No, he's Ok. I mean, I think he is. But I think he's in trouble.'

They both just stared in confusion.

She looked directly at Sally. 'Dougie Tate's got him.'

'Dougie Tate?' they said in unison, mystified but for different reasons.

'Who the hell is Dougie Tate?' said Mark.

***

Dougie was feeling quite chipper. The interruption had actually given him time to think of what else he could get out of her. The car was a definite. With that, he could drive to Portsmouth, get the ferry, and drive down though Spain. Then he could sell it. It might be tricky, what with not knowing Spanish and the road signs all being different. He'd have to be careful. A crash was the last thing he needed right now. He'd get as much cash as he could as well, and jewellery. There might be other stuff apart from the ring.

He'd phone again as soon as he could to make arrangements. In the meantime, everyone was getting ready to leave, which meant he had to go too. Sam was a little worried about the prospect of seeing his parents and Dougie reassured him.

'If you see them, you don't have to speak to them. Tell me. I'll make sure they don't bother you. If you don't want to go, I'll stay here with you. It might be better.'

Sam was not going to miss this evening for anything, though it wasn't only his parents that he was worried about seeing. He was also concerned that they'd bump into someone who knew him from Lewes, someone who knew about the swimming pool incident, which was obviously everyone under eighteen. More than anything, Sam wanted a fresh start with his new friends. He didn't want anyone calling him Sammy Skidmarks or laughing at him in front of Tizer and the rest.

He put on a black beanie, covering his blonde hair, and slipped the cardboard George Bush mask into his pocket. 'It should be alright,' he said. 'If I see my folks, I'll just move away. They can't do much.' He was a bit unsure of this; his fear of his mother endowed her, in his imagination, with almost superhuman strength. But he didn't want Dougie involved either. What did he think he was going to do? He wouldn't really hurt his mum, would he?

Although he was thrilled to be part of this new world, Sam was rather disappointed with what the Pranxsters had planned. It was all just a little bit tame. These people didn't seem to understand Lewes. What they had planned wouldn't be shocking to a crowd of people who regularly burnt effigies of the Pope and threw fireworks at someone in an Archbishop's outfit. Politicians, too, were regularly included in insulting tableaux. He was sure that George Bush had been done before by at least one of the societies.

The only part of the stunt that really interested Sam was when everyone put on George Bush masks. He'd heard of something like this happening before, up in London. People were calling it a 'flash mob', which sounded new and exciting. He wished he could think of something to make the rest of it all a bit more effective.

Out on the street, Sam tagged along after Tizer and the others and Dougie tagged along after Sam. The first stop was to be the Harveys Tavern. Not for drinks, they all had vodka in Red Bull cans already, and getting to the bar through the crowds would have been impossible. The Harveys Tavern was the first meeting place of the evening, chosen as a good spot for watching the barrel races coming down the hill into town.

The pub was already full inside and drinkers spilled out up and down the pavement and along to the Cliffe High Street. A line of people had taken up their position along the edge of the road in time for the processions and were jealously guarding their territory. The dusk was alive with hum of anticipation: yelled conversations over mobile phones and ring tones punctuated by the snap of firecrackers. All of the shouted phone conversations said the same thing: 'I am here. Where are you?'

Tizer and Janice spotted several people they knew and melted into the crowd. Dougie and Sam stood at the edge, looking at each other awkwardly. Sam wanted to join the others. He didn't know why he seemed to have got stuck with Dougie. He seemed to be a nice bloke, Sam thought, and he really appreciated everything that Dougie had done for him, but he didn't want to get stuck with the old man all of the time.

Also, he didn't want to admit this to himself really, as it made him feel like a bit of middle-class princess, but Dougie kind of put him on edge a bit. He made Sam feel a bit uncomfortable; the business about accidentally going into his parents' room felt wrong too. He knew he was being a real snob. If one of his so-called friends from school had walked into the wrong room by mistake he wouldn't have given it a thought.

Also, he couldn't quite shake off the feeling that Tizer and everyone else didn't really like Dougie, and that Dougie didn't like them. It didn't seem likely, as they all shared the same house and everything, but there was something not right, some kind of undercurrent that he hadn't worked out yet. If Sam was honest, and in spite of Dougie's helpfulness, he wanted to be on Tizer's side of any rift, not Dougie's.

His luck was in. After smiling at each other for a moment or two, Dougie nodded over towards Tizer.

'I've gotta make a call, kiddo. D'you want to go and hang out with Tizer for a bit? Don't go without me.'

Sam suddenly felt panicked and shy, but he pushed himself through the crowds to the edges of Tizer's group, where he stood looking hopefully from face to face. There was a girl who looked friendly and smiled at him. She was a bit dumpy but had nice eyes: kind eyes. For a split second he remembered how Eileen had looked at him when he was ill in the pool, and he blinked hard to remove the image from his mind.

Dougie slunk away to the far end of the car park, close to the river. He had to be quick. He didn't want Tizer moving off without him. He had a feeling that Sam would go too.

***

'What if he wants something we can't give him? I can't get hold of much money. Not straight away.' Mark wasn't sure if he could get anything out at all.

'God knows what he'll expect.' Emily took her purse from her bag and pulled out her credit cards. 'I can get 300 on this one. The Visa card. . . I don't think I've got a number for it. I think they sent one but I never used it. I'll go and have a look.'

She left the room, glad to be away from their anxious and confused expressions. It made it worse that no one had had a go at her. She almost wanted them to so that she could defend herself. She would point out that she didn't expect Dougie to do anything like that. She would never have told Dougie about the building plans if she thought he would attack anyone. Even this though, was beginning to sound a bit thin. Sally knew Dougie as well as she did. He had always been a violent thug. What else did she expect him to do? What on earth had she been playing at?

The Visa card number was nowhere to be seen. She dumped file after file on the floor and panicked, spreading the documents out and muddling them up until nothing made any sense and she gave up, a huge tear splashing onto a bank statement.

She turned around to see Sally and Mark standing in the doorway and looking awkward.

'I can get £300 on my overdraft' said Sally, and then bit her lip.

Emily knew how difficult this was for her to say and held back more tears.

Mark was looking sheepish. 'I can't do much. If it was when my redundancy had come it'd be Ok.'

'How much?'

Mark looked at the floor. 'I think the bank have heard about the redundancies. They've stopped the overdraft. I can try.'

Sally stepped over the pile of papers and sat down on the sofa bed. 'What d'you think he'll ask for? What about the police? Are you going to phone them?'

Emily grimaced. 'What do you think they'd be able to do? Anyway, I don't know how I'd explain it ... They could probably do me for soliciting GBH or something.' This possibility now seemed very real and frightening. 'Of course I would do if I thought they'd do any good. I doubt if there's anyone who isn't out at the bonfires.'

'You didn't ask him to kill anyone.' There it was; that was what Emily had wanted someone to say, but Mark wouldn't look at her when he said it. She was to blame for everything and she knew that he knew it.

The phone rang again and they stared at it in panic. Emily picked it up, still searching Mark's face.

'Hello' she said.

'It's me Emily. How are you doing?'

'What do you want?'

Dougie seemed taken aback at her brusqueness. 'Right then, let's get straight down to business. I need a car and money. And I want it now. I want to leave tonight.'

'Where's Sam? Is he alright?'

'He's fine, at the moment. We're mates. You got a fine boy there Emily.'

'You wouldn't hurt him.'

'You want to risk that, do you? Well, nice to chat, but I want everything now. Say ten grand. That should do it.'

'Don't be ridiculous. Where am I going to get that?'

'You want to watch who you call ridiculous. D'you know what your son thinks of you? Shall I tell you?'

Emily said nothing. For a long moment the only sound was the background noise of the crowd. A rocket went off somewhere at the back of the house and she heard it clearly though the phone at the same time. Dougie was in Lewes.

'I know you won't hurt him, Dougie. He's only a kid. You wouldn't hurt a kid.'

Dougie was obviously not going to be manipulated. 'If you can't get it all in cash I'm open to offers. I need as much of it as you can get in cash. But that diamond ring you've got. I'll have that for a start.'

'You won't hurt him,' she said again.

'Ok Emily, have it your way. Cards on the table: I'm fucked if I don't get out of here so I'll do whatever I need to, trust me. It was an accident. I didn't mean to do it. The bloke was just being an awkward cunt, excuse my language. But I've been in trouble before. Where d'you think I've been all this time? If they send me back it'll be forever. I'll never get out.'

'It's not my fault. You did it.'

'Bollocks. You'll pay up, Emily. I won't go back inside. Your son is a good kid. I like him, I really do. But I will fucking tear his head off and chuck him in the bonfire if I have to. I'll fucking tear his head off. And it'll be easy too. He's a good kid, Emily, but he's a fucking pussy.'

Emily made a little choking sound. 'I need to be sure of his safety before you get anything.'

'Fair enough. I'm a reasonable bloke. Definitely. So this is what's going to happen . . .'

31. REALISATIONS

Clare loved the Women's Barrel race. There was something about it that fascinated her: women in fancy dress performing such an undignified activity as running down the road pushing flaming metal barrels, their faces red even in the red light of the fireworks. She couldn't imagine what possessed them to do it. They always had such serious looks of determination on their faces and when, as inevitably happened, one of them tripped on the long skirt of her pioneer outfit, Clare was especially delighted.

Once the racers had passed, Clare turned to her daughter. 'Goodness knows what happened to your father. I know the bar's busy, but for heaven's sake.' She looked at her daughter, weighing a calculation. 'Clever of you to bring a coca cola with you darling. Do you want to go and find Daddy? Otherwise I'll be wanting a sip of your coke.'

Tamsin dissolved into the crowd as quickly as she could and Clare's dimples disappeared for just a second. Alcohol in the coke bottle, then. Before tonight she would have said that Tamsin was too much her daughter to let alcohol get the upper hand, but the business in the kitchen had rattled her. It was unsubtle. There were ways of doing things and that was not it. Naturally Emily had to be informed about what had happened to her son, and she did need to be brought down a peg or two, but that was not the way. It was embarrassing and now she needed to reclaim the moral high ground, to show Emily that Tamsin was the better behaved child.

It was about time that the girl was brought to heel. Just enough to remind her who was boss and to put a stop to future silliness.

***

'We can use the Cashpoint at the corner shop,' said Emily.

'Those machines cost one pound fifty a go! We never use them! Anyway, what will Sunil think if we all go in there and max out our cards?'

'Bloody hell Mark, do you really care? Honestly!' Emily was almost happy to feel in control again and to feel irritated with Mark for using the expression 'max out'. 'I can take out 300 from the savings account and 300 from the current account. If you two can get 300 each then that's twelve hundred, only just under nine grand left to go. Anyway, do you really think we're going to get near any other cashpoint in Lewes tonight?'

They found their coats and hats and trooped out, heads down. They were immediately struck by the absence of a familiar sight.

Mark's face went a ghastly grey colour. 'Oh god . . . the car. It's in the bloody garage, isn't it.'

He and Emily looked away from each other hurriedly, unable to cope with the despair in each other's faces. They trudged on to the shop.

Mark was right in that the shopkeeper had an embarrassing habit of commenting on his customers' purchases. 'Big night tonight, is it?' when they bought more than one bottle of wine, 'One too many last night?' when they bought aspirin.

This time, as they checked the money and handed it to Emily, he seemed too shocked to say anything other than 'Bonfire night tonight, eh? Bonfire night!' and rub his hands together looking worried.

They trudged back to the house and reconvened in the kitchen. Emily found a Tesco bag and put the money inside. She took off the diamond ring and then put it back on again. 'It'll get lost,' she said 'I'll put it in later.' She did not look at Mark.

'Will it be enough?' Sally was nervous that Emily would want something else from her.

'I can't think of anything that's worth anything. It'll have to be enough.'

They looked at the bag glumly.

'So now we just wait for the exchange, do we?' said Mark. 'This is bloody ridiculous. Even if he delivers Sam, it doesn't mean that Sam will come home with us.'

'No, I know. Dougie says he'll walk away leaving us with Sam. Obviously he wants to get away, that's what this is all about. So as long as Sam hasn't got that thing, you know, that syndrome where people start to like their kidnappers . . .'

'He won't want Sam to go with him will he?' Mark looked worried, a new, vile, possibility entering his head. He quickly dismissed it. 'No, you're right. He'll want to get rid of him. As long as he does leave. And he doesn't involve you in . . . things.'

'We'd better go,' said Emily. 'It might take a while to get there.' She took a last glance around to see if there was anything else that she could offer Dougie. The kitchen had never looked so messy, the granite worktop was covered in tea and coffee stains, a dirty dishtowel lay on the floor, one of the cupboard doors swung ajar revealing the mess within, and a plant wilted on the oak dining table.

She felt hopelessly ashamed that this was what all the fuss was about. How much of her life had she wasted on it, planning the refurbishments, trawling antique markets for exactly the right ornament and then dusting that ornament over and over and over again. And now someone had died over it all. The moral lesson was embarrassingly straightforward. Still, as soon as she got Sam back she'd give the place a good going over.

It was turning very cold outside. They could see their breath as soon as they stepped out of the door and all reached for their gloves and hats. Someone in the next street let off some crackers and a dog barked: a rhythmic and relentless hacking rasp.

They headed along the back roads towards the centre of town. The idea was to meet at the children's playground near the Pell's pool. Chosen, so Emily thought, because it was central but had several deserted roads nearby. It was also close to the river where James' body had been found. Emily did not think that this was accidental; Dougie had chosen it to remind her, and to scare her.

She was to go alone. The others would stay nearby, but not too near. She would tell Dougie what they had managed to get. If he was happy he would take Emily to Sam and then disappear, never to be heard of again. If he was not . . . Emily felt a cold shiver of fear. So it now seemed that Dougie's violent past was even worse than she had imagined. She had thought that James' murder must have been a ghastly accident, some kind of warning that had gone wrong, but now it seemed more sinister. He was a violent maniac who had been in prison for a very long time. She couldn't get the image of him from all of those years ago out of her head, flirting and waving while kicking someone on the floor. That was the sort of man he was and she wouldn't let herself forget it again.

Her hand went to her pocket for reassurance. The Sabatier vegetable knife was there, where she had put it.

***

Dougie realised that he was losing Sam to Tizer. Sam followed him everywhere, looking at Tizer with huge puppy eyes, agreeing with every word that he said. It was irritating and worrying too, he needed to finish all this off quickly before he lost Sam completely. Now he had to go and meet Emily, and take her to Sam, but he couldn't guarantee that Sam would be there if he left him alone for that long. For one thing it would take a while to get though the crowds and there were police everywhere.

'Sam, mate? I've got to meet someone. Bit of business to take care of. Will you wait for us?'

'Ok. Cool.' Sam was trying to listen to what Tizer was saying about Iraq. He felt really out of his depth. At school it had been enough to hate George Bush. Now it seemed that he needed to find out who Sunnis and Shias were, why they were fighting each other, and why it was our fault that they were.

'Sam! I mean it, mate. Stay here OK? It's really important. I want you to meet someone about a job.'

Sam gave up and turned towards Dougie. 'Give me your number. I'll text you if we move off.'

'Nah, don't worry, kiddo. I won't be long. Just . . .'

Sam was already patting his jacket pockets. 'Where's my phone?' The patting got more frantic. 'Shit! Where's my phone?' He spun from left to right, as if he thought someone was playing a trick on him and would give it back. The others looked at him and looked away, embarrassed. Tizer glanced at Dougie for a fraction of a second.

'We'll stay here' he told him, 'just make it quick' and then he turned away.

Dougie knew that he had no choice but to go. He gave Sam a last look and slunk off, pushing his way through the crowds on the high street until he found the alley leading to the back of the Harveys brewery. From there he turned around past the car park in the direction of the river bank.

He had just turned into a tiny alleyway when he caught sight of two policemen walking slowly towards him. He missed a step. What if someone had put two and two together about the leather jacket and they were already on the look out for him? He had a fraction of a second to decide, run or carry on. He chose to carry on and then immediately regretted his decision. He could have easily run back and then disappeared into the crowd. Now he had to carry on walking past them. Police in Lewes were notoriously chary of men walking around on their own. It was a family town. They would call him over and ask where he was going and where he lived. What would he say?

Now there was no point in running away. They would be able to catch him quite easily. His feet carried him onwards but his mind was looking for an escape route. It was hopeless.

The policemen had stopped talking now and were concentrating on Dougie. Still his feet moved onwards. He wondered about where to look. He decided on looking at the cops. A guilty person wouldn't do that, he reasoned.

They looked back. 'Evening,' said the taller cop, and they walked on past.

Dougie's legs gave a kind of shudder when they were safely behind him. It took all of his concentration to keep going at the same pace, but he did so, turning around to look only when he knew that the cops were far enough away.

The river bank was filling up with people waiting for the Waterloo bonfire. He stuck to the river's edge, his parka hood pulled around his face. Just up ahead he saw something that gave him a jolt. Under a tree near to the river bank was a small mound of flower bunches, still in their plastic. He approached near enough to smell their sweet, slightly rotting aroma. Floral tributes for rugby cunt, he thought. They were in the wrong place though. This wasn't where he had died. It must be where he had washed up. For a moment James' jellied eye presented itself to his mind and was brusquely blinked away.

There were quite a few bunches. People liked to join in when things like this happened. Dougie sneered and bent down to look at one of the messages. It simply said 'Why?' He stared for a moment. The question stumped him, and it took him a moment to trace the trajectory of the events, meeting Emily again, meeting her in the park, the realisation that he could help her, seeing a future that he realised now was just a stupid fantasy. She had strung him along. She wasn't even all that any more either. Not really.

He straightened up. Time to get going before anyone found him here. He walked on quickly, crossing the little metal bridge, past the place where he had killed James and on to the children's playground. Three girls sat on the swings passing a bottle back and forth. They looked at Dougie and he looked at them. He walked into the park and took one of the other swings, facing the girls. He swung back and forth, staring. They looked at each other and then, without a word, got up and left. Dougie carried on swinging, a little smile on his face. Emily would be there any minute.

***

Tizer went over to Sam. 'Did you leave your phone at Rosie's?'

'I don't know. I don't think so. I can't really remember when I last had it.' Then he remembered calling his mother and his cheeks felt warm. 'I haven't used it for a while.'

Tizer felt a pang of sympathy for this boy who seemed to have no friends, at least none who had called him while they had been together, and who he now realised had probably run away from home. He thought about questioning him again about the email from 'Mark' but remembered how the boy had snapped closed when he'd shown it to him.

He didn't know what to do. Should he phone this 'Mark', or was he the person that Sam was running away from. How would he know the difference? Maybe he could try and call him and sound him out. He couldn't be sure that this 'Mark' was OK, but he knew that Dougie definitely wasn't. The main thing that he could do really was to get him away from Dougie. He sighed. Responsibility weighed heavily on Tizer. It was all bringing him down.

'Let's go to the Lewes Arms,' he said loudly. 'See if the others are there.'

People drank up and got themselves together. Sam looked worried.

'You alright, mate?' said Tizer. 'Don't worry about Dougie. He'll guess where we're going. He'll catch us up.'

'Do you think it'll be OK? He told me not to move.'

'He didn't mean it. He probably won't come back. Don't fucking worry about Dougie, mate.'

'He'll definitely know where to go, won't he?'

'Course he will.' Tizer didn't know or care. 'He'll meet us there.'

Sam looked around one last time, hoping to see Dougie returning. For some reason that he couldn't explain he really didn't want to piss him off.

***

They walked in silence. Nobody had anything that they wanted to say to the others. Mark and Emily were grimly silent and Sally, though she wouldn't have admitted it for the world, was finding it all really rather exciting.

Here they were, the three of them, creeping around the back streets of Lewes, like a middle-aged Secret Seven. From a little way away they could hear the hum of the crowds and the constant rip of firecrackers, but the streets by the Pells were dark, illuminated only by the occasional coloured burst of ruby or emerald sparks. It was awesome. She would think about the 300 quid later. Emily was good for it.

'You stay here,' hissed Emily.

'We can't see the playground from here.' Mark didn't like it. He would have preferred to meet Dougie himself, but Emily wouldn't let him.

'Well, try to get nearer when I've gone then.' Emily was irritated. Having the other two along was just a bloody nuisance.

Mark opened his mouth to argue and then caught sight of Emily's face. He and Sally hung back and watched Emily walk down the hill towards the ornamental canal. A disturbed duck quacked and fluttered and then fell silent again.

Emily saw Dougie immediately. He had his back to her on the swing, a dark hanging shape, swaying gently back and forth. He did not bother to turn around as she approached.

'Hello Emily,' he said. 'Having a good bonfire?'

'Let's just get on with it, shall we?' she sat down on the next swing and noticed that she was shaking. The swing juddered and she had to hold herself rigid to stop it.

'You get straight to the point, don't you Emily? Direct, that's what you are. Ok then, what've you got?'

***

Tizer struggled with his conscience. At first he let Sam witter away without really listening, but he heard more and more things that worried him: Dougie's promise of finding Sam a job in the antiques trade, for instance. He knew exactly what that meant. Then Sam had tentatively mentioned finding Dougie in his parent's bedroom.

Tizer was silent for what seemed like a long while. Then he said 'Be careful what you say to Doug. He can be . . . a fucking nasty fucker.'

Sam gazed at him, confused. 'But he's a friend of yours, isn't he?'

'No,' said Tizer, 'he's fucking not. Look, Dougie's someone you can't get on the wrong side of, that's all. Be really careful. Alright?'

Sam now looked traumatised. He wasn't just thinking of the potential of harm from Dougie. He was wondering what Dougie might have done in his mother's room, and what she would do to him when she found out. She would kill him. He could absolutely never go home now. This was fine, he told himself. It was exactly what he wanted, wasn't it? Now, though, he didn't feel safe at the house in Elm Grove. He knew that his face would show how he felt as soon as he saw Dougie. What would Dougie do to him? What about this job he was supposed to be getting? What would happen if it was something dodgy and he said he didn't want to do it? In his mind's eye Sam was already in prison and sharing a cell with a gay gang member.

Tizer sneaked a glance at him from the corner of his eye and sighed. The karmic implications of doing nothing were too obvious. 'Go and talk to Janice for a moment, mate. I'll catch you up. I've gotta make a call.'

***

'So what have you got for me then, darling?'

'It's everything we have.' She passed over the Tesco bag. 'There's nothing else.'

Dougie peered into the bag and flipped through the money.

'Where's the rest?'

'You didn't give us much notice. What did you expect? It's going to make us overdrawn anyway.'

Dougie raised his eyebrows slightly. If that was true she hadn't been worth all the trouble. He had thought that she was rich, what with that house and everything. It was all show, then. Bloody middle classes, he thought. You never could tell.

They heard people approaching and Dougie hurriedly closed the bag. It was a large crowd of bonfire goers wearing red and white stripy jumpers. Their loud voices and laughter seemed surreal to Emily. Someone threw a cracker over the wall to the empty swimming pool and it bounced around, its bangs echoing and repeating relentlessly.

'Where's the car parked?'

Emily swallowed hard. 'It's in the garage. It's fucked. Honestly Dougie you have to believe me.'

He stood and loomed over her. 'You fucking lying bitch.'

'It is! It really is! It's been in for a couple of days. Look, you can go there and see it. . . it's in Franklin Motors, you can see it behind the gate. Go and look if you don't believe me.'

Dougie sank back onto the swing. They sat in silence while he took this in and amended his plans. When would things stop going wrong for him, he wondered. He felt cursed.

'Where's the ring?'

Emily looked down at the floor. 'I forgot it.'

'Bollocks Emily. I want the ring.'

'You'll have to come back to the house then. We can go there after I get Sam.'

'No chance. You give me the ring, then we get your boy. I'm getting in a bad mood now. You don't want me to take it out on the kid, do you?'

Emily let herself glance at Dougie for just a second. One hand held tightly onto the ring, the other grasped at the knife in the other pocket. She realised something: It was anger that was making her shake.

***

Sally and Mark hunkered down behind the wire mesh, trying to get a view of the park. Unfortunately someone had tried to clean dog mess off their shoes on the fencing and the smell was stomach churning, so they edged further and further away until they were much too far away to hear anything.

'I think I've trodden in it.' Sally was wriggling trying to look round at her shoe.

'Shh' said Mark.

They watched as Emily passed the Tesco bag over to Dougie. Even by watching his back they could tell that he was counting it out. Mark held his breath, hoping that it would be enough to satisfy him. Then there was what appeared to be a discussion. When Dougie stood up and loomed over Emily, Sally took tight hold of Mark's jacket. Then there seemed to be an impasse and the talking stopped.

At that moment Mark's phone beeped twice.

32. BUMPING INTO PEOPLE

'But you were a lesbian for political reasons, weren't you?'

The girl with the nice eyes and big bum was deep in conversation with Janice. Neither of them had noticed Sam's attempts to join in the conversation and now he backed away feeling totally out of his depth.

The crowd was breaking up as people moved off in the direction of the bonfire displays. Janice seemed to have forgotten him and Tizer was nowhere to be seen.

Sam tagged along behind them, far enough back so that there would be no chance of his being drawn into their conversation. A group of boys ran ahead, throwing a chicken carcass back and forth in what appeared to be practice rugby passes. Crackers popped all around and he was left further and further behind in the chaos of the crowd disbursing. He remembered the old warning from school about how people put fireworks in other people's hoods and drew his own tightly around his head.

Suddenly he realised why he was thinking of school. Walking towards him, but seemingly unaware of his presence, were a group of young people including John Watkin, Saul Adams, and Tamsin Grey.

Sam ducked into Bishop's Passage. What the hell was Tamsin doing with John and Saul? It was a totally impossible connection. Tamsin only hung around with people from Burgess Hill School for girls or Brighton College, people with rich mummies and daddies and second homes in other countries. The thought of her with his friends, talking about him, made him feel extremely worried. His enthusiasm for the planned demo at the bonfire was evaporating. He just wanted to get tonight over and get out of Lewes for good.

Still, he reckoned, Tamsin would probably go to one of the other bonfire sites, not the De Montfort one, where her parents would be. He made a quick decision and took the alley leading towards the castle. The back streets would be quicker, he thought. With his knowledge of Lewes he could get to the De Montfort site before anyone else.

***

Mark backed away from the playground, hoping that the ring of his phone hadn't drawn attention to their hiding place. Sally bobbed up and down as she tried to decide whether to follow him or remain hidden.

He didn't recognise the number. Hope and adrenaline constricted his throat.

'Hello,' he said.

'Hi,' said Tizer. 'Are you Mark? You left a message. It's Tizer.'

'Hi, yes, I'm looking for Sam . . .'

Tizer interrupted. 'Yeah, look. I know where he is. If you're a mate of his . . . He's hanging out with this geezer, Dougie Tate . . .'

'Do you know where he is right now? Sam, I mean.'

A rocket shot into the sky, showering red rain and screaming as it went.

'You're in Lewes, right?' Tizer hesitated. 'I don't know if I'm doing the right thing . . . Fuck! Fuck!'

'Please, said Mark. 'We're really worried. We just want to talk to him. You can be there if you want.'

'Oh fuck! He's outside the Lewes Arms.' Tizer hung up.

Mark stared at the phone, then he looked at Sally and back at the phone again. Should he phone Emily? Would she answer while she was with that man. . . probably. . . but would that alert him? He could just shout out to her, tell her to come away, but god knew what the psycho would do.

He beckoned Sally over and she ran towards him in a half crouch.

'Sam's at the Lewes Arms. You stay with Em.'

Sally opened her mouth to question him but Mark had already jogged away.

***

Emily kept both hands in her pockets. One hand still held the handle of the Sabatier 'professional' vegetable knife, the other played with her diamond engagement ring.

She didn't have a plan; she was just playing for time. She also didn't know why she had such trouble giving up the ring when she had handed over the money so easily. Her heart was thudding against her ribs, as if protesting at her own audacity. The ring really was a corker though, bought in better days and valued at nearly four grand only a year ago. Four grand was an awful lot of money and Emily was really very fond of it.

'Let's go then. Come on.' Dougie was irritated now, aware that she was being slow on purpose. He needed to move things along. Once he'd got the ring he could get to Julie's for his passport and his stuff. Then he could get back to Elm Grove and lie low until Gatwick got busy in the morning.

They walked up St John's Street, and then turned in the direction of the house. Emily was excruciatingly aware of Sally following at an inadequate distance.

Sally tried to hide behind cars as she shuffled up the road. An elderly couple passed by and looked at her with concern. She smiled at them, put her finger against her lips and nodded towards Dougie and Emily. They looked doubtful and gave her forced smiles in return.

Actually, though, Sally wasn't enjoying herself any more at all. Maybe she had started to sober up, but things seemed to have become more serious. She didn't like being left on her own. What if something happened? What could she do? If something happened to Emily she would feel responsible and everyone would blame her. Where the hell had Mark gone? This was his job.

She was also very annoyed. Emily set herself up as the sensible one, but she wasn't always. A vision flashed to the front of her mind: Emily on the first day of the school skiing trip, hurtling down a slope, her mouth set in a grim line and teachers shouting after her in terror. Then there was the time she'd punched a bloke who had pinched her bum. Now there was this. She'd got everyone into this mess.

She sighed and continued to follow Dougie and Emily. They appeared to be going back to the house. Dougie can't have been satisfied with what they'd been able to give him. Maybe he wanted the car after all.

She tried to concentrate on what to do next. Should she phone Emily or just shout at her from a distance? Cowardice won out and she took out her phone. She pressed Emily's number and could hear her phone responding further down the street. She saw Emily's hand reach towards her bag, then Dougie said something and she stopped, letting her hand drop back by her side. The ringing continued for a moment and then stopped.

With the skill and speed of a thirteen year old, Sally tapped out 'Sam at Lws arms. Mark gone thr'. She selected Emily's name and pressed Send.

She didn't hear the beep but saw Emily's hand, once more, reach towards her bag. This time Dougie let her, but when she took out the phone he snatched it away.

Sally moaned aloud. Why the hell had she done that? Stupid, Stupid. She snuck forward, one car at a time, catching a glimpse of Dougie and Emily between cars. Dougie read the text and looked stricken, he grabbed hold of Emily's wrist, and she tried to wrench it away.

Sally crept behind a Fiat Punto until she was level with them. For one second she prayed for deliverance from what she was about to do, then she launched herself, bellowing, at Dougie, smashing her fist hard into his crotch. He fell to the ground grabbing himself, writhing and groaning. While Emily was still staring with her mouth open, Sally grabbed the Tesco bag and pulled her away.

'Move!' she gasped. 'Quick! Sam's safe!'

With that, the two women bolted down the hill leaving Dougie still rolling on the floor and cursing.

Mark arrived at the Lewes Arms approximately one minute after Sam had left. He scanned the crowd outside, which had now spread to cover the adjoining streets. It was impossible. There were just too many people and too much chaos. Someone had set up a long line of crackers in a domino formation, reaching from the pub virtually all the way down towards the high street. One after another the fireworks cracked and sparked, setting each other off and adding to the cacophony of loud voices, intermittent rockets and assorted other fireworks.

He pushed backwards and forwards though the crowds saying 'Sorry, sorry' as he went. People were jostled and some angrily pushed back at him, sending him barging into yet more people until he felt like a ball in a pinball machine. Trying to look inside the pub was pointless. All he could do was stand in the door and shout 'Sam!' but in the relentless din the only people who took any notice were those who were standing right next to him.

He found a place against the wall, put his head back against it and closed his eyes in despair.

'For God's sake, Mark' said Emily, 'what the hell are you doing?'

Mark left his eyes closed for just one more second before facing his wife.

'He's not here. I can't find him. You look if you think you can do any better.' He looked past them and blinked. 'Where's Dougie?'

***

Dougie sat up and groaned again. Two men dressed as roundheads walked right out into the road rather than walk past him. His eyes narrowed in contempt as he watched them disappear down the road.

He pulled himself upright and stumbled, slowly getting his coordination back. There was no help for it. He had to go to the Lewes Arms. He had to get the money back, if nothing else. He had to get out before anything else went

226

wrong. He didn't believe in hitting women, as a rule. Not unless they were really asking for it, but given the opportunity he knew what he would do to those two bitches. He picked up his speed and ran at a half stagger in the direction that Sally and Emily had taken.

33. GUNPOWDER, DECEPTION AND SPITE

'Dougie will come straight here,' said Emily. 'Let's move.'

The blue and white striped Tesco bag seemed alarmingly vibrant in the red glare of the firework-illuminated darkness. Emily stuck it under her coat and then took it out again. It was too cold to leave her coat unbuttoned.

They headed up along the high street discussing whether they should split up to look for Sam or stick together. Sally refused point blank to be left alone.

Mark kept trying to call Tizer but they knew it was unlikely that he would hear it ring in the general din around them. Eventually he sent a text: 'S no longer at Lewes Arms. Please help, Mark.'

'Maybe he was having you on,' said Sally. 'You know, maybe he's trying to put you off the scent. If he's a friend of Sam's . . .'

Emily looked at Sally with annoyance, suddenly convinced that she was right and annoyed at not having thought this herself.

'No,' said Mark. 'You didn't hear him. He was Ok. Really.'

'Shit!' Sally hissed, cutting him off. 'There's that Clare. Damn, she's seen us. She's coming over.'

'Quick,' said Emily as she linked arms with the other two. 'Pretend you haven't seen her.' She pulled them towards the nearest alley and pushed them inside. Then they ran, as if they were ten year olds, until they were out of sight.

***

Clare stood quite still in the high street, people milling all around her.

They knew she was there and they had blanked her. Sally had obviously seen her and Emily had obviously pushed them down the alley so that they could avoid her. Clare became aware that she was grinding her teeth a little.

Tim turned around, wondering why she had stopped. 'Clare?' he said.

'Where's Tamsin?'

'Just over there with those boys. See . . .'

The street was emptying out a little now. The processions were over and everyone was making their way to one bonfire or another. Tamsin was leaning against a lamppost and laughing. She didn't seem to be taking much notice of the two boys she was with, looking out over the head of the short, hairy boy, as if hoping to spot someone more interesting behind him. One of the boys had apparently taken off his coat to give to Tamsin. A long parka was now draped loosely around her shoulders. Her gloved hands toyed with the tiny yellow handbag, which looked even more incongruous now that she had changed her trainers for wellington boots. She looked extremely cute and knew it.

'They're not her usual types, are they?' said Tim 'What's she up to? Do you know?'

'They're Sam's friends. She's trying to find out how he is. I'm worried about him, you know. I think we should do what we can to help.'

Tim gave her a sideways look and sighed.

Tamsin approached. 'Can I ditch them now?' she said. 'They don't know anything about old Skidpants.' She smiled over at the boys. 'Honestly Mum, if anyone sees me with them I'm dead.'

'Put your hood up then. If anyone sees you say you're doing your good deed for the day.'

Tamsin pouted 'What's the point? They don't know anything.'

Clare was getting fed up with this. Tamsin was rather too used to getting her own way.

'Stick with it for a while, darling. Don't be so obvious. They might find something out later. Don't burn bridges.

I've told you before; you never know what the future will hold.'

Tamsin's bottom lip stuck out further.

Clare relented 'Wait until we get to the bonfire. You can lose them in the crowd.'

Tamsin smirked and flounced back over to the boys.

***

Sally leaned towards Mark and read the text out loud.

'Soz. S prob at Demont bonf'. 'Sorry, Sam is probably at the DeMontfort bonfire,' she explained to Emily and Mark as if to elderly parents.

'Let's go then,' said Emily, giving her a look.

'What about that?' said Mark, gesturing towards the Tesco bag. 'Should we take it back to the house first?'

'I'm going straight to the bonfire. You take it if you want. Dougie seems to be able to get in the house when he wants to anyway.'

'Sally could take it and hide it,' said Mark.

'No way. You are not leaving me alone again.'

'That's that then.'

They were now at the far side of the castle on the grassy patch at the back of the old jousting green. There was a bench and a sheer drop overlooking the north of Lewes and out to the surrounding countryside. They could already identify a couple of bonfire sites in the distance, the burning torches gathering in the dark fields at the outskirts of town.

'There's the De Montfort site,' said Emily, pointing to moving lights massing in a field to the west. 'We should move.'

***

Dougie hurried towards the Lewes Arms in a frenzy of impotent rage. The implications of the last few minutes were hitting him in sickening waves. If he did not think of something soon he was finished. He was now almost completely broke, plus he had lost Sam, and had lost

230

Emily's money. Why hadn't he just taken the bag of money while he had the chance?

In spite of the still considerable pain he dragged himself towards the pub. If he could get there before they got to Sam he might still have a chance. Otherwise he would find Emily and get the money back somehow. He didn't care what he had to do. Sam was going to the De Montfort bonfire. Emily would be on her way there too. There was still a chance that he could get hold of the kid, or Emily, before they found each other.

34. BONFIRE PLOTS

There was an uneasy atmosphere at the De Montfort site. There was something out of kilter, something not quite right.

It was, even by the standards of Lewes bonfire, very overcrowded, and the balance of bonfire goers was a little bit off: the proportion of families was greatly exceeded by the number of young people of a certain sort, the sort that wears scruffy clothes and has unlikely hair styles.

A sharp observer would also notice something strange about the way that the different groups of young people greeted each other. They were quiet, cool and unusually serious. One boy of about sixteen laughed drunkenly, too loud and too long, and his friends backed away, embarrassed, not wanting to attract attention.

Parents with young children became vigilant, without knowing why or even realising that they were doing it. People watched each other rather than the final bonfire preparations behind the barricade.

Sam pushed through the crowd looking for familiar faces. No one had their face masks on yet, so it was obviously not the right thing to wear his, but he was frantically worried about seeing anyone he knew from Lewes. His beanie hid his blonde hair, though, and he held the hood of his coat close to his face. It was now so cold that this did not even look unusual. Most people looked like heaps of clothes with only their frosted breath to identify them as living beings.

At last he spotted Janice, at the front next to the barricade, identifiable only by her long matted hair. He pushed through the crowds towards her.

'Hi,' he said, looking round for Tizer.

'Hi,' she replied, then turned away.

'Where's Tizer?' Sam moved around with her.

'Haven't seen him since the pub. He'll turn up.' She turned again and started talking to someone else.

Sam hung around the periphery of the group, watching the crowd. There was some kind of activity by the trees at the side of the site. Sam guessed that this was where the George Bush effigy was being assembled. He made his way over to look. This was it, this was his chance to be part of something. He tried to put aside his disappointment at the lameness of the idea. He would ask what he could do to help, and maybe, next time, he could be more involved.

Several people looked up at him suspiciously as he approached.

'It's OK,' said someone that he recognised from the Lewes house: a spoon-faced young man called Gavin or Gareth. 'He lives with Tizer.'

Sam felt a swell of pride as people looked at him with a new interest. He crouched down gratefully. 'Where is Tizer? Do you know?'

'He went to get something.' Gareth/Gavin looked away, as if uncertain how much to reveal.

'He asked me to bring this.' Sam pulled the orange jumpsuit out of the rucksack.

'Ah!' the boy's spoon face broke into a tight, nervous smile. 'Excellent.'

The effigy was taking shape around them. Someone had just attached the stuffed arms to the torso and a couple of girls were giggling as they pulled a pair of trousers up stuffed legs. A slight looking girl who was sitting in a wheelchair stood up, did a little jig and sat down again.

'It's a miracle!' she cried, and everyone laughed.

Sam didn't get the joke and wondered why they were still dressing the guy in normal clothes now that the jumpsuit had arrived. Weren't they going to dress the effigy in that?

'Can I do anything? Can I help at all?'

The young man turned back to look at Sam, as if wondering why he was still there, then his expression changed, oscillating between contempt and a dawning interest. This kid was really young, but that would work in his favour if anything happened. Tizer wasn't there to say no. Why shouldn't the boy be the one to do the dirty work?

'You'd better put it on then,' he said, and threw the orange jumpsuit back at Sam.

***

At the other end of the De Montfort field, Tamsin was still stuck with John and Saul. Most of her attention was on her mobile: texting friends who had thankfully gone to the Cliffe bonfire and wouldn't be able to see who she was hanging around with.

John watched her as she occasionally looked up from her phone to dazzle them with a smile. He was fed up. He was cold but he didn't know how to get his coat back from Tamsin without looking bad. Also, Saul was being a total twat. Tamsin was very pretty, and obviously, if the situation presented itself . . . but somewhere in the back of his mind he knew that it was never going to happen. He and Saul would never, he realised with quiet sadness, be in the same league as girls like her. Listening to Saul was like torture. He was so embarrassingly over-eager. John felt like curling into a ball of shame as he stood, tongue-tied.

Anyway, she kept going on about Sam, as if she fancied him. John wasn't buying this, though. Sam was better looking than either of them, he supposed, but he wasn't part of the cool group at school. Sam wasn't good at anything that would give him extra kudos either: too uncoordinated for sport, not especially bright. Sam was just a really good bloke, and Tamsin, he knew, would not be interested in that, particularly as he had become a town joke after the swimming pool incident. He didn't trust her sudden interest and decided that he would not let her pump him for more information.

John turned his attention to the bonfire. The main effigy to be burnt today was a local property developer. John recognised the name on the banner from the local papers. Charles Brice was a popular figure to burn; Lewes people did not like changes to their cute little town and every new chain store or office building was fought against with great energy. Now the developers were considered directly responsible for the flood because they had built on the flood plains.

The massive Charles Brice was smiling insanely and waving a wad of money while sitting on the top of a model of the castle. A flooded Lewes was evidently below. The whole thing was over twenty foot high, higher now that it was placed on top of the bonfire.

'Shall we go down the front?' John was hoping that some of the heat from the bonfire would warm him up.

Tamsin looked round at her mother hoping to be rescued, but Clare just smiled encouragingly.

'You go on darling,' she said. 'Look, they're going to burn Charlie Brice from Brice & Co. How fun!'

Tamsin raised her eyes and trudged off with the boys. There was no escape to be had this evening. She resigned herself and began to look around. It was doubtful, but maybe someone interesting was there. She dabbed a bit of lip gloss on her pout and scanned the crowds.

***

'How the hell are we supposed to find him in this lot?' Emily pushed forward into the crowds, grabbing Mark's coat with one hand and Sally's scarf with the other.

They struggled on until they found a tiny gap in the throng. Behind them, a mother and two preteen girls waved sparklers menacingly.

'We should split up' said Mark. 'Take a different bit of the field. I'll do the left, you do the middle Em, and Sally, you do the right. Meet up by the barrier, over there by that tree, or as near as you can get.'

To his surprise there was no argument and the three set off immediately. Sally didn't mind so much now. Looking for Sam was something she could do. Facing Dougie Tate again was a different matter, but even if he caught up with them here, what could he do? Not much in front of such a huge audience anyway. Nevertheless, at the thought of him she tucked her hair into her coat and wrapped her scarf as far up her neck as it would go.

***

Tizer saw Dougie in a doorway, scrutinising the passing crowds intensely. He sighed to himself and made up his mind.

'Dougie,' he said, 'we were looking for you.'

Dougie stared at him with an expression that Tizer couldn't decode except to say that it didn't look good. Dougie face was blank but his eyes were blazing. 'Oh fuck,' he thought. He was going to have to be very careful.

'Where's Sam? He said he'd wait for me.'

'Yeah, I've lost everyone too,' he said. 'They'll have gone to the bonfire. It's nearly time to do the stunt. D'you want to walk up there?'

They moved off quickly, Dougie pushing through people so aggressively that, with Tizer travelling in his wake, they made good time up the hill. At last, Tizer drew level with Dougie.

'I didn't want to tell you at the house, mate . . .'

Dougie gave him a sideways look.

'Sam's got people looking for him. Family, I think. He's only a little kid.'

'So what? What are you saying?'

'Just that . . . maybe he . . . he's a bit young . . . d'you know what I mean?'

'No, I don't know what you fucking mean.' At any other time Dougie would have asked Tizer if he was calling him a nonce. At the moment though, the priority was to get Sam back. He turned to Tizer, frustrated that he couldn't just headbutt his stupid ginger face. 'I know Sam's parents, right? I know his mum from years back. She's a total fucking bitch. He's better off out. I'm telling you, this woman is a fucking monster. Got his balls on a string round her neck.'

'The bloke I spoke to, he must be his Dad. He seems ok.'

'Well she's got his balls too.'

'Fuck,' said Tizer. He didn't know what to do now. Poor Sam didn't seem to have many options. He still thought that he was better off away from Dougie though.

'She knocks him about too,' Desperation was making Dougie inventive. He was pushing his luck now, but it seemed to be working. 'She's an alkie.'

'Fuck!' said Tizer again. 'I didn't fucking realise.'

'No. You didn't bloody think.'

Tizer subsided. They were nearly at the bonfire site now and he hadn't a clue what to do.

***

The boys with the chicken carcass were still at it. Sam watched in irritation as they passed it back and forth. Typical moronic rugby types. How long could they keep this up for? Then the carcass fell into a slick of mud and they all moaned at the end of their game. One of them, an overmuscled boy with a nasty expression took a run up and kicked it. The others soon joined in. Sam felt uncomfortable, but he didn't know why. It was dead, just a dead chicken, and one of his favourite foods was roast chicken. This, somehow, seemed different though. The desecration of its lifeless body offended him in an inexplicable way.

Sam slipped the jumpsuit on over his clothes, and then put his coat back on over the top for warmth. The girl in the wheelchair suddenly jumped off. There didn't seem to be anything wrong with her at all, but the chair became the focus of intense activity. Sam got closer so that he could see what was going on.

'What are you doing?' he asked one of the girls.

She gave him a grin. 'We're making the electric chair. Isn't it you? Aren't you going to do it?'

Sam smiled back. He still wasn't sure exactly what he was lined up for, but this was a bit more like it. Everyone was busily attaching fireworks to the wheelchair. Rockets were being taped to the backrest, Catherine wheels adorned the chairs wheels. 'George' was eventually seated and more fireworks were stuffed into his pockets and clothes.

It was still a tamer stunt than he would have liked, but the electric chair idea was at least visual. It would make an ok photo, provided the fireworks went off. Also, it was a slightly sick, which moved the whole stunt just a little bit away from the sort of thing that went on during a normal Lewes bonfire. It still wasn't enough though. It needed to be more offensive, more visceral. 'Visceral' was a word that he had learnt recently and liked a lot.

He suddenly had an idea.

'Ok' the spoon-faced young man called him over. 'This is the plan: At exactly 9.30 a fight will break out over there.' He nodded towards the middle of the crowd. 'At 9.33, when the cops move in to sort it out, everyone will put on their masks. The guys having the fight will have De Montfort stripy jerseys on, so they can melt into the crowd. These guys' he gesticulated to the girls with the wheelchair, 'will help you move the fence so that you can get the chair though. Then you just have to run like hell and get it as near to the bonfire as you can and light this rocket' he pointed to a massive rocket nestled between 'George's' legs and pushed a lighter into Sam's hand. 'Run back into the crowd after and get rid of the jumpsuit. So that's it really. What do you think?'

Sam didn't know what to think. He was too terrified. So he was supposed to be a Guantanamo prisoner sending George to the chair. Quite neat. If it went well, he would be a hero. If not . . . It all seemed very well organised, but would everyone really do their part at exactly the right time and would everything really go ok?

'Ok,' he said. 'But can I suggest something?'

35. FIREWORKS

Tizer pushed through the crowd after Dougie. He probably wouldn't be able to stop Dougie getting to Sam now, but he could at least make sure that he was there too, and he could try to talk to Sam.

Dougie looked around. 'Where're your mates?'

'By the tree.'

They ploughed on. Tizer looked at his watch. It was nearly time. The crowd was falling eerily quiet. There were a few loud hoots and giggles.

'Dougie,' Tizer tugged at Dougie's parka, 'put your mask on.'

A long sharp whistle blew three times and a cheer went up throughout the crowd. All around them, people pulled on George Bush masks, some shop bought and moulded into the shape of a face, some photos cut from magazines and some just black and white enlarged photocopies held on with string. PC Roberts, who was standing by the barrier, stopped chewing gum long enough to fire a quick series of statements into her radio.

The results were better than Tizer could have envisaged. The black and white images in particular lent the event a surreal air. The crowd erupted into whoops and cheers, cameras flashed and those without masks looked around, puzzled or worried. Amongst these was Tamsin, furious now that she did not know what was going on and, for once in her life, had been left out of the loop.

Someone started to sing 'Don't wanna be an American Idiot' and the rest of the crowd tried to join in.

'Now!' shouted a young man in the middle of the crowd, and groups of other young men whooped and rushed at each other as if in the mosh pit of a concert.

'Now!' hissed Janice as she pushed Sam towards the barrier.

'Now!' yelled a bonfire boy from behind the barrier. A second bonfire boy lit a fuse and they backed away while the first rockets shot into the sky and screeched off through the blackness.

Suddenly, Sam found himself on the other side of the fencing. The bonfire was hot and he was confused by the sparks and bangs all around him. He looked up briefly at the sea of George Bushes and then ploughed on, pushing the wheelchair towards the bonfire. The property developer effigy was now sparking off fireworks in all directions and Sam put his head down to push the final yards. Then he reached for the lighter.

Through all the confusion something in Emily's mind jogged at the sight of the orange jumpsuit and the skinny figure inside it. Before she could stop herself she screamed 'Sam' and pushed to the front of the crowd.

Dougie looked around and saw Emily a few feet away but unreachable in the crowd. He saw the Tesco bag swinging on her wrist and lunged towards it fruitlessly.

He followed the direction of her glance and saw Sam, running, pushing the wheelchair and pursued by an overweight female cop.

Now everyone in the crowd was watching the action behind the barrier. The policewoman caught up with Sam, and following a short tussle managed to bend him over the wheelchair as she reached for her cuffs.

'Look!' said the girl next to Emily. 'Look at its head!'

In the struggle the mask had fallen off the effigy to reveal a chicken carcass, wings upwards like makeshift ears. All around people started to laugh. Now the tableaux looked almost obscene: Sam was bent double, his face in the effigy's lap, while PC Roberts appeared to mount him from the rear. Cameras flashed all around.

Emily strained towards the barrier. This was so unbelievable dangerous she couldn't believe her eyes. All around, fireworks continued to shoot and whirr. Multicoloured sparks flew from the fireworks and flames

241

flicked from the bonfire which was now nearly fully alight and massive, throwing its heat out far into the crowd. She heard a frightened voice above the general din; 'The wheelchair's got fireworks in it' and people started to push back against her, straining to get away.

She looked around in desperation. Further back in the crowd she could see Sally and Mark with Clare and Tim. She managed to catch Mark's eyes, but he looked desperate. There was nothing he could do from there, and now the weight of the crowd was pushing him backwards.

Tamsin, Saul and John were still further along the field, crushed up against the barrier.

'Isn't that Sam's mum?' said John. They watched as Emily scaled the barrier and then ran, with an uncoordinated lack of grace, towards the wheelchair and the struggling couple. 'And that's Sam!'

John groaned as he recognised the slight figure in orange. What the hell was Sam doing now?

'Oh-my-god' squealed Tamsin, immensely cheered. 'Sam's mum's going to fight the cop!'

Emily reached PC Roberts and pulled the neck of her jacket, prising her away from Sam.

PC Roberts, trained for such attacks, used her right leg to kick out backwards into Emily's knee. Unfortunately for the policewoman, she skidded in the mud and missed her target. She steadied herself, holding onto the wheelchair, but Emily and Sam took their chance and ran towards the barrier.

'What the fuck!' screamed someone, 'what's happening to the head?'

The crowd now fell almost silent as they watched in awe. The firework-stuffed chicken head started to bob. Then it seemed to hop a bit. Then it jumped off its neck and lay in its lap, still twitching. At last, it gave a kind of heave, before leaping into the air and exploding.

Bits of skin and flesh flew out in all directions. PC Roberts took the brunt of the downpour, hot meat and fat welding itself to her uniform and only missing her face by inches. Those in the front row also suffered. Tamsin, despite turning her back in good time, put her hood up a few seconds too late, not noticing that it was already full.

Emily looked around briefly. The wheelchair was now alight and fireworks were sparking off in all directions. She pushed Sam over the barrier and then slung herself forward, scrabbling until welcoming arms helped her over.

Then she saw him. Dougie made a grab for the Tesco bag, losing his mask in the process. Emily snatched the bag away, holding it above her head as she pushed backwards through the crowd. Her other hand clasped the knife in her pocket, ready. Dougie jumped up towards the Tesco bag, snatching wildly in the air, before falling back onto Emily's knife.

At that moment, the wheelchair sparked into life, crackling and flickering as the hidden fireworks caught light. A shell exploded with a thunderous boom, drawing a neon dandelion in the sky. Then a stray rocket took off at an angle, skimming over the head of the crowd, just clipping the edge of the Tesco bag with a trail of red fire.

Amongst the many photos that appeared in the papers on the following day, one made most of the front pages: it showed hundreds of hippies wearing George Bush face masks, jumping in the air to catch money floating in a crimson sky.

Dougie slunk away, defeated, and with a sharp pain in his behind. His hand moved automatically to the pain and came away covered in blood.

An old man in a wheelchair looked at him curiously then tugged the jacket of the woman standing next to him.

'Look Janet, it's the toilet man,' he said.

The woman looked confused.

'The man who came about the toilet. You know. . . on the day we were burgled.'

As the summoned police backup descended on the field, Dougie was almost relieved to walk into their waiting arms.

36. ASHES

Jenny picked up another of James' shirts and put it on the ironing board, pulling it until it was stretched tight.

She had not forgotten. The last time she had done this was the night that James had disappeared. At first she was shocked and disturbed at how the methodical act of ironing shirts brought that night back to her. She remembered exactly how she felt, how she had been thinking about work and how absolutely trivial her thoughts had been. Then she fell into a reverie, pleased to remember these trivial thoughts, happy to recall the mundanity of everyday life, a life that had now blown away like dust.

The cacophony of the main firework displays brought her back to earth. She took the pile of freshly ironed shirts and stacked them onto the ironing board. She would take them to the Oxfam shop as soon as she could. There was no point in hanging on to them.

Now she had nothing else to do and she stared helplessly around. Suddenly, she couldn't stay in the house another night. She knew that Vero would not welcome her back at her father's house but she just had to go somewhere where there was life around her.

She had parked her car a few streets away so that Clare would think that she had already gone. This also meant that she was outside the road blocks set up for bonfire night and would be able to leave if she wanted to.

She looked at her watch. If she was going to go she had to do so immediately, before the firework displays and bonfires finished, and everyone in the world was trying to get out of Lewes.

She ran to the bedroom and picked up the small suitcase that she and Clare had packed earlier. Then she headed for the front door. She felt like she had forgotten something but shrugged the feeling off. It wasn't as if she couldn't come back. By the time she had closed the front door behind her and walked to the street where she had parked the Audi, she had forgotten all about it.

***

The first job that James and Jenny had planned for the house was to strip the walls and then totally rewire and plaster. The fact that the wiring was several decades old was evidenced by the Bakelite switches, so old that they were almost fashionably retro, except that, of course, no one wanted antique wiring.

Up-to-date wiring systems would have shorted out when the iron, which Jenny had forgotten to turn off, fused. In this case though, the iron just sent out a Catherine wheel of little sparks, several of which landed on the crisp, dry, mountain of shirts. Here the flames licked and played until the mountain toppled, falling in a blazing cascade onto the wooden floor below.

It being bonfire night, nobody took any notice of the crackling noises and the flashes of light until it was too late and the flames had spread to Emily and Marks' house. Once there, the fire consumed the house from the bottom up. Each floor collapsed on top of the other onto the basement kitchen.

Clare and Tim fared better. Clare was to complain for years about the smoke damage and the cracked glass in the conservatory, but by the time the fire brigade was eventually called, and had made its way through the crowds, they were the only ones who had a house to come back to.

37. A YEAR LATER

The flat was fine. Her share of the insurance would cover most of it and she could fit it out with a couple of trips to IKEA. Sam could sleep in the study if he wanted to visit. Her probation officer was OK with the move. Best of all: nothing needed doing. She could move straight in.

Brighton would be a new start. You never knew what would happen. Anything was possible. Well, maybe not anything, not at her age, and with a criminal record. She stopped herself. That was too negative. Women of her age weren't quite past it any more. Or was that only in soap operas?

She turned off up the London Road, heading for Sally's for hopefully the last time. Just ahead she could see a couple who were probably around about her age. For a split second, Emily felt cheered. The woman was dumpy and the man's hair was greying, but even from a distance she could tell that they were happy. The man had his arms right around the woman's shoulders, which were shaking with laughter. Their faces mirrored each other in smiles.

The man was Mark. He looked up, only registering the car and Emily when they were safely in the distance. Emily's mouth set into a smile, then she turned the Ramones up to full to volume and stamped on the accelerator.

ABOUT THE AUTHOR

DM Stone lives in Lewes with her husband and at least one dog.

ACKNOWLEDGEMENTS

Many thanks to the many posters on the Lewes Forum who gave me encouragement and ideas. Special thanks to Deelite and Webbo.

Also thanks to Viva Lewes Magazine, in particular Beth Miller and John McGowan.

To the WIPers, specially FR, I miss you and thanks.

Most of all, thanks to M, J and D.

14022334R00147

Printed in Great Britain
by Amazon.co.uk, Ltd.,
Marston Gate.